she said, her whispered demand intense with the maelstrom
of feeling whirling through her.

His lips quirked into a teasing smile. "Show you what,
milady?" His gaze beckoned her, enticed her to lean closer
to him.

Did she have the courage to continue what she'd started? A
simple glance at Padrig's face was all the answer she needed.

"Show me how to kiss, if you please," she said, in the
haughtiest tone she could contrive—though she mitigated
that offense with a smile.

"There are many kinds of kisses." He nuzzled her cheek,
then touched his lips to her ear. "You've only to tell me what
you want, milady," he whispered. "I am yours to command."

Unfamiliar desires engulfed her; her body demanded
something, but she'd little notion precisely what it was she
wanted. What she needed.

All at once the answer came to her. She wanted *more*...!

* * *

For My Lady's Honor
Harlequin Historical #794—March 2006

For my Lady's Honor

SHARON SCHULZE

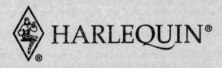

HARLEQUIN®

TORONTO • NEW YORK • LONDON
AMSTERDAM • PARIS • SYDNEY • HAMBURG
STOCKHOLM • ATHENS • TOKYO • MILAN • MADRID
PRAGUE • WARSAW • BUDAPEST • AUCKLAND

ISBN 0-373-29394-1

FOR MY LADY'S HONOR

Please address questions and book requests to:
Harlequin Reader Service
U.S.: 3010 Walden Ave., P.O. Box 1325, Buffalo, NY 14269
Canadian: P.O. Box 609, Fort Erie, Ont. L2A 5X3

To my son Patrick and his wonderful wife:
May your life together always
be full of love and laughter.

And in loving memory of my grandmother,
Clara Willey—for card games, Sunday dinners
(and wrestling!) and making each of us feel like
the most special person in the world.

Chapter One

~~~~~

The Welsh Marches, 1222

Lady Alys Delamare slid her head out of the blanket and greeted the brightening sky with relief. After a nigh sleepless night—during which she'd scarce dared move upon her pallet lest her maddeningly observant escort notice her restlessness—she couldn't wait to be quit of her bed and on the road once more.

Another day of their journey meant another day in the company of the ever-irksome Sir Padrig ap Huw.

Yet it also brought her another day closer to bidding him farewell.

'Twas a shame the nagging voice inside her head—speaking for the part of her that took a reluctant pleasure in Padrig's teasing ways—had taken on a sad tone at the thought of their inevitable parting.

She'd plans for her life, plans that didn't include an attractive young knight…no matter how appealing she found him.

She peeked over at Padrig's bedroll. 'Twas empty.

By the Virgin, she'd swear she'd heard him every time he'd so much as shifted on the ground in the night! How had he managed to rise without her noticing?

He's a skilled warrior! Who knows what the man is capable of?

Alys squirmed free of her bedding and stood, tugging at her twisted undertunic and giving a shimmy to settle the garment. Ignoring the stout boots and bliaut on the ground beside her, she edged around Marie, her maid, who continued to snore unabated.

Mayhap Marie had drowned out the sound of Padrig's leaving. She bit back a laugh. 'Twas possible, for the young woman could nigh wake the deaf at times, she made such a racket.

Once away from Marie, Alys focused instead on the beauty of the morning. Thick grass covered the clearing, soft and cool beneath her bare feet. The sensation sent a shiver of pleasure through her; she could scarce remember the last time she'd had the chance to savor the feel of the earth against her skin.

A smile on her lips, she crept from the clearing and, following a faint path through the trees, entered the forest.

Her unbound hair, mussed from sleep, caught in a low branch. She paused to free herself, the fresh scent of pine adding to her awareness of the world around her—and of herself. She felt vividly alive, conscious of her body in a strange new way.

Her senses alert, Alys heard water splashing. Following the sound, she hurried along the path until she reached a small pool surrounded by trees and rocks.

A pool occupied by a muscular, naked man.

He faced away from her, the water barely hiding his buttocks. Moisture shimmered on his tanned skin, accentuating his strong arms and back. He swept his hands through his wet hair, smoothing it back to lie, dark and wavy, to his shoulders.

She couldn't mistake that hair. 'Twas Padrig.

Blessed Mary save her! She'd always thought him handsome, but she'd never imagined he looked like this.

Her mouth dry and her gaze intent upon Padrig, Alys stole closer to the edge of the pool. She'd no intention of bringing this mesmerizing scene to an end any time soon by catching his attention.

He stretched his arms over his head. The muscles in his back and shoulders flexed, drawing her attention to several dark, intricate designs on the smooth flesh of his shoulders and upper arms.

They appeared to be drawn upon his skin. She'd never seen such a thing—what could they be?

Padrig began to slowly walk away from her, toward the other side of the narrow pool. Startled from her fascination, Alys knew she should do something to make him aware of her presence, but instead she lingered at the edge of the forest, motionless and silent, to savor this unexpected pleasure for as long as possible.

Padrig's lips curled in a smile as Alys continued to lurk near the water on the other side of the pond. Her startled gasp when she'd seen him would have given her away even if he hadn't already heard her moving through the trees lining the path. He should have spoken, or shifted deeper into the water once he'd known she was there, but he couldn't resist the provocation to tease her.

How far could he go, he wondered, before she'd do something to let him know she was there?

He stretched his arms skyward and took another step

away from Alys and closer to the far edge of the pool. He had to fight the temptation to turn around, to see the expression on her face as she watched him. He could feel her eyes upon him, the intensity of her gaze nigh a physical caress over his flesh.

A caress that was causing an all-too-real reaction, he noted wryly. Mayhap he'd better move into deeper water after all; he didn't need to have her run screaming back toward their campsite, sending her maid into a tizzy and his men scrambling to protect her.

But what if she didn't react that way? For all he knew, she might even now be removing her own clothing to join him in the water....

Closing his eyes for a moment against the yearning *that* image brought to mind, he reluctantly shifted his thoughts instead to Lord Rannulf's reaction should Padrig take such base advantage of a young lady in his care.

Jesu, had lust unbalanced his mind? Lady Alys was a noblewoman—a *virgin*, he had no doubt.

If Lord Rannulf didn't have his head for such insolence—or some other part of him a bit lower, he thought with a chuckle—the lady's father would certainly take exception should Padrig attempt to steal her innocence.

Pah, as if Lady Alys would want the likes of him anyway!

Though her continued silence did make him wonder what she was about.

Unable to resist one last taunt, Padrig took a step back, until the water covered him to just above his hips, and turned.

"Can I help you with something, milady?" he asked evenly. 'Twas difficult to maintain a neutral air once he saw Alys, however. The mere sight of her sleep-tousled hair, combined with the way the soft fabric of her gown clung to her lissome form, sent his body into instant rebellion against his strength of will. The expression on her face—soft, curious, her gaze intense as it grazed over him—was impossible to ignore. Despite his attempt at restraint, he could not suppress an equally heated response.

He moved deeper into the water at once, lest he flaunt his reaction to her; he'd no wish to embarrass her or himself.

She wet her lips with her tongue and raised her hand to smooth down her dark chestnut hair, a tide of color tinting her cheeks. "Nay, sir," she replied, her gaze meeting his with a hint of challenge. "I was simply curious. I wished to explore a bit before we resume our journey."

"And was your curiosity satisfied, milady?" he asked.

Her lips curved into a faint smile. "Not yet, Sir Padrig." She moved closer to the water's edge. "Though I believe if I'm patient enough it will be."

Padrig drew in a deep breath and reminded himself she was an innocent maiden who didn't realize how her actions and words might be interpreted. Though he willed himself to cool down, his body would not obey. 'Twas a miracle the water around him hadn't begun to boil from the heat pouring through him!

How could he make her leave?

"'Tis said that patience is a virtue, milady. I've no doubt you're a virtuous lass—"

"'Tis also said that virtue is its own reward," she pointed out. She stepped onto the rock-strewn rim of the pool, her bare feet shifting on the slippery stones. "I'm not certain I believe 'tis true, though. Have you ever noticed that the most virtuous people you meet seem the least happy?"

Aye, he could not disagree with that. He closed his eyes for a moment as memories swept through him. His own mother, Lord rest her, had been an intensely virtuous woman—yet to her, life had been a constant misery of disappointment and sorrow. No one and nothing could ever meet her standards; he'd stopped trying when he'd scarce the years or wisdom to understand the impossibility of it. Only by the grace of God—and his cousin Lady Catrin—had he escaped that torment.

He'd often wondered, in the years since his mother's death, if she'd simply died of frustration that the world fell short of her measure.

While he'd been momentarily lost in the shadows of the past, Lady Alys had made her way around the pond. Her gown hiked up to her knees, she waded through the shallows, her face alight and her lips curled into a winsome smile that set his heartbeat racing.

"What are you doing?" he demanded. By the rood, but he wished he were dressed! He felt at a distinct disadvantage, trapped here in the water while Lady Alys, all unknowing, tempted him nigh beyond endurance. The gauzy fabric of her gown—naught more than her undertunic, he'd vow—clung to her where she'd got it wet, the thin material outlining her curves and heating his blood further.

His mouth dry, his mind numb, Padrig sought in vain for the words to deliver himself from this situation. In her innocent dishabille Lady Alys was seduction personified; now that he'd seen her thus, he doubted he'd ever again be able to treat her with the deference a lady of her station deserved.

"The water is so soothing," she said, ignoring his question.

Soothing? Was she mad?

He drew in a deep breath. There was nothing *soothing* about the look in her eyes—no, nor little of the innocent, either, he noted.

His pulse thrummed harder. Damn the woman! She knew precisely the effect she was causing, he'd warrant.

Damn *him,* for finding that truth so exciting. He took a step back, in the futile hope of hiding his rampaging body.

"Lady Alys—" His voice sounded strange even to his own ears.

"Aye, Sir Padrig?" she asked, her tone light with merriment as she followed him. "Was there something you wanted of me?"

He bit back a groan. "Go back to the camp," he said flatly.

The glow of mirth brightening her eyes faded, replaced by embarrassment. A bright tide of pink swept up her face and she looked away from him.

"Milady—" He'd not meant to upset her, only to bring a halt to her teasing before it went too far.

Her shoulders set in a rigid line, Lady Alys spun on her heel, lost her footing, and, letting out a shriek, came tumbling into Padrig's arms.

Chapter Two

Padrig caught her as she fell backwards. She barely even touched the water—a testament to his knightly prowess, no doubt. Whatever the reason, Alys was glad of it, for in spite of her taunting prowl through the pool, she'd no desire to immerse herself completely.

He gathered her close and hiked her up into his arms. She gasped at the touch of his wet flesh, for despite the icy water and the slight breeze wafting gently over them, Padrig's fiery skin smoldered through the linen of her gown as though the fabric didn't exist. Hot, firm muscles lightly dusted with dark hair and the sensation of Padrig's chest and stomach against her was nigh branded upon her body for all time.

"I ought to drop you right here," he muttered. He raised her slightly away from him, still holding her easily within his grasp. "'Twould be no more than you deserve."

"Don't you dare!" Alys shifted in his hold and wrapped her arms tight about his neck lest he try to make good upon the threat, although a swift glance at his face confirmed her suspicion that he'd not actually do so.

The movement brought her face close to his. Her mouth tingled with the need to touch his, to test the contrast between the dark whiskers on his jaw and the surprising softness of his lips. Mouth dry, she swallowed and dragged her gaze down before she gave in to temptation.

She should have glanced away instead, however, for everything within her view tempted her.

And she could not look away.

She had to dig her fingers into his shoulders to keep from stroking the smooth, tanned flesh within her reach. 'Twas a feast for her senses; she felt nigh drunk on the feel of him, the fresh scent of his wet body, the warmth radiating out from him to envelop her like a cloak. 'Twas as though they were linked together by invisible bonds. She glanced up and met his eyes—a mistake, for they smoldered with a heat fit to match that of his skin. She dared not hold his gaze, for fear she'd lose her will completely if she did.

Closing her eyes, she shook her head to clear her muzzy thoughts, the movement tugging sharply at her hair where it was caught between their bodies. When she drew away from him to free herself, a feeling of loss rushed over her. The sensation, though painful, brought her to her senses; she wriggled loose and dropped into the water with a splash.

'Twas so cold! The water closed over her head for but a moment before Padrig hauled her up and out of it, but 'twas enough to clear her wits. A tide of heat rose to her face as her actions replayed themselves in her mind.

What had she been about, to tease and taunt him as she had?

Alys found her footing, rose and swiped her wet

hair out of her eyes. Backing toward shore, she risked a glance at Padrig, then whirled away from him in shock.

He'd come after her, leaving the protective cover of the water. He stood before her in all his naked glory—and by the Virgin, he *was* a glorious sight. Fully aroused, his wet body gleamed in the early morning light.

Somehow she forced her reluctant feet into motion, *away* from him, toward the camp.

Unlike her journey to the pool, this time she noted nothing of her surroundings. Instead all she could see in her mind's eye was Padrig, her only thought a question pulsing repeatedly through her brain.

How in God's name could she become a nun now?

Padrig watched Alys stumble away from him and along the path with mixed feelings. 'Twas for the best that she'd left, no doubt—but by the rood, how he wished she'd stayed!

He grinned. The Lady Alys he'd observed at l'Eau Clair—though he'd not seen her much, 'twas true—had led him to believe her to be vague, distracted, scarcely aware of her surroundings. She'd surprised him this morn, her actions and her words both, for she'd been quick-witted, clever and enticing.

He had noticed her very soon after his return to l'Eau Clair several weeks ago. She was a comely lass, petite but curvaceous, her dark chestnut hair and light amber eyes a striking contrast to her alabaster skin. Something made her stand out among the young ladies in Lady Gillian's household, though he could not say what made that so, for more than a few of them were beautiful.

Still, when he'd tried to speak with her on several occasions, she'd scurried away with scarce a word to him—she'd barely even looked his way.

When he'd asked about Lady Alys, he'd been told by Hugh, one of the other knights in Lord Rannulf's train, that she was nigh a lack-wit, scatterbrained to the point where Lady Gillian despaired of teaching her much of anything. She appeared cautious of men, so that none had managed to lure her into the slightest indiscretion— though not for want of trying, Hugh had added with a wry laugh. It had soon become apparent, though, that Lady Alys seemed lost in a world of her own, unaware of most everything and everyone around her.

Not worth the bother.

A day ago, he might have agreed—reluctantly, 'twas true, for he'd continued to be drawn to her.

Yet now… Now he could only wonder which woman was the real Lady Alys.

He bit back a laugh. He had no doubt which he'd rather she be!

Though in truth, it should matter naught to him whether she were a woman, a horse, a missive to be conveyed. So far as he was concerned, delivering her safely to her father's care should be a responsibility he must fulfill.

Nothing more.

Yet he'd never before felt anything stronger than a sense of duty toward *anyone* he'd been obligated to escort, to protect.

Nor should he now, he reminded himself sternly, no matter how sweet, how enticing the provocation.

Padrig waded to the side of the pool where he'd left his clothes and sword, relishing the sensation of the breeze on his damp skin. His body had finally begun to cool, now that Lady Alys was no longer there to tempt him, though the desire she'd stirred still simmered low in his belly and thrummed through his blood like the hot, dark embers buried deep within the heart of a banked fire.

He'd do well to ignore that craving until it disappeared, rather than let his continued exposure to the lady rouse it to fever pitch again. A man in his position couldn't afford to give in to his passions whenever he encountered a pretty maid.

He'd never had trouble keeping himself in check before, a fortunate thing, as all too often the women who caught his attention were as far beyond his reach as the moon.

The same could be said for Lady Alys. She was far enough above his station that any attention from him could be considered bold arrogance on his part, at the very least.

And if his suspicion about the reason her father wanted her back was true, he'd be an idiot, indeed, to allow himself the slightest interest.

He wasn't about to become a fool now. He tucked his shirt loosely into his braes, picked up his sword and dagger and headed for the path Lady Alys had taken through the trees. He'd yet to meet a woman who was worth more than a moment's thought anyway.

Why, then, had he already spent so much time thinking about her?

The camp was astir by the time he returned, some of his men busy loading and saddling the tethered horses, others gathered near the ashes of the previous night's fire to break their fast.

Of Lady Alys he saw no sign, though her maid lingered by a thicket on the far side of the clearing, her expression troubled, her hands waving about in agitation as she spoke to someone within the bushes.

Her mistress, no doubt.

He wondered what reason Alys had given for her state of soggy dishevelment. He glanced at his men. Had anyone realized that he and Lady Alys had been away from the camp at the same time, and that though they'd returned separately, they were both wet?

His own damp state was less apparent than hers had been, but it scarce took much imagination to consider…

His face grew hot, as it had not since his youth. Thankfully no one could guess what they'd been doing, nor would they realize his lapse in judgment as he'd taunted Lady Alys with his words….

With his nakedness.

Jesu, but he must have been mad, to have treated a noble lady thus!

Nor would anyone ever imagine—for he could scarce believe it himself—that Lady Alys had also done her innocent best to tease *him*.

He shook his head and forced away the nagging sense of guilt that plagued him. They'd done nothing amiss. 'Twas the knowledge he'd behaved badly plaguing him, nothing more.

Nay, no one would expect such behavior of Lady Alys—and he'd shown naught but the slightest, most general interest in her. They were more apt to believe she'd fallen into the pond on her own—for 'twas precisely what they'd expect of her, after all—and that he'd had to rescue her.

Padrig crossed to his baggage and drew out a dry shirt, turning away from the men nearby as his face grew hotter still, in anger this time. What must it be like, to have everyone assume the worst of you? To be treated as though you were nigh brainless?

His stomach knotted—not from hunger, but because he recalled all too clearly what it was like to be the focus of attention, to be watched, weighed and found wanting.

To be the cause of jeering and mockery.

For the most part it had been silent attention in his case, but he'd been aware of it all the same. His fear mounting as he waited for his body to betray him, to fold in upon himself for lack of breath, his strength flown with his last lungful of air.

How could he fight in battle, be a warrior, when he didn't know when next he'd be stricken?

He'd won his spurs despite the hurdles the ailment placed in his path, working hard to become physically powerful, to hone his skills till he could hold his own against all opponents. Through strength of body and of will, he had proven the naysayers wrong.

And been fortunate enough to outgrow the weakness—so he hoped. It had been several years since he'd last been set upon by the malady.

Pray God it never returned again.

Enough! Such thoughts belonged in the past, buried deep, nigh forgotten, where they couldn't slink forth to weaken him.

He'd dressed and armed himself while he'd been lost in thought. A glance up at the brightening sky told him 'twas past time they were on their way. He looked around the campsite, noting that his men had finished their preparations and appeared ready to leave.

Where was Lady Alys?

He crossed to where he'd last seen the maidservant. There wasn't so much as a path through the trees here, though the underbrush was bent where the women had trod upon it.

He'd no intention of going into the forest after them, however. He'd rather not even imagine Lady Alys's state of dress—or undress. He felt unsettled enough already from the morning's earlier events; no sense making matters worse.

A low murmur of voices sent a wave of relief through him, swiftly followed by impatience. He moved aside several leafy branches and moved into the trees—but not too far. "Milady!" he called. "'Tis past time we were on our way. Come along now—I doubt you want me to come in after you." He grimaced as soon as the words left his mouth, for the image that rose to his mind set his pulse pounding as wildly as it had during their encounter by the pool.

Jesu, but he was a fool!

Branches rustled, the sound moving closer, though he still couldn't see the women. "We'll be but a moment more," Lady Alys called. "Sir Padrig?"

"Aye."

She'd thought 'twas he. Taking a deep breath, Alys tucked the quill, tiny ink bottle and small piece of parchment she'd been clutching into the leather pouch she used to carry them and tied it to her belt at her hip. Giving the small bag a pat, she squared her shoulders and crept along the near-imperceptible path until she could just see Padrig's dark blue surcoat through the thick boughs. She could not continue to hide within the forest's comforting embrace any longer, she thought, wishing herself nigh anywhere else but here.

Nor hide within the confines of her mind's eye, either, she added silently as she settled the pouch more comfortably on her belt.

She peered through the bushes at Padrig, her coif askew, the neck of her gown still unlaced and her cheeks hot. Sweet Mary save her, had she truly seen this man naked? Been held within his strong arms, her flesh pressed against that muscular body?

Though she took several deep, calming breaths, her heart raced faster—with embarrassment or excitement, she could not tell. Whichever it was, she could not meet his gaze. "You need not wait for us here," she told him, forcing herself to step away from the thickest bushes and infusing her voice with a confidence she did not feel. "We're nearly ready."

"Are you?" He reached out with both hands and took hold of the loose laces dangling down the front of her gown. "I see your maid forgot these." Fixing her with a steady look, he gave a slight tug.

She glanced up, unwittingly captivated by the mischief glinting in his blue eyes, dragged in a shaky breath and took a step closer.

Had she gone mad? What was she doing? His presence alone drew her to him—her will to resist gone, her wits askew, her strength of mind faded away to a near-silent voice of protest sounding somewhere deep within her addled brain.

She stood motionless before him, scarce able to breathe as he slowly tightened the strings, his knuckles lightly skimming her ribs, then working their way up to delicately stroke the sensitive skin of her throat.

He knotted the laces of her bodice, his hands lingering a moment once he was through.

Were his hands shaking, or was it her own body trembling?

Step back, Alys, step back now.

Move away from him before you do something even more stupid.

Her legs refused to obey her mind's summons to move, but her hands…her hands rose despite her will, settling atop Padrig's.

His were strong, warm, hard—so intriguingly different from her own. Tightening her fingers, she drew in a deep breath, filling her lungs with the scent of him, and gave herself over to madness.

He leaned closer, his warmth surrounding her. His gaze moving over her face felt like a caress; watching *him*—the flush riding high along his cheekbones, the contrast between his bewhiskered face and the softness of his lips—heated her blood and made her heart pound so hard 'twas a wonder he could not hear it.

She raised one hand and set her fingertips questing, brushing over his mouth before settling along his jaw. If she edged a bit closer…

"Milady, where—" Marie burst from the trees behind her and banged into her, knocking her into Padrig; the armload of clothes the maid had been carrying flew everywhere.

He caught Alys before she could fall and reached out to steady Marie on her feet.

They stood there staring at each other for but a moment before the maid took hold of Alys's arm and nigh wrenched her free of Padrig's hold. "Release my mistress at once, you churl!" Marie snarled.

Chapter Three

Alys jerked her arm free of her maid's grasp and, grabbing the woman by the hand, dragged her back toward the bushes. "Marie! What are you about, to speak so to a knight?"

She turned her back to Padrig and tried to focus her attention on the maid instead. Her heart pounded and her body shook, a combination of Padrig's recent nearness and being startled nigh out of her skin by Marie. 'Twas all she could manage to keep her voice from quavering.

The maid's face went pale for a moment, then, glancing past Alys to Padrig, her expression firmed into a mask of determination. "A knight he may be, milady, but it gives him no right to be touching you." She shook her head and glanced from Padrig to her mistress. "Nor to be looking at you the way he does, either."

Whatever did Marie mean? How he looked at her…? Curiosity outweighing unease, Alys shifted so she could see Padrig, as well.

He met her gaze, his blue eyes steady, his expression impassive, but she could hardly fail to notice the faint tide of pink tingeing his neck and face. "I beg your pardon if I have offended you in any way, Lady Alys," he said, his tone formal. He bowed and stepped back, gesturing toward the clearing and his waiting men. "If you are ready now, we must be on our way."

Thankful he didn't seem to expect a response to his apology—she scarce knew what she would have replied—she smoothed her skirts and nodded. "Of course. We'll be but a moment more." She bent to pick up her belongings, scattered on the ground around them, motioning him away when he would have helped.

Her thoughts were jumbled enough as it was; she didn't need to add the image of Padrig handling her damp shift to the brew.

He hesitated but a moment before he nodded and strode off.

Despite her best intentions to ignore him, Alys clutched the clammy linen in her hands and watched him until he joined the others.

Padrig glanced up at the clouds thickening overhead, scudding fast across the darkening afternoon sky. He'd hoped to keep going until near nightfall, by which time they should have reached one of the villages along the way, but it appeared they'd need to find shelter sooner than that.

They'd been fortunate the past two days, for the sky had remained clear and the roads dry. Though they'd resumed their journey this morn far later than he'd planned—and the blame for that lay as much with him as with anyone—they'd made excellent time.

Lady Alys and her maid had kept up with his men,

an unexpected surprise, but one he was grateful for. Perhaps she was simply eager to reach her home—or to be rid of him, he thought wryly. Whatever the reason, he was pleased with their progress. The journey to return Lady Alys to her parents should take four more days, if they could continue on as they had thus far.

Not quite a punishing pace, but close, he thought guiltily. The faster he delivered Lady Alys to her father, the sooner he'd be away from the unexpected, intense distraction she presented.

Yet his frustration with himself—with his weakness—was no reason to drive the others into the ground. He'd need to keep a close watch to be certain he wasn't pushing too hard.

He'd dealt with distractions before, he reminded himself, and managed to do what he had to do.

Though he'd never before met a distraction quite like Lady Alys Delamare.

A powerful gust of wind buffeted him, pressing his clothes tight against his body and whipping his hair about his head. Muttering a curse, he shoved the unruly locks from his face and scanned the forest.

He could see no place to stop and take refuge from the weather here. The trees loomed close on both sides of the narrow road, the growth so thick it hemmed in the path with a nigh-impenetrable barrier. They had little choice but to stay on the road until it led them to a village, a clearing—any place where they could hole up until the storm passed.

Given the way the trees had begun to sway, he'd no desire to remain where they were. Once the downpour began in earnest, the wind and rain could very well uproot trees or send branches flying.

The air was heavy and damp, awash with a tension he could feel skittering over his skin. Even the horses seemed aware of it. His own destrier, bred for battle and chaos, took exception to a puny flock of birds bursting out of the bushes and nigh unseated him before he got the jumpy beast under control.

He peered back over his shoulder at the others. Moving apace, they were clustered together right behind him, their mounts appearing as unsettled as his own. "Come on—hurry," he shouted as he nudged his horse to a faster speed.

The sound of Padrig's voice startled Alys from an intensely pleasant daydream, one of many that had kept her mind's eye focused firmly inward as she'd ridden along in Padrig's wake.

Mostly focused inward, she admitted to herself. She could scarce blame herself for taking notice of Padrig on occasion, since he rode just in front of her.

Of course, she'd paid no attention at all to the rest of their party. Despite their proximity, they simply did not intrude upon her awareness.

Fortunately her patient mare, Arian, was used to bearing a distracted rider upon her back. 'Twas ever thus for Alys when she rode—her head would settle firmly into some tale or another, and she'd lose sight of all but the glorious world she carried hidden away within her imagination.

Her fingers itched to at least make note of the bits and pieces, the details swirling through her brain, to record them before they faded from her mind, but she *was* aware enough to realize now was neither the time nor place to do so.

She bit back a growl of frustration; it might be days

before she'd the privacy and the opportunity to write down all that she had spinning about in her mind.

How could she sort through the tumult of thoughts, the sheer chaos setting her mind akilter, otherwise? To be so close to attaining her heart's desire, and to find herself so easily tempted from her long-held dreams… She needed to concentrate, to refocus her attention where it needed to be.

Patience, she reminded herself. She ought to have developed a bottomless fount of that virtue by now, for she almost never had the chance to write when she wanted to…nay, when she *must.*

To use her tales to settle her mind.

'Twas a compulsion as strong as the need for food or sleep at times, a siren's call she could not ignore.

In the peace of the cloister she'd be free to—

The wind whipped round her, startling her from her musings, tearing loose her veil and sending her unbound hair whirling about. She caught the gauzy fabric before it flew away and slipped it off, finally clear-headed enough to pay heed to her surroundings.

Cool air nipped at her skin, a shocking change from the earlier warm damp.

When had it become so dark? Surely 'twas not nightfall already?

They were trotting along at a rapid pace, the gait jarring, too swift for the narrow, rutted track. She hadn't understood what Padrig had shouted earlier, but he must have been urging them on. Despite her distraction—or perhaps because of it—Arian had gone faster to keep pace with the others.

The wind gusted hard now, tearing loose leaves and small branches that battered at them, making it difficult to sit upright in the saddle. The sky grew ever darker, filled with a strange dusky half-light that sent an icy chill of foreboding down Alys's spine and dragged her firmly into the present.

The road widened. Padrig shouted again, his words muffled, barely audible in the howling storm. However, his intent was clear when he spurred his mount to even greater speed.

Everyone did the same, until they were all thundering along the track. Alys tightened her legs and hung on, wrapping one hand in her mare's mane and clinging to the reins with the other.

The rain began then, a cascading deluge that made it nigh impossible to see or hear. Water pooled on the hard-packed road in a matter of moments, concealing the uneven surface and forcing them to slow their headlong pace. 'Twas as though the clouds had opened wide overhead, a frigid, pounding torrent that drenched them to the skin at once.

They slowed, then halted; the horses, tense and uneasy, sidled about. Alys could hear the others, but though she knew they were close by, she could scarcely make out where they were in the murky gloom.

Arian twitched and sidestepped, demanding all her attention. The leather saddle was slick, and Alys's clothing a sodden, heavy weight to drag her out of it. She tightened her grip on the reins and murmured soothing nonsense to the poor mare, who shifted, soaking wet and quivering, beneath her. It did no good, however, for surrounded as they were by the squalling storm, 'twas doubtful the animal could hear her—or would have cared if she could.

Lightning blazed overhead, a volley of thunder rolling over them almost at once. Alys's mount squealed and reared up. Hooves sliding in the mud, the frightened beast flailed sideways. Alys caught a brief glimpse of Marie's pale, terrified face beside her as their two mounts crashed into each other.

Arian, panicked beyond any hope of restraint, began a maddened dance, bucking and slipping on the muddy track. Praying aloud, Alys fought for control, but 'twas all she could do to remain in the saddle.

Lightning split the sky again, so close the flash was blinding. The thunder was a force itself, a pummeling wave that shook the ground, and sent Alys lurching sideways to cling, shaking wildly, to the slick leather seat.

Her heart pounding hard in her chest, she tried to right herself. Muttering a curse, she dragged herself upright just as, with an ear-splitting crack, a massive tree fell toward her.

"Go!" Alys shouted to Arian, slapping the reins against the mare's neck and digging in her heels. Hooves scrambling for purchase, Arian gave a valiant leap forward, only to come crashing to the ground beneath the tree's weighty branches.

Bright pain shot through Alys's head, and she knew no more.

Chapter Four

Her limbs leaden, her vision a blur, Alys came to her senses, sprawled flat on her back beneath a veritable thicket of fallen trees and the icy lash of rain. She opened her mouth to call out, but gasped and choked as a torrent of water poured over her, carrying with it bits of bark and leaves that clung to her face and filled her mouth. Coughing, she tried to rise, but her strength was no match for the mass of branches and debris pinning her down.

Last she remembered she'd been in the saddle, riding hard as the storm raged around them...urging on Arian to avoid a falling tree....

She blinked her eyes to clear her vision, yet still she could see naught but a deep, shadowed darkness all around her.

Where was Arian?

And the others? They'd been riding close together, racing to outrun the storm's fury. How many trees had come down? It felt as though she were buried beneath a veritable forest!

By the sainted Virgin, what had happened?

Marie had been nearby, her own mount frightened, out of control. There might have been still others as close to them—she hadn't been able to see much of anything through the rain-filled gloom.

Pain washed over her, emanating from her back and shoulder and radiating outward, pulling her firmly into the present with a vengeance. It hurt to so much as breathe. She could tell she'd any number of scrapes from head to toe, for each one stung like fire beneath the force of the pelting rain. A dull throb from her ankle told her she'd at least one other injury.

Taking shallow breaths, she sought for calm and focused her senses. She tried to free her right arm; she could not make it move, though the attempt sent a surge of stomach-roiling pain washing over her. Swallowing back a gasp, she wriggled her other arm from beneath the branches and shifted it enough to push aside her sopping hair and wipe her eyes.

The deep, harsh rumble of thunder mixed with the sound of horses squealing in terror and voices sharp with alarm surrounded her. She could see little through the rain-filled darkness until a flash of lightning split the sky, giving her a moment's glimpse of chaos.

It seemed as if she was buried amidst a thicket of fir branches, the scent of pitch and needles sharp and nauseating. Had the entire forest come down around them, to create this dense jumble? She caught flashes of movement along the edge of the pile—men and horses both, it appeared—so clearly not everyone was ensnared within the tangled mass.

She heard whimpering and moans close by, and held her breath for a moment to listen. The whimpering ceased at once—had she been crying and hadn't known it?—but the moans continued, coming from somewhere near her, off to her right.

She wasn't the only one injured…or trapped, as well?

The realization brought her no comfort; instead it sent a wave of dread coursing through her, fear that Marie might be injured, that others might be hurt. Her heart beat faster, lending her the strength to try again to move—using her left arm this time, since her right would not obey her. Teeth gritted against the pain wrapping her from head to toe, Alys shifted, barely turned to her side within her prickly cocoon.

"Marie!" she called, her voice little more than a faint, uneven squeak. "Where are you?"

She drew in a deep breath, ignoring the pain as she sought to control the way her entire body shook, and reached out, trying to shove her arm through the tangle overhead. "Marie! Sir Padrig—" A flood of debris and water filled her mouth again. Sputtering, she turned her head and spat, then tried again. "Padrig…anyone…I'm here."

His sense of dread growing by the moment, Padrig concentrated on digging carefully through the huge tangle of trees that spilled across the road and into the forest. What he really wanted was to tear at the mound with his bare hands, to rip it all away until he found everyone and knew they were safe.

Lady Alys was missing, as were her maid and three of his men. They had to be trapped somewhere within this morass, though he hadn't any notion precisely where to start looking.

The situation appeared grim. The horses of those

missing were gone as well, save for Lady Alys's mount.
Her mare had evidently bolted free; unfortunately in the
confusion no one had noticed where she'd been before
the trees collapsed. She now stood, shivering and lame,
away from the mess with the rest of their horses and the
pack animals.

No help there.

Though twelve of them had set out from l'Eau Clair,
their company was badly depleted. Besides those unac-
counted for, only four of their remaining number had escaped serious harm, including himself. One of his men
was dead, man and mount both crushed beneath the
trunk of a massive tree. Two others were badly hurt,
though it was difficult in these circumstances to determine just how severe their injuries were.

It had taken but a few moments after the falling trees
had settled before those of his men who could move had
regrouped in the road ahead of the collapse. They'd escaped misfortune only because they'd been at the front
of the column and had already passed over that stretch
of road.

When they'd made their way around the tangle
blocking the road, they'd found the injured men and the
pack animals on the other side. After hastily treating
their hurts and settling them as best they could out of
the rain and away from danger, they went to look for the
others.

It was nigh impossible to see much of anything in the
fitful light and pouring rain. He'd called out for the missing at once; they all had as they'd frantically begun to
search, till he realized they'd never hear a response over
their own shouts and he'd called for silence. But only the
unremitting rumble and crack of thunder, accompanied

by the sporadic, ear-splitting sounds of more trees crashing down close by, disturbed the relative silence.

Lightning continued to flash—over them, around them, everywhere, it seemed—the erratic light a fitting accompaniment to the hellish chaos surrounding them. Though daunting, nonetheless it *was* their sole source of illumination. A mixed blessing, for as long as the storm continued, they—and those yet to be found— were also at greater risk of further injury.

Between the accident, the constant barrage of thunder and lightning and the driving rain, the horses were cold, soaked, their nerves on edge.

He and his men were in little better state.

"Sir Padrig—over here," Rafe, his second in command, shouted from the opposite side of the jumbled trees. "Hurry!"

Padrig dragged aside the cumbersome branch he'd disentangled from the pile and hastened to his side. Rafe lay draped over a massive tree trunk, his body half-buried within its thick boughs.

"Have you found them?" Padrig asked as he reached him. "Who? How many?"

"Quick, sir—grab my feet," Rafe gasped. Padrig caught hold of him just as he began to slip away and, bracing himself, held the other man steady. "I've got a cloak in hand," he added. "I think I've found one of the women—'tis too fine a cloth to be one o' ours."

Jock and Peter, the other two men, had arrived hard on Padrig's heels; they immediately set to work shifting away the maze of branches surrounding the tree Rafe lay draped over while Padrig kept hold of him. Once the worst of the debris was cleared away, Padrig maintained his grip on Rafe even as he climbed up onto the fallen tree, as well.

"Lady Alys?" he called, leaning over to peer down into the stygian darkness. He shifted to pin Rafe's feet in place with his body and one arm. Reaching down into the gap in front of Rafe, he skimmed his free hand through the space and came up empty. "Damnation!" Abandoning that fruitless act, he moved back a bit and caught Rafe by the ankles again. "Marie?"

The only sound coming out of the opening was Rafe's raspy breathing. Coughing, Rafe squirmed lower on the tree, cursing as his boots slipped from his feet and he slithered downward.

Cursing as well, Padrig flung the empty boots aside and grabbed the back of Rafe's tunic with both hands. Bracing his legs against the rough trunk, he gave a mighty heave and hauled Rafe upright, barely keeping them both from falling headfirst into the void.

"I can't believe I lost her!" Rafe flopped onto his back and lay gasping in the downpour. Spitting out a mouthful of water and bark, he sat up. "By Christ's toenails, everything's so slippery you'd think 'twas ice fallin', not rain." He picked up one of his boots, shook it out and rammed it onto his foot, jerking the lacings taut before knotting them. "I held on tight as I could manage," he said, disgust tingeing his voice, "but I could scarce get a hold o' her to begin with." He tugged on his other boot and tied it. "Let me have a moment to catch my breath, Sir Padrig, and I'll give it another try."

"At least you found her," Padrig reassured him. "'Tis a start."

He sprawled next to Rafe, mind awhirl. While he was heartened by Rafe's determination, he couldn't help but wonder what they'd discover once they rescued the woman who lay buried here. The fact that she'd made no sound at all when Rafe attempted to lift her out was not a good sign.

Should he assume she was dead, and go back to looking for the others?

He straightened, horrified. *There* was a thought to make his heart stop, whichever woman was the victim.

Jesu, if it were Alys...

Gone in an instant, her lovely smile and unexpected wit snuffed out—

He refused to consider such a notion, lest the hideous thought become reality.

He'd not abandon her—nay, anyone—to such a fate.

Despite his efforts to calm himself, his hand trembled a bit when he raised it and swiped it over his face. What if someone else came to further harm while they struggled to search here?

He could set Peter and Jock to work elsewhere while he and Rafe looked in a different place.

Yet what if the woman trapped beneath them was not dead, but instead was unconscious, or injured too badly to speak?

They could not ignore her; rather they must get her out as soon as possible and treat her injuries.

He shook his head and focused his racing thoughts. Jesu, mayhap they should wait till morning to search further, when presumably the storm would have passed, the sky would brighten and they could see what in God's name they were doing!

He dismissed the notion as soon as it formed. They could not wait so long. Glancing up at the storm-filled sky, he judged it was barely dusk now. Though it felt as if it had been an eternity, and it was nigh impossible to gauge from their surroundings, in truth he doubted much time had passed since the storm's wrath split their world asunder. In any case, 'twas too cold and wet to leave anyone exposed to the weather for a moment longer than necessary.

They needed to get the injured men they'd left huddled beside the trail to shelter, as well.

He shifted and peered down into the gaping opening. At least they knew there *was* someone here, though they could not see who it was. 'Twould be best to deal with what they knew, before venturing off into the darkness again.

He bit back his frustration and breathed deep as though he were readying himself for battle. The urge to jump up and escape into the night was nigh overwhelming. 'Twas as likely he'd find answers there, lost among the destruction, as he would by muddling along here.

He scarce gave the traitorous thought life before he forced it from his mind. 'Twas only that it had been so long since he'd felt so helpless, adrift in a sea of uncertainty—and the weight of command sat heavy upon him, foreign, unfamiliar.

Thank the Lord, the cold and wet hadn't affected his breathing. Given their ill luck to this point, he'd expect no less. However, he couldn't help adding a prayer of gratitude for that favor to the heartfelt pleas for God's mercy that he'd already sent heavenward.

He'd rather have an enemy to fight, by God, someone he could face over a shield, battle with a sword, a demon he could slay and be done with it.

Biting back a mocking laugh, he shoved his dripping hair back from his face and sighed.

He ought to know by now that nothing was *ever* that simple.

Calmer now, he considered how best to conquer this obstacle. Rafe had caught hold of her, but it seemed he was too small to keep a grip on her. Padrig swung around on the tree and began to tug at his sopping boots, working them off and tossing them aside before unbuckling his belt and knotting the leather tight about his waist.

"What're you doing?" Rafe asked.

"I'm taller than you are," Padrig told him. "If you or Jock grab my belt and hang on to me, mayhap I can get a good grip on her and haul her up. I doubt I can pull her straight up through the debris without her getting entangled worse, so whichever of you isn't holding on to me had better crawl up here and do what he can to help ease her out." He hefted himself back up onto the tree. "Meanwhile, Peter, you go and see if you can find any sign of the others."

"Aye, milord," Peter said before disappearing into the gloom.

Rafe and Jock had no sooner situated themselves behind Padrig and begun to ease him down into the gap when shouting cut through the rumble of thunder.

Padrig barely caught himself from tumbling into the morass when Jock and Rafe loosened their hold on him and turned to answer Peter's frantic cries.

Padrig hauled himself up and sprawled over the rough bark as Peter came into view.

"Milord, come quick!" Peter stumbled to a stop before them. "'Tis Lady Alys, milord—I've found her, and she's alive!"

Chapter Five

A man shouting close by startled Alys, setting her heart thundering faster in her chest and making her limbs tremble even harder than they had already—despite all her efforts to bring such cowardly behavior to an end.

She knew 'twas not cold alone that made her shake so badly. Fear was as much her enemy as the cold, should she give in to it.

"I'm here," she cried, her voice sounding faint even to her own ears. Disgusted by her weakness, she gathered herself to try once more. "Hello, I'm here! Please don't leave!"

Thunder boomed again, rendering the reply indistinct, but the muffled thud of running feet and the muted sound of additional voices soon after the din faded away gave her hope that rescue was at hand.

As she'd lain there, numb with both pain and cold, her right arm useless, it had taken nigh all her resolve to stay alert and keep calling for help...to force her body, protesting all the while, to shift as much as she could within the tightly interlaced shroud of branches enveloping her on the faint chance she might wriggle her way closer to freedom.

'Twas only by reminding herself of the valiant people whose tales she'd worked so hard to chronicle during her years at l'Eau Clair that she found the fortitude to continue fighting against the sapping lethargy that threatened to overwhelm her. Whether brought on by the icy rain, her injuries, or a combination of both, she didn't know, for her knowledge of healing ways was sparse. But whatever the cause, she *did* know 'twas dangerous in these conditions to fall asleep.

Better to allow her anger free rein, to let it work to help her. How it galled her to lie here nigh helpless, waiting to be saved!

The voices grew louder, though she could scarce make out what they said. "—be back in a trice," she heard, followed by what sounded to her straining ears like retreating footsteps.

"Nay, don't leave!" she cried. "Please—please, come back."

No answer met her plea; she could hear naught but the storm.

She must be patient, she reminded herself, disgusted by the feelings of panic she could not completely suppress. For all she knew, many others could be trapped as well, in circumstances far more dreadful than her own. There were people out there searching; they'd not leave her here any longer than they must.

She *could* endure this! Think of Lady Catrin, she told herself, wounded by bandits, with none but Lord Nicholas to help her. Remember Lady Gillian, abducted by an evil kinsman and spirited away from Lord Rannulf, from her home and all she held dear…. Did these intrepid women give up? Nay—they remained strong, did whatever necessary to help themselves.

At the least, she could wait patiently for however long she must.

And in the meantime, she'd try again to work her way out. She'd one useful arm, hadn't she? What more could she need than that?

Despite her resolve, however, tears streamed down her face, startling her with their warmth. 'Twas such a contrast to the utter cold suffusing her from head to toe that it made her shudder more violently. Sweet Mary, how the slightest movement hurt…but she refused to give in to the pain. She'd withstood it till now, she could not let it overwhelm her.

Seeking distraction, she concentrated instead on her surroundings as she carefully worked her arm about in the narrow space enclosing her. 'Twas impossible to move anything much out of the way, but by dint of gritting her teeth against the pain and pressing her arm against the dense jumble of branches, she was able to increase the space around her.

'Twas still not much room, barely enough to shift so that her head rested higher than her feet and she could almost pull herself into a half-sitting position. Nonetheless, the simple fact that she'd made this much progress inspired her to keep at it in spite of the pain.

Alys had no idea how much time had passed, but it appeared the storm had finally begun to fade, the rumbles of thunder more distant and farther apart, the rain lessened from a pounding torrent to a soft, pattering shower.

Other sounds rose to replace the storm's fury. Boughs

creaked and snapped as they were moved about, debris crunched beneath booted feet. Voices wove through the sounds; though she could not clearly understand the words, the mere sound of them—the sense of resolve they conveyed—lent her strength, gave her faith that this ordeal would soon be over.

Lightning flashed yet again, however, followed almost at once by the deep boom of thunder and a series of sharp cracks as wood splintered. She stopped moving and held her breath for a moment to listen as the sounds faded away, lips moving rapidly in a near-silent prayer. Thankfully she heard no panicked cries of pain, nor the crash of more trees coming down close by.

The rumbling had barely ended, however, before she realized the lightning had filled her timbered prison with a brief, eerie glow so bright she was able to briefly distinguish individual branches piled overhead.

Anticipation flared higher—there had to be less debris piled atop her than before, if she could see so well!

Who would she find there, she wondered, once the rubble had been cleared away and she'd been pulled from the pile? Were there others trapped as well, or injured?

Was Marie all right? Though she could not distinguish individual voices, what she could hear sounded nothing like a woman's higher tone.

Which could mean nothing more than that the men had already settled the maid someplace safe.

And what of Padrig? He'd been riding at the head of the column…had he been the first to fall?

Abruptly on the verge of panic, Alys caught her breath, disgusted by her weakness. What was wrong with her? By the Virgin, had she grown maudlin from lying here so long?

No more! Calling herself a fool, she closed her eyes for a moment and prayed that *all* their party had escaped the storm's wrath unharmed...that she'd find within herself the will to do whatever she must.

Calmer now, her strength of will restored, she opened her eyes, clenched her teeth against the renewed pain and resumed her task. Though she tugged and pulled with all her might, one-handed, in so little space, she could make little additional headway into the thickly packed tangle of limbs along her side. Nigh growling with frustration, she shifted to lie flat on her back and thrust her left hand up into the thick mass overhead.

All of a sudden the entire mound above her shifted and disappeared, sending a torrent of cold water and debris spilling over her. Temporarily blinded, she gasped and coughed as she sought to catch her breath and clear her vision.

When a warm hand captured her own, she couldn't help but shriek.

"Alys? Milady, is it you?" Padrig asked, his tone urgent as he shifted aside more branches with his free hand. He kept hold of her, the feel of his fingers clasped tight around hers as comforting as an embrace. "Jesu, are you all right?"

She'd inhaled so much water—especially when she'd screeched—'twas a wonder she hadn't drowned, but it mattered not a whit. "I am now," she said, still gasping a bit, her voice little more than a croak.

Grinning like a fool, realizing she'd no doubt sounded like one for shrieking when he'd touched her hand, Alys tilted her face into the clear cascade of rain and let it wash away the bark and needles clinging to her skin. She turned her hand within Padrig's until they touched palm to palm, their fingers intertwined. "Thank you for finding me," she murmured, tightening her grasp.

He shifted to sit on the edge of the mound and leaned closer, his face scarcely visible in the faint light. What she saw there, however, pushed aside her joy at being found, replacing it with the fear that had haunted her captivity.

"What of the others, Sir Padrig?" she asked. "Where is Marie?"

In her urgency she tried to sit up, the movement wresting a cry of pain from her before she could suppress it. "Have a care, milady," he cautioned. He wrapped his arm about her; with his assistance, she pulled herself up so they were face to face.

Sir Padrig somehow maintained his hold on her as he eased himself over a sturdy tree trunk and down into the hole with her. Tears of joy pooled in her eyes; she blinked hard till they were gone, for she did not wish to appear weak before him.

She'd far rather keep such vulnerability locked away, lest he think her naught but a pathetic fool.

"Don't worry about the others, milady," he said, his manner calm and reassuring, his face kind.

Yet there was a fleeting look in his eyes...

This close, even in such poor light, she could tell there was something he sought to hide—but 'twas there, then gone, in an instant.

"You'll see the others soon enough once we get you out of here," he told her. "Meanwhile, let me see how *you've* fared in this disaster." His gaze had shifted away from hers as soon as he began to speak.

Increasing her misgivings. Something was obviously amiss.

Since he hadn't given her a direct response, he'd simply have to hear her question once more—and yet again, if necessary, until he answered her.

Her stomach in a knot, she tightened her grip on his hand until he looked at her. Once she was certain she had his attention, she asked, "What of Marie?" She infused her voice with Lady Gillian's quiet tone of command and hoped 'twould be effective. "Have you found her? Is she alive?"

Chapter Six

"What of Marie?" she'd asked again.

Lord save him from a tenacious woman! By Christ's bones, why must she ask such questions now, when 'twas *her* safety paramount in his mind?

"She is alive," he told her, his tone abrupt.

"God be praised," she murmured. "Thank you, Sir Padrig."

Guilt weighed upon him at her words, at the relief so evident in her expression, but he brushed the useless emotion aside. "Now, milady, will you please let me take care of you?"

There was scant room for him in the niche Lady Alys had created around her, evidently by her actions as she'd attempted to dig her way out. That she'd done so much under such horrendous conditions was impressive; that she'd not been able to do more—given that she appeared to him to be extremely determined, made him worry about the extent of her injuries.

He supported her weight with one arm as he wriggled into the narrow space alongside her. "Rafe," he called over his shoulder, "Lady Alys's cloak is sopping. See if you can find a blanket or something to wrap her in. If there's anything that's not dripping wet, it would be an improvement. And bring some wine or ale, if there's any to be had."

She rested her head on his arm and sighed. "'Twould be such a pleasure to be warm again."

The way she felt next to him made Padrig's heart trip and his chest tighten, the sensation completely different from the way he felt when his breathing bothered him. She leaned against him so easily, as if it were the natural thing to do—as if she trusted him to make all right.

By the rood, there was a formidable—nay, a truly alarming—notion!

Taking a deep, calming breath, he shoved that idea far back into the recesses of his brain where he'd not be aware of it. Instead Padrig forced himself to focus upon their surroundings.

The pit Alys lay in was deep; the top would likely reach to mid-chest were he to stand up. She must have been terrified, held captive within its dark, wet confines for so long.

Any guilt he felt over the extension of that time because of the decisions he'd made, he must wait until later to indulge.

If she'd been frightened, or still was, she scarce showed it now. Her voice, while weak and scratchy— no doubt from calling for help—otherwise seemed steady and sure. Her expression, what little he could see of it in the meager light, held joy at being found.

Joy mixed with what was obviously pain, he noted with a swift glance at her strained appearance once he'd settled down into the confined space alongside her.

Careful not to jostle her, he slipped his arm from behind her, watching her closely. Her entire body tensed and she began to list away from him before he caught her and gathered her close again.

Sucking in a sharp breath, she buried her face against his shoulder. She held on to his hand all the while, her grip fierce, as if she drew something—strength, or comfort, perhaps?—from the contact.

His touch as gentle as he could make it, he slipped his hand free and held her upright within the cradle of his arms, shifting them both into a more stable position. With a bit of maneuvering he sat and stretched his legs out before him, leaning back against the same tree he'd slipped over to join her, and drew her down to rest against his chest. "Where are you hurt, milady?"

She pressed her cheek so hard into his linen surcoat, 'twas likely she'd carry the impression of not only the coarse fabric, but also of the mail hauberk beneath it, crushed into her flesh. Stirring slightly, she mumbled something unintelligible into his neck, her breath cold against his own none-too-warm skin.

He drew together the sodden strands of hair plastered to her face and swept them aside, resisting—barely— the urge to bury his fingers within the lavender-scented mass. Instead he cupped his palm about her cheek and tilted her head slightly, so he could see her when she spoke. His gazed fixed upon her, he bent close and asked again, "Lady, where are you hurt?"

Even in the dim light, he could see how she gathered herself, composing her features into a semblance of calm, swallowing and clearing her throat before she replied. "I'm not certain—though I hurt everywhere, or so it seems," she murmured, her mouth curving into a faint smile, her voice stronger than it had been when he first found her.

"I'm not surprised," he told her. "You were buried beneath enough wood to build a fortress. Did you hit your head? Are your limbs sound? What of—"

She placed her fingers over his mouth to silence him. "I believe I'll have to get out of here and try to stand up before I can give you a full accounting of all my aches and injuries."

"We'll get you out soon," he assured her.

"Why don't we try now?" she asked. "With your help, I'm sure I could climb out."

"You couldn't even sit up straight but a few moments ago—what makes you believe you can stand?" he demanded, shaking his head at her foolhardiness. "Besides, I've got no place to put you once you're out—not yet, at any rate. We'll see what Rafe has to report before we do anything more."

"Do you think I can get any wetter? More rain is hardly like to harm me at this point, Sir Padrig," she told him, her voice tart. "I'm no delicate flower to be battered by wind and rain—"

Footsteps crunched nearby, interrupting her tirade—for which Padrig was grateful. Where was the quiet young woman he'd been told had scarce two thoughts to rub together?

Not that he'd actually believed she was like that, but still—

"Here you are, sir." Rafe leaned over the edge of the hole and handed Padrig a bundle of cloth wrapped in oilskin. "I couldn't find any wine or ale, milady, but this here will warm ye straight to your toes," he assured Alys as he held out a wooden flask.

Moving carefully, she took it, gifting Rafe with a slight smile and a nod. "Thank you, Rafe," she murmured. "Whatever it is, it will be most welcome. Though I'm wetter than a fish, I'm very thirsty." Despite her brave front, Padrig noticed her arm shook as she lowered the flask to her lap.

"There's plenty there, milady—the flask is full—so have as much of it as you like. And don't let Sir Padrig take it all, either," Rafe warned, chuckling. "He's been known to be a trifle stingy when it comes to the sharing o' drink."

"Indeed." Alys's body quaked with laughter and she craned her head around, her eyes questioning.

"I'll try to restrain myself for your sake, milady," Padrig assured her with mock seriousness. "Never let it be said I did not treat a lady with every consideration—the best tidbits at table, the most comfortable seat, first chance at a goblet of wine or mead—"

"Ah, but who gets the last sip?" Rafe asked, eyebrows arching to emphasize his point.

"The lady, of course," Padrig said, laughing. "'Tis one of our knightly responsibilities. 'A noble lady shall have the best of everything, first to last,'" he quoted in a portentous voice, his gaze on Lady Alys to judge her reaction to their banter. Amusement brightened her expression, faded the shadows in her eyes. "Is that not the way of it?" he asked Rafe.

"Aye, Sir Padrig, it is. He has manners better than many a fine lordship—some o' us call him 'milord,' milady, right to his face. He doesn't seem to mind it. So you needn't worry too much about this rogue's ways, milady—at least for the nonce." Rafe grinned, his teeth showing bright amidst his dark whiskers in a sudden flash of lightning. Once the thunder faded he told her, "You'll not have to put up with him for much longer. We're readying a place for you to rest out o' the weather. We'll be finished with it in a trice. In the meantime, you've naught to do but settle yourself here and trust Sir Padrig to make you more comfortable." Nodding, he clambered out of the hole and disappeared into the shadows once again.

Chuckling, Padrig called out his thanks, then turned his full attention to Lady Alys once more. After peeling off her sodden cloak and tossing it out of the way, he spread the blanket over her, then covered as much of the blanket as he could with the oilskin. Tucking it all around her, he gathered her close against him.

Though he might be near as wet as she, at least his body still threw off some heat. Hers, on the other hand, radiated an icy cold everywhere they touched.

He uncorked the flask and sniffed the fumes rising from it before sampling the powerful liquor. 'Twas strong enough to peel the hide from an ox! With any luck 'twould do her some good, however, for it had most definitely sent a wave of fire flowing in its wake.

As long as she didn't choke on it.

Raising her head a bit, he held the drink to her lips. "Careful now," he cautioned. "I'm not precisely certain what this is, but I assure you it's far more potent than any wine."

She took a small sip, gasping and coughing for a moment. "Aye, 'tis not wine," she told him once she'd caught her breath again. "I've had such drink before. 'Tis a favorite of my father's. The Scots make it." She closed her left hand over his, brought the bottle to her mouth and drank again, then, surprising him, swallowed

still more. She took a deep breath and let it out on a hic-
cup and a sigh. "Sweet Mary save me, but in truth 'tis
the devil's own brew!"

"Then I pray 'twill lend you some of its fire to warm
you, milady."

Letting her hand drop into her lap, Lady Alys closed
her eyes and slumped into Padrig as her tension eased.
He took one last sip of the liquor and corked the flask,
balancing it by his side should Lady Alys have further
need of it.

She lay curled against him as though she would crawl
inside his very being to seek his warmth. "I told you before that I don't know the extent of my hurts." Her voice
slurred a bit, as if she hovered on the cusp of sleep. "I
do know, though, there's something wrong with my
right arm." She raised her head slightly from his shoulder and met his gaze, her eyes huge in her pale face. "It
will not work at all—and it hurt terribly when I did try
to move it."

"Indeed." Mind awhirl, Padrig did his best to maintain an impassive mien and to keep his body from revealing his dismay.

Damnation! He had a very good idea what the trouble with Alys's arm might be. If he was correct, 'twas
something he could make right, but the process would
likely be very painful for both of them.

For her especially, for he knew from personal experience the gut-wrenching agony caused by settling a
dislocated shoulder back into its proper position.

The thought of causing Alys such pain, of using his
strength against her, of manhandling her delicate body,
made his stomach twist.

"We'll look at your arm, and your other hurts as well,

once we get you out of here. Rafe will be back soon,"
he assured her. "We'll move you to shelter, get you dry
and warm." He nestled her more firmly under his chin
and pressed his face into her hair, the scent of her filling
his senses once again. "Do you feel any warmer yet?"

"Aye," she told him, though she sounded as though
she held her teeth clenched tight together as she spoke,
making him doubt she told the truth.

Still, what more could he do but hold her, try to protect her, keep her safe until his men had made some sort
of shelter?

Aye, Padrig, a mocking voice within him chided, *'tis
a terrible burden, is it not, to hold such a lissome creature so snug within your embrace?*

To his surprise, 'twas tenderness he felt flowing
through him, not lust. To hold a woman so close with
no other intent than to provide comfort and care was to
him a foreign emotion, no question of that.

Yet there was a rightness to the feel of Lady Alys in
his arms…a sensation as right and true as the feel of his
sword held firm in his hand.

By the saints, the day's misfortunes had turned him
into a maudlin fool! In truth, he felt no more than any
decent man might—his knightly duty to care for those
weaker than himself.

'Twas naught more than that.

He closed his eyes for a moment before forcing himself to ease his grip on Lady Alys.

Absolutely nothing more.

His thoughts now firmly under control, Padrig gathered Lady Alys a little nearer, brushing his palm over
her forehead, then cupping her cheek. Her skin still felt
cold, although she'd a tinge of pink riding high on her

cheekbones. Mayhap the color was a result of the liquor she'd drunk, rather than any returning warmth—though the faint brush of her breath against his fingers seemed less chill than before.

Still, 'twas such a slight improvement. Further concern edged its way into his already uneasy thoughts. Despite his efforts to warm her, Lady Alys continued to shudder and shake within his hold.

Jesu, she must be frozen to the very marrow of her bones!

He needed to get her out of this pit now, but he dared not move her alone. Any movement that jolted Lady Alys's arm or shoulder would be excruciating.

But he dared not keep her here any longer, either. In addition to her injuries directly attributable to the storm's fury, she could have developed an inflammation of the lungs, or some sort of fever.

By the rood, for all he knew Lady Alys might have injured her head as well; she had not asked about her maid since they'd first uncovered her. Though he might not know her well, he knew well enough she'd never have forgotten about Marie.

He glanced down at her face. She appeared to be asleep, her features slack from exhaustion…and mayhap a bit from the strong drink, too. Whatever the reason, he'd not find a better time to get her out of this hole. "Alys," he murmured, brushing his fingers over her cheek. "Milady?"

She nestled deeper into his embrace, the innocent movement filling his unruly body with an unexpectedly intense heat. Aye, 'twas time—past time—to get them both out of this morass.

He loosened his hold on Lady Alys and repositioned

her to sit upright across his lap, her weight slumped against his arm instead of draped over his body. Shifting, he pulled himself up with his free hand so he could peer out over the rim of the hole.

The rain had slackened noticeably in the brief time since he'd climbed in here with her. Unfortunately, the sky had not cleared much. Scattered moonlight broke through the scudding clouds, the fitful light providing scant illumination—and now the storm had died down—there had been very little lightning in the area to lend its questionable assistance, either.

A dubious blessing; they need not worry so much about being struck down by a bolt from above any longer… yet the price of such security was to be struck nigh blind instead.

'Twas ever his share of fortune, he thought with a wry chuckle—to be blessed on the one hand, and cursed on the other.

But mayhap their luck was about to improve. They ought to be able to kindle torches now. Lord knew they could use them! He couldn't see much as he gazed out over the expanse of destruction, only vague, shadowy movements shifting about off in the distance.

He'd absolutely no notion who or what he saw—there was as much chance 'twas their horses he was watching as it was his men.

He took a deep breath and tamped down his frustration; this night seemed endless, maddening, a test of his leadership he feared he'd fail.

He'd not let things come to such a pass, he vowed silently.

The sun had to rise sometime soon—but he'd not wait for it. 'Twas time—past time—to get things moving.

To get Lady Alys out of here, to make certain she and the other injured were out of the storm and tended to.

Now.

Chapter Seven

"Rafe," Padrig muttered, grown impatient with waiting. "Damnation, where are you?"

"Right here, sir," came the reply from just the other side of the pit.

Clutching Alys to his chest with one arm, his free hand grasped firm about his knife hilt, Padrig leapt into a half-crouch.

"Christ on the cross, man, but you gave me a start," he said. Exhaling sharply, he let his dagger drop to his feet and lowered himself to sit again. His heart still thumping hard, he eased Lady Alys's limp form down to rest against his chest and drew the blanket higher about her throat. She settled into his lap as if she'd done so many times before. Softening his voice, he added, "I didn't even hear you draw near."

"I tried to stay quiet, sir, so as not to disturb the lady if she'd settled into sleep." Rafe climbed up onto the mound, perched on the edge and gazed down at her.

"I don't know that much of anything will disturb her at the moment." Padrig shifted her body a bit, so she rested in a more comfortable position. "She didn't so much as twitch when I jumped up."

"Poor wee lamb," Rafe said quietly, shaking his head. "Just look at her, all bruised and battered—and no doubt hurt in other ways as well, like the others." He reached into the leather bag hanging from his belt and drew forth a small cloth-wrapped bundle. Unfolding the material, he revealed a candle stub, tinder, flint and steel, the lot of which he held carefully cupped within his hands. "'Tis a miracle she was able to stay awake and call for help, without a doubt."

"'Twill be a miracle, indeed, if you can manage to start a flame under these conditions." Padrig watched as Rafe leaned forward from the waist, using his upper body to shield the tinder from the drizzle. "But a welcome one, nonetheless. Here, let me help." He wiped his hands on the blanket edge and picked up the oilskin, raising it to form a makeshift canopy over Rafe's hands.

Rafe struck the flint and steel a number of times before he ignited the tinder, then the candle wick.

"Well done," Padrig murmured as the wick burned with a steady light. "Could it be that our fortunes are finally about to improve?"

"We can but hope, milord," Rafe replied.

The faint flame glowed bright as the sun after so long in the dark. The light was a blessing, for the longer Lady Alys remained asleep, the more concerned Padrig grew about her condition. At least now he could get a better look at her.

She had remained limp in his hold when he'd jumped up, sat back down—even now she hadn't so much as stirred or in any way seemed to take notice of either their conversation or the candlelight.

"Let's hope she's hardier than she appears." Padrig smoothed his hand over her disheveled hair and let it rest for a moment on her cheek. Was her skin warmer, or did hope alone make it seem so? "I assume you've a place ready for her?"

"That we have, milord." Rafe pointed to the east, where the devastation had been the worst. "Just along the edge o' the new clearing. Figured since all the trees've already come down, it should be as safe a spot as we're like to find."

Padrig nodded his approval. "Good work! See if you can find a safe place for the candle and lend me a hand raising her out of here, would you? We might as well get her to the shelter while she's sleeping so soundly. We'll not get a better chance."

Rafe stashed the candle beneath an arching branch and climbed down to help Padrig.

Careful to jar her as little as possible, Padrig slid out from beneath her. "I pray she stays asleep. If we're lucky, she won't even notice we're moving her. I don't believe there's any way to get her up over the edge without hurting her." He settled her right arm gently across her stomach. "From what she told me, I'm afraid her shoulder is out of the socket."

Rafe winced, and looked unconvinced. "I don't know about that, milord. She'd have to be more than asleep to bear the pain—she'd have to be flat out insensible!"

"You'll need to be very careful then," Lady Alys warned them, startling them both when she slowly eased out of Rafe's hold and sat back against the side of the pit. "For I'm wide awake now and in full command of my senses, more's the pity. And thanks to your lovely candle, Rafe, I'll see whatever you do."

* * *

"I take it you couldn't get her to drink all o' the whiskey?" Rafe muttered to Padrig. "She must have a head hard as an ox! By my reckoning there ought to have been more than enough liquor in that flask for such a dainty lass to drink herself into a stupor," he said, his amazed expression so comical, Alys couldn't help but chuckle. "Aye, one so deep 'twould last for days!"

Even the minor act of laughing sent spiky shards of pain lancing through her. Slightly breathless, she told them, "This 'dainty lass' knows better than to take more than a few swallows of that devil's brew. Even if I could buy myself a brief period of oblivion from the pain I feel now, it still wouldn't be worth the agony I'd go through later."

"Milady, I doubt there's any way we're going to get you out of here without hurting you," Rafe warned. He picked up the flask, opened it and held it out to her. "Please—have some more. As much as you like! You might as well go ahead and—"

Ignoring the flask—no easy feat when the smell wafted all around them—Alys cut him off with a shake of her head. "Nay," she said firmly, the mere idea of swilling that much liquor making her stomach clench. "I said I'll not have any more, and I meant it."

"But milady—just this once—" Rafe met her gaze and evidently saw she would not back down. Sighing, he lowered the flask. "'Twould truly be for the best if you'd go ahead and drink." Meeting her scowl with one of his own, he held the whiskey out to her once again.

"Enough, Rafe." To Alys's surprise, Sir Padrig reached out and took the whiskey and cork from Rafe, stoppered the flask and set it down out of the other man's reach—but within hers. "If she says she'd rather not, we cannot force her." He met her gaze, his own steady, reassuring. "She's no child, to be cajoled into going against her own wishes."

"I got quite thoroughly drunk on my father's whiskey just once," she said, hoping if she explained, Rafe would accept that she'd valid reasoning behind her decision. "I was such an idiot once I drank it, and the aftereffects were so bad, I vowed then never to subject myself to such an embarrassing experience again. As a general rule, 'tis easy enough to avoid it."

Rafe's single-minded determination that she avail herself of the whiskey to dull her pain, however, did make her wonder. Precisely *why* did he think she'd need it? She hurt now, 'twas true, but 'twas not so bad as to be unbearable.

Did they think something was so wrong with her that she couldn't bear to deal with it? By sweet Mary's grace, what were they trying to protect her from?

Mayhap, she pondered with a frown, they thought her a weak, cowardly woman, unable to bear the slightest pain or misfortune.

She bit back a wry laugh at the idea. Men! If they'd ever any idea how strong women really were, they'd no doubt be terrified.

She should simply ask them what they were so concerned about....

Or was she better off not knowing?

Whatever they had in mind, she *had* heard them say they were moving her out of this pit. At the moment, getting out of this vile place was all she cared about...and was as far into the future as she would allow herself to think.

She didn't know how much longer she could continue to sit here and hold herself together. It took all her energy to simply carry on a conversation and try not to shake as if she were about to fall apart.

"If you'll help me, milord," she began, holding out her left hand to Sir Padrig. "I'd like—"

All of a sudden she could feel her chest tightening, her breath coming in short, hard gasps, her heart thundering until she thought 'twould burst. She tried to bring her right hand up to her throat to ease the tightening noose of muscles choking off her air, instead setting off a wave of agony as her arm remained limp at her side.

"Alys!" His voice sharp, his touch firm, reassuring, Padrig caught hold of her by the waist and hauled her up from where she had slumped against the wall of the pit.

She heard Padrig telling Rafe, "You needn't have tried so hard to get her to drink more whiskey. All you needed to do was *talk* her into insensibility!"

Then sight and sound faded away.

"Jesu, what a stubborn wench," Rafe muttered. "Not a bad thing, I suppose—"

"Unless you're trying to work around her stubbornness," Padrig pointed out. "Then no, 'tis not good." He tugged at the blanket and wrapped it around Alys, careful not to jostle her. "And given that we don't know how long our good fortune will last this time, we shouldn't waste another moment." He hoisted her up in his arms and got to his feet. "Let's go."

"You don't think she'll awaken again anytime soon, do you?" Rafe asked.

Padrig settled Alys more comfortably in his grasp. "Who knows? I wouldn't count on her remaining quiet for long, though." He gazed unseeing out of the pit for a moment, then shook his head. "'A quiet wench, though 'tis doubtful she's any sense at all rattling around her pretty head,'" he muttered to himself, transferring Alys up into Rafe's arms. "Not bloody likely."

"Milord?"

Padrig made a sound of disgust and bent to retrieve his dagger, slipping it into its sheath and adjusting the strap tied about his thigh. "You'd think I'd know better by now than to believe a word that pompous twit Hugh de Tremont says."

"What are you talking about?" Rafe asked. Picking up the flask, he uncorked it and took a long swallow, then held it out to Padrig.

When Padrig shook his head, Rafe slid home the stopper and climbed out of the pit.

Padrig scrambled up to join him. "I was repeating one of the lies Hugh told me about Lady Alys," he said, not bothering to hide his disgust. "He did his best to make her sound nigh brainless whenever he spoke of her."

Rafe snorted. "Hugh is an ass." He gazed down at Alys's face for a moment, as though weighing whether or not he should speak, then glanced at Padrig and shrugged. "I'm not surprised," he added. "The lecherous sot has been trying—without any success whatsoever that I could see—to get under her skirts. Hasn't quit since he came to l'Eau Clair last year. So far as I know, she's scarce seemed aware of him at all." He grinned. "'Tis clear to me that Lady Alys is a most discerning woman."

His heart suddenly lighter than it had been all night, Padrig laughed and reached out to take Alys back into his arms. "So it would appear, if she's kept him at bay all this time." Careful of his footing, he began to make his way over the pile of debris. "Now that you mention it, I had noticed he deems himself quite the gallant. How could I have forgotten? From what I've heard, there's hardly a woman in the entire demesne he's not tried to bed—except for Lady Gillian, of course."

"Do you think he's got that much sense?" Rafe asked with barely suppressed amusement. He tucked the flask into his tunic, picked up the candle and caught up with Padrig, grabbing Alys's sodden cloak as he passed by the spot where Padrig had tossed it earlier and flinging it over his shoulder.

"Sense—nay?" Padrig sidestepped down the side of the mound and waited for Rafe. "Self-preservation? Perhaps. 'Twould be more than his life is worth to anger Lord Rannulf."

"Or Lady Gillian, given her ability with a blade," Rafe added reverently. "She could defend herself right well, I'd wager."

"Indeed," Padrig agreed.

Though he doubted Rafe had any notion just how skilled with weapons the women of that family were.

Lord knew, he would never forget the sight of his cousin, Lady Catrin—who was Lady Gillian's cousin, as well—wielding *his* sword, standing alone against several outlaws after she'd tricked him into leaving for help...

So that he could live to fight another day, she'd told him later.

Padrig shook off the memories and cradled Alys a little closer in his arms. She remained motionless and silent, but from the sound of her breathing, she'd settled into sleep, not a swoon, thankfully.

They picked their way toward the shelter, even the meager light from Rafe's candle a help as they wended through the mess of toppled trees and uprooted brush littering their path.

"Lady Alys spurned Hugh's advances, then?" Padrig asked, finding himself surprisingly eager to turn the conversation back to the woman in his arms.

"Aye—several times in public, so rumor has it. Truth to tell, I doubt anyone would expect any different." Rafe frowned. "She's always seemed a shy little lass. Talks more with the older men, ones who've been around since before Lady Gillian and Lord Rannulf wed. Strange, that. Could be she likes 'em well-seasoned—"

Suddenly he stopped and grinned. "Did you show any interest in Lady Alys?"

Padrig paused, as well. "I asked Hugh about her, nothing more than that," he replied, trying to think back to the discussion. Had he asked about any other women? He couldn't recall.

Rafe clapped him on the shoulder. "With Hugh, it wouldn't take more than that. In his eyes, he's God's own gift to womanhood—and every other man is his competition. Aye, you got him worried, and he tried to distract you from paying her any notice."

"Worried? About what?" Padrig asked, completely baffled.

"That you'd ruin his chances, of course. A strong, handsome fellow such as yourself, newly returned from foreign climes, rumored to be a bruising fighter—"

Padrig snorted and started moving again, but Rafe kept on talking even as he kept up.

"—I can see why he'd be concerned. He's not really as successful with women as he likes to claim."

"There's a surprise," Padrig muttered under his breath, eliciting a nod from Rafe.

"So how can he compete with you, a mysterious warrior the ladies are waiting to discover?"

"Mayhap it isn't only Hugh who is a fool," Padrig scoffed. "By Christ, how did you come up with such nonsense?"

Rafe laughed. "'Tis none of my making! I heard some o' Lady Gillian's young ladies talking about you. Including Lady Alys," he said, his grin widening. "Could be that Hugh heard them, as well—they were making no effort to be quiet."

By the saints! Padrig felt a flush of embarrassment heat his face. Given the speed with which gossip usually spread throughout l'Eau Clair, 'twas nigh a miracle that he'd heard naught of this before now.

Yet he couldn't help but be amazed by the thought that a group of women—noble ladies, no less—had found him worthy of discussion.

And what should that matter to him? Despite the fact that he had several noble relatives, he himself sat far lower in rank. He was a landless knight, nothing more. Clearly some misunderstanding had occurred, for in the ordinary way of things, he'd hardly have a slew of ladies in pursuit of him.

No matter how "mysterious" they found him to be, he thought with a rueful smile.

Still, he couldn't help but wonder what Alys—*Lady* Alys, he reminded himself lest he get too full of himself—what had she thought? What, if anything, had she added to the discussion?

Rafe stopped; Padrig did as well, noting that while they'd been involved in their most peculiar discussion, they'd made it to the shelter. Rafe had paused just outside the makeshift hut.

In the eerie glow of the candle, Rafe's knowing expression shone all too clear. He moved closer. "Wouldn't you like to know what Lady Alys—"

"Nay," Padrig cut him off, ignoring the intense desire to hear what Rafe was obviously eager to share.

"Sir Padrig—" he goaded, "—I *did* hear her, you know."

"No," Padrig said flatly.

Rafe turned away from the shelter and faced Padrig, his manner more serious. "I've seen how you look at her, milord... Jesu, if you could only see how you look at her now."

When had Rafe turned into the devil, to taunt and test a man nigh beyond endurance?

He'd not give in, no matter how strong the temptation.

"Enough," he growled. Turning from the other man, he tucked Alys more firmly against his chest and ducked to enter the hut.

Chapter Eight

Sheer anger—at himself, at their situation, at God Him-self—lent Padrig energy enough to carry him through the remaining hours of the seemingly endless night. Shortly after he and Rafe had brought Lady Alys to the hut, Jock and Peter carried in the last two of the missing men—both badly injured by the storm, and chilled to the bone by the weather besides.

Their party now numbered eleven: four unharmed; four badly hurt, including Marie; and three, including Lady Alys, whose injuries fell somewhere in between.

Once they'd gathered everyone together in the shelter, Padrig, Rafe, Jock and Peter did what they could for their battered comrades. With Padrig tending to the women—an awkward experience he'd rather not repeat any time soon—they got everyone out of their sodden clothing and bundled them up in whatever dry cloth they could find in the baggage.

Fortunately the packs were wrapped in heavy hides, and had escaped the worst of a soaking. Every piece of clothing, bedrolls, spare saddle blankets—even the rags for cleaning armor were put to some use.

Padrig had stripped off his surcoat and mail hauberk. 'Twas a relief to be rid, even for a brief time, of the cold, wet garments. Clad in a shirt and tunic over his still-damp braes and boots, he felt considerably warmer than he had in his armor.

They needed a fire. However, though they might have trees in abundance, wood dry enough to burn was in very short supply. Amazingly they found a small cache of it buried beneath a pile of brush, along with the last man they rescued—who was not too seriously injured.

Somehow Rafe scraped together enough wood to build a fire. Protected within a circle of stones in the back corner of the shelter, scarcely big enough to heat a pot of water, nonetheless its flames threw off a welcome glow of light and a small pool of heat. They'd not get very warm or dry from it, but it provided them with hot drinks to help warm up the injured.

The mere sight of it helped to brighten a truly dismal night.

Considering the paltry light of their few candles, the crude conditions and their meager store of supplies, they treated the injured as well as they could, but Padrig feared they'd not done enough.

Everyone was so cold and wet! In addition, the injured men, Lady Alys and her maid all needed more care than they had resources to provide. 'Twas too long a journey to go back to l'Eau Clair; they needed to find someplace nearby to seek shelter and aid.

Right now he couldn't say for certain where they'd ended up. Under the current conditions it was nigh impossible to take note of any sort of landmark—they might be in an area he'd have easily recognized before, and he'd not know it now.

Once the sun rose and he'd had a chance to scout the area, mayhap he'd have a better idea of their location, and thus what options they had.

In the meantime, he could do naught else but take care of his charges and pray.

Until he'd fulfilled his duty, relaxing his guard in any way was not a luxury he could allow himself.

Not that he'd have been able to rest anyway.

But once they'd set up their patients on their make-shift beds, Padrig sent Rafe, Jock and Peter to get what sleep they could while he kept watch. Everyone else seemed to have drifted into some sort of rest; 'twas fairly quiet now that the storm had moved on, with only the occasional distant rumble of thunder accompanying the soft patter of rain on the branch-covered roof. Every so often someone would groan or snore, but other than himself, it appeared everyone had settled deep into slumber.

Perhaps he could use the time to collect his thoughts and work out some sort of plan for the morrow. Now that he'd the opportunity, however, his mind—full to over-flowing with worries and possibilities—would not cease its headlong whirl.

Sighing, he sprawled on the ground beside Lady Al-ys's pallet so that he faced her, stretched out his legs, and reached over to smooth his hand along the length of her hair where it lay spread atop the covers. He gently worked his fingers through the tangles, savoring the softness against his skin. It calmed him to touch her. He found it soothing, reassuring in some strange way.

He didn't understand it, and he knew 'twas wrong of him to make free with her person—especially without her knowledge or permission—but he could not resist the impulse to do so. Perhaps all he felt was the comfort of human touch. If so, mayhap his touch brought comfort to her, as well.

He hoped so.

He choked back a bitter laugh. It suited him to believe so, more like.

Still—for the moment, where was the harm in it?

He stroked the back of his hand over her forehead before cupping his palm about her cheek. Thankfully her skin had finally warmed, her breathing had become slow and even. Whatever her other hurts, she'd at least escaped becoming sick from lying out in the cold and damp for so long.

Lady Alys stirred beneath his touch, shifting awkwardly within the bedding before opening her eyes. She glanced around the shadowy structure before her attention came to rest on his face. "Padrig," she murmured. "Where are we?"

Her voice, husky with sleep, skittered along his spine like a caress, making his body—nay, his entire being—take notice of her in a manner that was completely inappropriate.

Yet wholly tempting.

Especially when combined with the dark, smoky look in her amber eyes as her gaze met his.

Lord save him! Padrig snatched his hand back from Alys's cheek as though she had suddenly burst into flame. Moving slowly, he sat back on his heels, his hands resting on his knees. "'Tis the—" He sounded like a croaking frog; he cleared his throat and tried again. "'Tis the shelter my men built."

She nodded and tried to pull herself up to sit against the crude wall, but stopped in mid-movement, grimacing. Her breathing uneven, she motioned to her right arm, which remained resting across her torso. "Could you help me up?" she asked.

"Of course." Feeling like a fool for not realizing what she'd been trying to do, he dropped to his knees beside her, reached out and eased her arm to her side.

She cradled it against her body, supporting it with her left hand.

Though 'twas clear that moving hurt her, she let him clasp her about the waist and shift her.

By the rood, why hadn't he thought to bind her arm so its weight would not pull at the joint? If he'd done it when she'd been sleeping so deeply, he might have spared her this pain.

'Twas too late to worry about that; instead, he'd do what he could to fix the situation. Still holding her, he looked around for a length of cloth, a shirt—anything he could use to fashion a sling.

A strip of linen left over from binding wounds caught his attention, tossed aside on the floor. Snatching it up, he knotted it into a rough sling and carefully positioned her arm within its folds.

Though her body tensed and her breathing roughened for a moment, amazingly she hadn't cried out. He'd seen hardened warriors nigh in a swoon to have their arm moved at all under such conditions.

Lady Alys continued to surprise him—not necessarily a good thing, since the more he learned about her, the more he wanted to know.

A man like him didn't need to know anything more about a young noblewoman save that she was above his touch, in every way that mattered.

He'd do well to remind himself of that fact every chance he got.

"Thank you." Alys closed her eyes for a moment as if to compose herself, then opened them, met his gaze and sighed. "'Tis strange, is it not, to thank someone for doing something you know will be awful? Still, this does make things a bit more comfortable."

"If I'd done it earlier, you might have slept more soundly." Still supporting her, Padrig rearranged her blankets, concentrating on smoothing them out and making certain her feet were well covered rather than on watching her face. "You might still be asleep."

"I must have rested long enough, for I feel wide awake now." She laid her left hand atop his, bringing his restless fidgeting to an end. "I'm glad to be upright, Sir Padrig, and to be free after lying pinned for so long in that mountain of trees."

He allowed his gaze to rise, to alight on her lovely face, and felt any intelligent words—words he could say without sounding an idiot—fly straight out of his head. "I'm glad we found you," he finally managed.

Of course you're glad, you stupid fool, he berated himself. *What else would you have done—left her there?*

If he weren't careful, he'd soon be sounding as pathetic as Hugh.

Wasn't *that* a disquieting notion!

Evidently she saw nothing wrong with his response, however, for she relaxed against him. "'Tis warmer and drier here—and the view is certainly better, as well," she added, her lips curving into an almost imperceptible smile, her gaze settling on his face with an intensity it took all his attention to ignore.

That look, combined with the way it felt to hold her, set thoughts he'd no business thinking rushing to his brain—as well as to other, more unruly parts farther south.

By the saints, she should know better than to look at him that way!

"Is that so?" he replied, even as he regretfully mustered his common sense and withdrew his support, easing her out of his grasp. Straightening his legs, he settled himself beside her pallet, once again facing her. "I believe I can put your arm aright once there's light so I can see what I'm doing," he told her.

"I know." She met his questioning look, her expression solemn. "I drifted in and out of sleep while you were carrying me—I heard bits and pieces of your talk with Rafe."

Damnation! Which parts had she heard?

"Did you?" He tried for a neutral expression and hoped his face didn't flush with embarrassment. "Then you know it will hurt like the devil to reset the bone in the socket."

"It hurts like the devil now," she said, her tone tart. "I doubt you could make it much worse."

The teasing temptress had clearly fled in the face of painful reality.

And 'twas obvious she'd scant notion just how painful reality could be.

"I'm more concerned about whether you can make my arm work again," she added. "I use my right hand far more than the left."

"I'm certain we can do that," he reassured her. "For now, though, why don't you rest until morning?" *Please sleep,* he silently begged. *Only then—perhaps, if I'm lucky—will I be able to resist you.* "Everyone is asleep at the moment—including Marie," he added, knowing without a doubt 'twould be her next question if he gave her the chance to ask. "There's naught else anyone can do for now. Once it's light, we'll need to get moving, find a place to stay nearby. You'd be wise to sleep while you can."

Alys leaned toward Padrig, watching his face carefully in the uneven candlelight. "What of you, Sir Padrig? Will you rest?" To judge by the variety of expressions flickering over his face and in his eyes, 'twas as if some battle raged within him.

Whatever could it be?

"Someone must keep watch," he said simply. She couldn't mistake the weariness roughening his voice. "Come, milady—shall I help you back onto the pallet?"

She'd slept enough for the nonce; mayhap if she sat there quietly, Sir Padrig might get some respite, even if he could not relax his vigilance any more than that.

Though she doubted 'twould do any good to suggest such a thing. "Nay, milord, I'm more comfortable sitting like this. But I thank you for the offer, and for all your help."

"'Tis my duty to watch over you, Lady Alys. Lord Rannulf would expect no less of me than that."

And Sir Padrig would always expect more of himself, she'd wager.

Something about the dim light and near quiet of the small, shadow-filled hut after the violence of the storm made Alys think of the enveloping depths of a bed with the curtains drawn. The sense of intimacy surrounding her and Padrig made it seem they were alone here—sitting close together, speaking in low, hushed tones... Awareness of the others scarcely intruded upon them. 'Twas a seductive cocoon wrapped about them; she didn't want to do or say anything that might destroy it.

Though she'd like to continue talking with him, she could see he'd be more at ease if she did not.

She wriggled into a more comfortable position against the roughly-woven wall of branches. "Good night, milord."

"You should not call me that," he said harshly. "Rafe only does so as a jest."

"Rafe does it because he respects you, Sir Padrig. He thinks you a noble man, as do I." She met his gaze calmly, willing him to see the truth of her words.

'Twas clear from his stunned expression that she'd surprised him, whether with her reason, or Rafe's.

Hoping to relieve his worry about her, at least, she lowered her eyelids and sought to slow her breathing. She'd feigned sleep before, as a child—she knew just how much to close her eyes yet be certain she could see him through her lashes.

Hopefully 'twould serve to make him believe she'd drifted off.

Since her arm still ached and throbbed in reaction to her stupid, unthinking attempt to move it, Alys sought instead to distract herself by centering her attention upon Padrig.

This close, she could see the shadowed exhaustion that leached the healthy color from his tanned skin. He sat near enough that she could have leaned over and rested her head against him again—could just as easily have kissed his lips, had she dared be so bold.

Her heart raced at the thought. Oh, how she was tempted!

What would he do, were she to throw caution to the wind, make her imaginings real? He'd not wish to hurt her, her body nor her feelings—she knew that much about him—so he likely wouldn't push her away.

But would he accept such a caress from her?

He's a man, Alys, a little voice in her mind mocked. *When have you ever known a man to refuse a woman's attentions?*

Lord knew, men sought women's notice often enough—practically any way they could get it, if her own experiences with them were any indication.

The look she'd seen in Padrig's eyes earlier, when she teased him in a way quite foreign to her nature, said he returned her interest. He'd been watching her as well, his blue eyes dark, yet the weariness etching his handsome face made it look as though he wore the weight of all the world's sorrows upon his wide shoulders.

Could she help ease some of that weariness, distract him from his worries for a few brief moments?

Should she try?

His touch, before he'd withdrawn it from her so abruptly, had been firm, assured. Yet his gaze held a cautious quality, one she didn't expect to see in the man she'd begun to know.

Almost as though he expected her to take him to task.

For what, she couldn't imagine.

It was not his fault they'd been caught in the storm's fury. 'Twas ill luck, bad timing, misfortune, nothing more than that.

Even so skilled and diligent a knight as Sir Padrig must accept that every day brought events beyond anyone's power to change.

Or perhaps she was attributing her own emotions to him. After all, if not for her own unrelenting desire to join the sisters at the Abbey of St. Bridget, none of them would have been traveling upon this particular road just at the time when a vicious storm arrived.

However, she refused to believe either she or Sir Padrig had anything to do with their current situation. All life was in God's hands, surely. 'Twas presumptuous, indeed, for anyone to suppose they could influence the Lord's plans.

She nearly smiled at the odd turn her thoughts had taken—to leap from wondering about kissing a man to pondering God's mysteries was a strange journey, indeed—but she caught herself in time. Padrig would have noticed, since he'd scarce moved or shifted his gaze from her since she'd said good-night.

The power of his scrutiny weighed upon her, warming her from the inside out, quickening her pulse and breathing, making her aware of her body in new and enticing ways. Her mouth ached for the touch of his lips; she wanted to feel the brush of his fingers along her cheek again, the caress of his hand in her hair.

She'd never before noticed the way her clothing felt against her skin, or experienced the hot, tingling sensations that centered in her breasts and her belly and made her yearn for...

For him.

All of that from a look—when he didn't even know she was watching him.

Of course, perhaps that was why he dared to look at her thus.

Everyone around them was asleep, she reminded herself. No one save Padrig would know if she were to "awaken" and test her newfound boldness on him.

Nay—*with* him.

Did she dare?

She peeked at him through her lashes, noting the strength of his features, the temptation of his tall, lean body...an image she could recall in vivid, naked detail.

She drew a deep breath and her heart pounded fast and loud.

Aye, she dared...

It took but the slightest change of position to shift closer to Padrig, but even so, he'd noticed and moved to catch hold of her.

"Milady, are you all right?" he asked, his hands clasping firmly about her waist to steady her when she swayed in his grasp.

"Aye, Padrig. I am now." Words she'd intended to sound enticing had come out solemn instead, but she could tell when she looked into his eyes that he understood what she'd meant by them.

She raised her left hand and settled it on his cheek. The prickle of whiskers along her palm sent heat blazing through her. How would it feel to graze the more sensitive skin of her lips over his face? A shudder passed through her at the notion.

Padrig's hands slid up from her waist, stopping just below her breasts, his hands splayed along her ribs, their heat like a brand upon her flesh.

She glanced up, her gaze meeting his, held captive by the intensity in his dark blue eyes. He caught her hand in his, but made no effort to move it away. Instead he wove their fingers together. "Alys?"

"Padrig?" She'd no trouble infusing her tone with a teasing note now.

"Be sure you want this," he murmured, his voice low, rough. He brought her hand to his lips, but rather than placing a kiss on the back of it in the usual manner, he turned her hand over and swept the caress across her palm, then pressed his lips to the spot on her inner wrist where her pulse raced.

She slipped her hand free of his and rested her fingers on his lips. "I'd not have started this if I wasn't sure," she whispered.

Smiling, she brought her mouth to his and kissed him.

Chapter Nine

Alys pressed her lips to Padrig's and was immediately overwhelmed by sensations. His mouth was so warm, softer than she'd expected it would be.

And the fact that he was kissing her back was incredibly beguiling.

For all her imaginings about kisses, despite all the times she and Lady Gillian's other young ladies had discussed kissing, she'd truly very little notion how to go about it. Touching her mouth to Padrig's was exciting, but she knew there had to be more to it than this simple caress.

Clutching a handful of his tunic, she drew back just enough to see his face. "Show me," she said, her whispered demand intense with the maelstrom of feeling whirling through her.

His lips quirked into a teasing smile. "Show you what, milady?" His gaze beckoned her, enticed her to lean closer to him. Careful of her arm in its sling, he stroked one hand up and down her side in a leisurely caress, spreading heat from her waist to her breasts. He'd buried his other hand in her hair, his fingertips moving lightly, teasingly, upon the sensitive skin at her nape.

It seemed since she'd been so daring as to kiss him, now he expected her to be bolder still.

Did she have the courage to continue what she'd started?

A simple glance at Padrig's face was all the answer she needed.

"Show me how to kiss, if you please," she said in the haughtiest tone she could contrive—though she mitigated that offense with a smile.

"There are many kinds of kisses." He nuzzled her cheek, then touched his lips to her ear. "You've only to tell me what you want, milady," he whispered. "I am yours to command."

Unfamiliar desires engulfed her; her body demanded *something,* but she'd little notion precisely what it was she wanted.

What she needed.

All at once the answer came to her. She wanted more.

More of life, of excitement, adventures of her own to write about someday when she was old and gray.

How she would survive *more,* she couldn't imagine—but she was certainly willing to try.

First, however, she must reach out and grab hold of what life was offering her.

For once in your life be bold, Alys. You may never have another chance like this.

She drew in a deep breath, calmed herself—a little. "Show me how to kiss you as a woman kisses a man," she whispered, watching his face as she spoke.

"We are man and woman, and we just kissed," he said, the amusement dancing in his eyes making a mockery of his innocent tone. He brushed his cheek to hers. "Was that not what you wanted?" The vibration of his voice against the side of her neck made her insides clench and shivers run down her spine.

"I never knew you were a tease, Sir Padrig," she chided before adding tartly, "I do realize there's more to it than that."

A bit shaky, she rested her head on his shoulder for a brief moment, reveling in the feel of strong muscles beneath his shirt even as she was tempted to poke him in the chest. Why must he compel her to tell him exactly what she desired?

Mayhap he thought she wouldn't do it.

He was about to be surprised.

She straightened and met his gaze. "Very well, milord. Show me how lovers kiss," she commanded. She traced her fingers over his mouth. "Every detail, if you please."

Though his expression never changed, his chest shook.

"You're laughing at me!" she accused, outraged.

"Nay, milady—'tis only that this is a most wondrous ending to an absolutely terrible day. I'm simply amazed at my good fortune." He stroked her cheek, his palm coming to rest at her throat. "I'm just happy."

The warmth of his hand, combined with his words, sent heat spiraling along her flesh to center somewhere in the region of her heart.

Could *she* claim some responsibility for his happiness? Should she?

She knew she could hold Padrig responsible for the way she felt at this moment—poised on a precipice, feeling as if she could fly away from her everyday, mundane existence into this new world that Padrig introduced her to.

She didn't know whether she should trust the sensation. Should she see where it might take her? If she did, would the results wipe her mind clean of all coherent thought and lead her astray?

Sweet Mary save her, when had she become so timid?

Alys savored the faint taste of Padrig clinging to her mouth, and knew she wanted more.

Adventure, Alys, she reminded herself, her pulse pounding as anticipation flowed through her. *You will never have a chance for anything exciting to happen if you don't give living your own life a try.*

"You're happy?" she asked, nearly cringing at the eagerness in her voice.

"Aye, truly." Lips curved in a smile, he cupped her chin in his hand and lowered his mouth till it was next to hers. "Don't you know 'tis every man's dream, to have a beautiful woman ask for his touch?" Brushing his lips over hers, he added, "I'd be delighted to show you how to kiss, Alys, any way you'd like. Or to teach you anything else you'd like to learn." He nipped gently at her lower lip, then soothed the spot with a light stroke of his tongue. "'Twould most truly be my pleasure."

"And mine," she murmured against his mouth.

Eager to experience the excitement of these new ways of touching, she kissed him the only way she knew, hoping he'd show her more.

He did not disappoint her.

He stroked his thumb over her lips. "Part your lips, sweeting," he murmured. "Let me in." Tracing his tongue along their outline, he tilted her head to allow him better access to her mouth.

Alys was quick to follow his lead, hoping he'd experience the same excitement she did as she echoed the caress.

He touched her slowly, as carefully as if she were made of spun sugar, his tongue painting a delicate trail of fire as he taught her a lover's kiss.

Swift to learn, she kept pace with him, but soon 'twas not enough to merely touch mouth to mouth. She couldn't bear to stop touching him—his hair, his neck. Even to simply rest her hand on his chest and feel the thundering of his heart gave her pleasure.

It made her forget about their surroundings, made all her aches and hurts fade away.

There was only Padrig and Alys, huddled together in the dark, encircled within the rising warmth of their bodies and the intensifying passion that pulled them into its web.

Padrig took his time, the leisurely rhythm of his caresses apparently designed to drive her into a frenzy of impatience. Every nuance, every thing he taught her led her deeper into passion.

Though he kept a tight rein on the tempo of their loving, the intensity of it grew with each touch. Finally she could stand his torment no longer. Eager for more, she sought to take the upper hand, to hasten the pace of their kisses.

He allowed her control for a moment; then, groaning, he framed her face with his hands and eased his mouth from hers, resting his forehead on her cheek. "Jesu, but you've a frightful power, milady," he murmured against her skin. "I vow you'd make a saint pay no heed to the hope of salvation."

He thought *her* powerful? He made her forget nigh everything save the pleasure he brought her!

'Twas a wonder she was aware of anything at all. Her world had closed in until it encompassed them, her awareness only of Padrig, the sight and smell of him, the restrained passion of his touch.

Her flesh tingling, her body resting against Padrig's as comfortably as if they'd held each other this way a thousand times before, Alys had to concentrate on simply breathing until she felt some measure of control flow through her.

Then, in command of herself once more, she set about to make the magic happen again.

Yet it seemed they'd scarce touched before Padrig caught her wrist in one hand, cupped her chin in the other, and eased away from her once more. "Enough, Alys," he whispered sharply when she tried to shift back into his embrace. "By the rood, you're dangerous! Don't tempt me past endurance."

Raising his head slightly, Padrig glanced around the hut, letting out his breath in a sigh when he brought his gaze back to her. "I cannot believe how swiftly you make me forget we're not alone."

Alys flinched at the reminder, for she, too, had forgotten. Her face heated. What if anyone had awakened and seen them?

Though she didn't know what Padrig felt, when they'd kissed she'd become powerfully aware of him— overwhelmingly so. Nothing else existed, even her pain forgotten. She and Padrig had been wrapped about each other so closely that she doubted either of them would have noticed much of anything.

Save perhaps if the storm had returned in full force, or the hut had collapsed around them.

He wove their fingers together and brought her hand to his lips, brushing a kiss over the pulse in her wrist and sending her heartbeat soaring. He watched her all the while; he must have seen something of her thoughts in her expression, for he stroked his other hand along her cheek, then smoothed her hair back from her face. "I'm certain no one saw a thing, milady," he reassured her. "We'd surely have heard them moving about."

"I don't know that I would have," she confessed, her face growing hotter at the admission.

"Do you think any of this band of ruffians would have stayed quiet? They'd have had *something* to say, I promise you." He chuckled, the low sound skittering along her skin to settle deep within her belly.

She drew in a sharp breath as the sensation drifted through her body in a wave of yearning. Her gaze never leaving his, she turned her head and pressed a kiss into his palm.

Moving swiftly, he shifted beside her, drew her half across his lap and into his arms, and took her lips.

His mouth was fiery hot, consuming, undeniable. Alys could scarce keep up with him as he ensnared her with a kiss completely unlike their earlier ones.

He swept her along with him into a passion so straightforward, she could not mistake the depth of his response. If he was determined to overwhelm her, he accomplished his goal with ease.

Then just as abruptly as he had caught her to him, he released her and, cradling her in his arms, set her back upon her pallet.

"Padrig?" she gasped, unable to catch her breath.

Muttering curses, he raked his hand back through his hair and shook his head as if to clear it. "I'm sorry," he said quietly. "I should not have—"

She lashed out at him with her left arm. The blow caught him in the chest, the impact sending a jolt straight across her back. That pain was insignificant, however, compared to what she felt inside. "Don't you *dare* apologize," she snarled.

"But—"

She poked him in the arm, less hard this time. "No, Padrig—not for anything."

Alys slumped back against the rough wall, grimacing at the pain that continued to resonate through her torso now that her attention was not distracted by Padrig's touch. "You've done nothing to apologize for," she repeated. "Not just now, and certainly not earlier."

Now that they were not touching at all, the sense of loss she felt nigh overwhelmed her. Exhaustion, pain, confusion—all conspired to bring tears to her eyes, tears she refused to shed.

Instead she blinked hard, refusing to meet Padrig's curious gaze.

He, however, ignored her attempt to distance herself; he leaned close enough to continue their low-voiced conversation without danger of being overheard.

"All right—I'll be truthful, then," he whispered. His eyes were fixed upon her face. What he sought to find with his intent gaze, she could not guess. "I'm not sorry we kissed, nor for anything else we've done, though no doubt I ought to be." He brushed his nose lightly against hers and straightened slightly. "However, I *am* sorry you're hurt, that we're not alone and that we had to stop just now."

He reached down to the ground and pulled a rock nearly the size of her fist from beneath him. "Though under the circumstances—" he cast a glance over his shoulder at the men sleeping nearby "—'tis most likely just as well I sat on this."

Taking her hand, he placed the jagged stone on her palm and closed her fingers about it. "Here, milady— your chastity belt." He laughed shakily. "Or your savior, more like."

"What?" she asked, confused.

"If I hadn't landed on *that* in a particularly sensitive area, I doubt I'd have been able to stop unless you told me to—or until the others pulled me off you."

Chapter Ten

Padrig held Alys's fingers closed tight over the stone and counted himself a most fortunate man.

Thank God she didn't seem to recognize—would hopefully *never* know—how close he'd come to completely losing any sense of restraint just now.

What the devil was wrong with him?

He'd never been so swept away by a woman. Jesu, even as a youth eagerly beginning to indulge his passions, he'd never been so out of control as to lose all awareness of his surroundings, of all rational thought.

And to do so under such circumstances as these…

In truth, he must be going mad.

He glanced at Alys—so brave in the face of pain, so bold when challenged by an impudent knight.

Her lovely face, her expressive eyes…those lips capable of surprising him with both words and deeds…

What a sweet madness it had been!

He gazed into her eyes yet again, and realized he could distinguish their amber color, could see her features, the scratches on her face, more distinctly than he'd been able to a few moments earlier.

While they'd been so involved with each other, a new day had begun.

"'Tis growing lighter." Still holding her hand cradled within his, he reached out with his free hand and swept the disheveled mass of her hair away from her face, his fingers lingering within the thick, silky strands. She leaned into the caress, intensifying his desire—and his regret that this was apt to be the last chance he'd have to touch her as a lover would. "The men will likely be stirring soon."

They'd little time left before the responsibilities of the day would fall upon them all.

What should he say to her? What should he do to bring an end to what must remain naught but a brief interlude between them, something that *must never* happen again?

In the harsh light of day, Sir Padrig ap Huw was a soldier in the service of Lord Rannulf FitzClifford— Lady Alys Delamare's loyal servant for the nonce.

Nothing more than that.

He'd do well to remember his place, for both their sakes.

However, Padrig thought, casting a swift glance out the narrow doorway of the hut—the sun had not made its way into the sky quite yet.

Until this night was completely gone, he vowed, he would remain Alys's tutor—in one way or another.

Silence yet reigned in the shelter, but he expected someone would be up soon. 'Twould be wise to prepare accordingly.

He hadn't let go of Alys's hand when he'd given her the stone; he released her now and settled beside her on the ground, sitting so it appeared as though he'd been examining her arm.

He didn't dare touch her again, for 'twas obvious he had little control where she was concerned. Instead he let his gaze settle upon her as he wished his hands could, lingering over each feature of her face, stroking the dark river of hair flowing over her shoulders and bosom.

Her indrawn breath, and the color rising to tint her cheekbones, told him she felt the phantom caress. "Padrig, what are you doing to me?" she whispered, her voice faint, pleading.

"I cannot touch you as I wish to—as I did before. But I want you to know I don't regret what we shared." Her hand, still clasped tight around the rock, lay in her lap; he glided his fingertips over the back of it, the touch come and gone in an instant. "I thank you for the gift of your kisses, Alys. I shall treasure them always."

Before he could say more, he heard voices. Glancing back over his shoulder, he saw Rafe sit up, heard someone else speak.

He turned back to Alys. "Always," he whispered.

Rising to his feet, he left her and went to check on his men.

By the time Padrig, Rafe, Jock and Peter had cared for the injured, armed themselves and left the shelter to go investigate their situation, the sun had come up and brightened the sky to full morn.

As was so often the case after a storm, it was a light-filled and glorious day.

Every joint and muscle protesting loudly, Alys made her way to Marie's side to check on her once more before venturing outside. The maid lay in a deep swoon, her body covered with bumps and bruises, several bones unmistakably broken.

Worse than that, though, was the long, nasty gash running from her temple up onto the top of her scalp. Padrig didn't believe her skull had been cracked, but it was difficult to recognize such an injury. Whether it was or no, there was little they could do for her beyond setting her broken bones and cleaning and binding up her wounds. They'd no healing herbs or soothing tisanes to ease her ills; they could only watch her closely, pray for her recovery and hope that nothing they did caused her further harm.

Between her dislocated shoulder and twisted ankle, along with myriad scrapes and bumps, Alys felt like one huge bruise. She moved gingerly as she made her way to the entrance of the ramshackle hut, careful to avoid the trees propped on either side to support the roof.

All she needed was to knock into it and send the entire building down atop the poor souls inside!

Considering that the men had gathered the materials and constructed the shelter in the midst of a terrible storm, with scarce enough light to see their hands in front of their faces, the structure was a marvel.

Under any other circumstances, however, 'twould be considered a collapse waiting to happen. Remembering how often she'd leaned her full weight against the wall as she rested upon her pallet, 'twas a wonder the entire hut had not fallen down atop them then.

When she added the possibility that she and Padrig had bumped into that wall several times besides— though she couldn't vouch for that fact, since she had little recollection of anything save what they'd been doing—'twas a miracle, indeed, that the shelter had remained standing throughout the night.

Just thinking about the hut coming down and bury-

ing everyone was enough to send a shudder of horror
rushing though her.

Even if she'd not been completely distracted by Padrig and his "lessons" in the last dark hours of the night,
she knew she wouldn't have been able to sleep. Every
time she closed her eyes for longer than a moment, she
felt transported back to the stygian depths of the mound
where she'd been trapped.

She was tired, yet she didn't know if—or when—her
fear of being closed in would end. Until then, she didn't
think she could close her eyes long enough to sleep.
What little rest she'd gotten before Padrig had carried
her here had been the result of exhaustion, the cold and
a dose of whiskey.

Once he'd settled her in the shelter, where she was
dry and warmer, she'd awoken. The hut, small and dark,
had reminded her too much of her earlier resting place
for her to relax and sleep again. If it hadn't been for the
comfort—and in all honesty, the distraction—of Padrig's presence at her side, she didn't think she'd have
been able to remain there until the sun rose.

Once it was light, thankfully, her fear had begun to
ease. Still, she'd sit out in the sun gladly, and savor
every bit of its warmth and comfort.

Mayhap then she'd be better prepared to face her
next trial—when Padrig returned, he planned to reset
her shoulder.

In the meantime, she'd rather think about anything
else but that.

How were the men faring in their search of the area?
She wished she had been able to ride out with them, for
she was familiar with the demesnes of several holdings
along this route. Somewhere in the vicinity her father

held two small manors in his own right. She'd visited them several times before, and she'd once attended a hunting party at another keep nearby.

Glancing out at the complete devastation surrounding her sent a rush of cold through her, chilling her to her bones. 'Twas eerie to see such complete destruction, the piles of wet, blasted trees glistening in the warm sun, clouds of moisture hovering low to the ground all around them like some hell-born miasma.

'Twould take a sharp eye, indeed, to recognize anything in conditions such as this.

Of course, there might not be anything at all left to recognize after the storm. Still, 'twas possible she could have helped.

She prayed they would find *something* familiar and realize where they were—or at the very least, happen upon a village or manor—for they were in desperate need of someplace where they could find shelter and aid.

After the men had ridden out, Alys had done what she could for the injured, giving them water and food, talking to them so they'd know they were not alone and checking their injuries.

Though to her shame, in truth she knew little about how to treat them.

She should have paid more attention to Lady Gillian's training in the healing arts, and less to daydreaming and collecting information for her stories. Even once she began her new life, when she joined the abbey, 'twould be useful to know—

Dismay filled her. Had she ruined her chance for the future she'd wanted for so long?

Jesu, what had she done? After her bold behavior with Padrig—behavior she could not make herself regret one bit, to her shame—would the abbess be willing to take her on as a novice?

Did she still want to *be* a nun?

Mayhap the true question was—had she ever wanted to be one?

She'd never had a vocation to serve God—that lack she'd freely admit. Yet if she joined the order, she would be doing the Lord's work in some form.

Her primary reason for joining the order, however, was purely selfish. It was the only place she knew of where she would be free to continue her writing. Indeed, at the Abbey of St. Bridget writing was encouraged. It could even be considered a requirement. As with some of the monasteries, the purpose of this convent was the compilation and dissemination of knowledge.

They wrote and copied books.

When Alys had heard of their objective, she'd been overjoyed. A place where she would fit in, be able to continue her work. A place where she could discover more about the world far beyond her tiny corner.

She ought to have been able to join them several years ago. Her father had already found a well-connected husband for her sister, and her brother had wed an heiress from a noble family of higher degree than their own.

Surely after having twice developed such valuable bonds by marriage, her parents didn't need *her* to further their ambitions.

Yet they'd refused her request to join the abbey, had gone so far as to send her nigh to the other end of the Marches to foster with Lady Gillian at l'Eau Clair.

They'd said 'twas to give her a good education in the arts of housewifery, to broaden her prospects by giving her the chance to meet other young nobles.

Young noble *men*.

'Twas to broaden *their* opportunities to form more noble bonds, more like.

And to move her far away from home, where they wouldn't have to listen to her constant entreaties.

Once she'd gone to l'Eau Clair she'd kept up a steady stream of letters to sustain her campaign, but there was no guarantee they'd read any of them.

Indeed, she doubted they had. They'd been amazingly skilled at ignoring her in person. How much easier must it be to simply toss her missives into the fire unread?

After all, it wasn't as if they needed to worry about her, or concern themselves with her well-being at all. They'd placed her with Lady Gillian FitzClifford. What more could any sensible parent have done for their child?

Lady Gillian's familial ties extended all the way into Ireland and Wales, while within England she had connections to several of the most noble households in the land. She was also known far and wide for her ability to train young noblewomen to be skilled chatelaines.

A woman trained under Lady Gillian's tutelage made a fine wife for a man of the highest degree.

'Twas all too likely her parents anticipated that after a while in Lady Gillian's world, Alys could make a match with some high-born fool they could manipulate.

Why, then, had they sent for her to come home now?

She'd believed they'd sent for her because they'd finally yielded to her pleas and arranged for her to enter the abbey.

Now she could only wonder how she could have been such a fool.

Had she let her desires blind her to reality once

again? It had ever been her way, to see only what she wished to, rather than what truly was.

Now, however, the possibility she'd finally attain her heart's desire seemed to grow smaller the more she thought about it.

Had they made arrangements for her to provide them with another high-born son by marriage?

By the Virgin, if that were the case, what poor fool might they have chosen to be her husband?

She swiftly considered possible choices, though she could think of few likely candidates.

One thing she did realize, however.

No matter who the man was, she knew he would never be a simple knight such as Sir Padrig ap Huw.

Alys sat out in the sun, letting it ease her aches and trying without success to secrete the memory of Padrig's kisses deep in her brain. Her ankle, thank heaven, was not broken, but it twinged with pain when she walked, else she'd have tried to pace away her agitation.

Her fingers itched madly for pen and parchment. 'Twas as well she could not write, for otherwise she'd surely have been compelled to note what they'd done, how she'd felt and what she'd thought of the experience.

Lacking the opportunity to record her thoughts had never stopped her from thinking about what she'd write once she got the chance, however. Other than going back into the shelter to look after the others, she spent most of the time until Padrig's return doing what she'd promised herself she would not do.

Reliving the moments in Padrig's arms.

Ah, she'd drive herself mad if she kept up such foolishness!

She welcomed the sound of approaching horses, glad of the chance to think about something—nay, *anything*—else.

Padrig and the others rode into the clearing. It seemed they'd been gone forever, though a glance at the sky showed the sun had not yet journeyed a quarter of its path to midday.

They'd plenty of daylight left to move on to someplace better than this one.

Assuming such a place still existed, she thought, then took herself to task for her cynicism.

They halted at the opposite edge of the clearing and hobbled the horses to graze along the grassy verge.

Rafe and Padrig appeared deep in conversation as they approached, but grew silent as they neared the shelter. Jock and Peter unsaddled the horses and followed them soon after.

Alys remained seated just outside the entrance to the shelter. Her aching body had stiffened despite the sun's warmth, and she feared she'd collapse at their feet were she to try to stand.

Wouldn't *that* be a lovely way to greet Padrig? As it was, after everything they'd shared last night—after her obsession with the topic all this morn—she scarce knew if she'd be able to so much as look at him without turning red as a cherry.

Would Rafe be able to see that there was something different between them?

"Lady Alys, well met!" Rafe cried, making an elaborate obeisance as he and Padrig stopped before her. Padrig's bow, while far more reserved, was well within the bounds of courtesy.

She suppressed a sigh of relief; she'd not been certain what his manner would be toward her now, though it didn't seem his nature to expose what was private between them, nor to treat her with disrespect.

Besides, when they'd parted, they'd been on civil terms. She worried over nothing, as usual.

The other two men reached the hut, nodded courteously to her and went inside.

"'Tis good to find you up and about," Rafe told her, dropping down to sit on the ground across the doorway from her.

Padrig dragged a short piece of tree trunk closer, brushed it off and offered it for her to sit upon. "Here, milady—this will get you up out of the dirt."

She still didn't dare try to get up. "Nay, I'm fine here," she said, motioning for him to take the seat. "I doubt I could get much dirtier, and I'm too comfortable to move."

Though he sent her a look she couldn't interpret, he sat down on the log.

"It feels wonderful to finally be warm," she said. "I wish I could have brought the others out here into the sun as well, but I didn't dare try to move them. I did check on them and do what I could for them." She motioned to the ground nearby, where she'd spread out all the wet clothing she'd found piled just inside the doorway. "I managed to get these out here, though. I believe most of this lot is almost dry already."

"You shouldn't have been working at all, milady," Padrig chided. "You're in little better condition than the others who are hurt."

"I'm able to stay awake and to move about. I'd say that puts me in far better shape, Sir Padrig. Even with one arm bound to my body like a millstone." Alys sent him a stern look. "Unless 'tis that you don't believe a lady should dirty her hands?" she asked with a challenging glare.

He shook his head, his lips twisting into a wry smile. "Acquit me of that offense, milady. I've lived a long while around noble ladies who work so hard, they'd put a slave to shame." He stretched his legs out before him and sighed. "I've no doubt that they—and you—could keep up with any knight, should you wish to take up a sword and join us."

"You'll get the chance to prove your mettle soon enough, milady," Rafe told her. "It will take all our resources to leave this hellish place."

"Did you determine where we are?" she asked eagerly. In her excitement she straightened her back, sending a sharp bolt of pain along her spine. Undaunted, she winced, but kept talking. "You cannot have found other people, else you'd have brought them back with you. But do you know of any keep or village nearby?"

"Have a care, milady." Padrig stood and moved to her side. Ignoring her questioning look, he bent down and swept her up into his arms, sending a flush of heat to her face and making her heartbeat soar. "Aye, we know, more or less, where we are." He stood and turned to cross the clearing. "I believe there are settlements of some sort in the area—"

"Actually," Rafe cut in from behind them, "you may know more about that than we do, milady."

"Do you need me to ride out with you?" Mayhap that was why they were heading toward the horses. While she didn't much look forward to riding in her present condition, if she could be useful, she could endure it.

"It's been several years since I've traveled this route, but I'm sure I'll recognize something."

"Nay, milady," Rafe said. "We've a fairly good notion where we are. But if you could tell us anything at all about the manors hereabouts, 'twould help us decide where would be best to go."

Alys squirmed about in Padrig's hold, trying to peer over his shoulder at Rafe.

"Alys, stay still," Padrig murmured. "'Tis awkward carrying you with your arm in the sling. I don't want to hurt you."

"You had no trouble holding me before," she whispered so only he could hear. Her cheeks flushed with heat as soon as the words left her lips. "Dear God in heaven, I cannot believe I just—" She buried her face against the coarse linen of his tunic. "I don't know why I said that."

"Hush, sweeting." His back to Rafe, he pressed a kiss to her hair. "'Tis never any trouble to hold you."

"Lady Alys," Rafe called, jogging a few steps to catch up to them. "Are you all right? You didn't answer."

"I jostled her a bit and hurt her arm," Padrig told him as Alys kept her face pressed to his shoulder. "She'll answer you in a moment, won't you, milady?"

Hoping her flush had faded, Alys raised her head and nodded.

"That's good." Rafe nodded. "I figured we'd want to learn anything you know soon, before you—"

Padrig shook his head to cut off Rafe before the other man could finish. Alys took one look at Padrig's uneasy expression and immediately tried to wriggle free.

"Before what?" she demanded.

"Alys, Rafe didn't mean that the way it sounded," Padrig began, his tone similar to that of a parent about to dole out some sort of punishment.

"Actually, I did mean just what I said," Rafe pointed out. "It makes no sense at all to wait till after to ask her— What if she swoons? We'll get no answers from her then."

Alys caught Padrig's jaw in her hand and made him meet her gaze. He paused in the middle of the clearing, his blue eyes dark with some turbulent emotion, the muscles of his jaw like a rock beneath her fingers. "Whatever it is you're talking about, I'm not going to like it, am I?"

Closing his eyes briefly, he shook his head. "No, milady, you will not." When he opened his eyes, his expression was fierce. "Nor shall I. I must slide your arm back into the socket—and there's no way to do it without causing you a great deal of pain."

Chapter Eleven

Alys's face might have been pink with embarrassment a few moments earlier, but 'twas pale as milk now. Padrig hadn't realized it was possible for the color to drain from a person's face so swiftly.

Yet her expression was composed, her touch firm as she cradled his jaw. "I know you'll do your best not to hurt me," she said. Her gaze met his, her amber eyes serene. "Rafe has the right of it, though. If I'm to tell you anything important, I had better do so beforehand. I fear I'll be little more than a gibbering idiot once you've finished with me."

Her courage astounded him, although he should not be surprised by anything about her. Lady Alys Delamare was an amazing woman.

He'd do well to remember that fact.

He started walking again. "Rafe will assist me, if you don't mind. 'Twill be easier for both of us if someone holds you, and I didn't think you'd want one of the others to do it."

"That's why you're moving me away from the shelter, isn't it?"

Padrig nodded. "We'll give you as much privacy as we can. As it is, I'll need to remove your gown. You'll be covered by your undertunic," he assured her.

"Ye needn't worry, milady." Rafe gave her an encouraging smile. "I can keep my eyes shut tight the entire time. I'll not see a thing."

Something about what Rafe said, or the way he said it, had made her chuckle. That was good; if they could keep her amused, distract her attention a little, mayhap she'd not be so apprehensive and tense.

"'Tis his usual custom when faced with a partially-dressed woman," Padrig said, straight-faced.

Rafe nodded and squeezed his eyes closed in an exaggerated manner. Then, popping them wide open, he winked at her.

Alys giggled, then laughed at his antics.

"You'd best hold his hand good and tight, as well," Padrig warned her, "for I vow he'll be as nervous as a bride on her wedding night."

They'd reached the far side of the clearing. Padrig stopped near an old log fallen along the edge of the forest and lowered Alys to her feet beside it, steadying her as she stood. He untied the knot holding her sling in place and, supporting her arm with his free hand, unwound the strip of linen and let it drop to the ground.

Alys stood watching his every move, her gaze intent, her face so pale he could see the faint smattering of light freckles dusting her cheekbones. She grimaced, slipping her hand beneath his to hold up her right arm.

Padrig held Alys's gaze as he reached for the strings tied loosely at the neckline of her gown. The tails of the knot had wound into a tangled mess; muttering a curse, he began the tedious chore of unraveling it.

Rafe spun on his heel and stood with his back to them, positioning himself so that he shielded her from view, should anyone look across the clearing. "You may need to help me get about, Lady Alys, for I cannot see a thing. Got my eyes closed up tighter than a virg—" He abruptly cut off the word.

He'd spoken a heartbeat too long, in Padrig's estimation, since 'twas clear from Alys's suppressed laughter and raised eyebrows that she knew exactly what inappropriate comment the irrepressible rascal had been about to make.

Judging from her reaction, however, Rafe had not offended her. Far from it.

Perhaps that had been why he'd done it. Though Rafe could not see Alys, she *was* smiling, and a slight tinge of color brightened her skin.

"Thank you, Rafe," Alys called.

Aye, thank you, Padrig echoed silently. 'Twas precisely what she needed just now.

She glanced up at Padrig, her eyes alight with amusement. Leaning close, she asked, "Come, Sir Padrig— how can you remain so serious?"

"He's a serious fellow, milady," Rafe called over his shoulder. "All Welshmen are, 'tis a well-known fact. Think of it. When did you last see a Welshman smile? And when you add the fact that he has spent a good long time— How many years were you with Lord Connor at Gerald's Keep, milord?"

Padrig shook his head, but went along with Rafe's jabbering. "'Twas nigh seven years."

"Sir Padrig spent nigh seven years—dear God, man, *seven years?* However did you stand it—living among the Irish? They are a most grave and solemn lot, so I've been told. 'Twill be a wonder, indeed, if we ever see him smile again."

Padrig bit back a laugh. "Mayhap 'twas you who spent years in their midst! I doubt there's anywhere else in the world where you'd find so many silver-tongued devils spouting their nonsense." He settled his face into a solemn expression, though he didn't doubt his eyes gave him away. "'Tis almost enough to drive an honest Welshman to drink."

"Speaking of drink—you didn't happen to bring along that flask, did you? I could use a drink right about now. A man needs something to occupy him if he's to stand about, waiting." Rafe paced back and forth, keeping his back to them. Halting, he demanded, "What are you doing, milord? 'Tis taking an uncommon amount of time for what ought to be a simple task."

"My lacings are knotted," Alys told him. "I'm not any help, and Sir Padrig can't get them untied."

Rafe hummed a brief snippet of a lively tune, ending it as abruptly as he'd begun. "Do you know, milady, I believe Sir Padrig should shut his eyes, as well. He has already proven he can get you in and out of your gown—or is that out, then in?—without looking at you at all. Clearly, the fact that he can see you now is holding him back. Is that the problem, milord?" he teased.

Padrig ignored Rafe's mocking question, instead focusing his attention on the unwieldy knot. He'd had no trouble with the lacing when he'd tied it—in the dark—during the night.

"What is he talking about?" Alys asked, her whispered demand no less intense for lack of volume.

She swayed on her feet. Padrig caught her carefully about the waist and lowered her to sit on the log, her back propped against a fallen tree. "'Tis nothing," he muttered without meeting her eyes. "Just ignore him." His callused fingertips seemed huge and clumsy as he plucked at the narrow strings.

She rested her injured arm in her lap and closed her left hand around his wrist. "If it was nothing, you'd have tossed some jest back at him." A bright tide of color rose to her cheeks. "Is he right? Did you undress me last night?"

Padrig glanced up at Rafe, who'd evidently seen the wisdom of moving far enough away from them to give them privacy—as long as they spoke quietly. Turning, he knelt before Alys and took her hand. "I brought you into the hut dripping wet, yet when you woke, you were dressed in dry clothing. How did you imagine that came to pass?" He toyed with her fingers, looked up at her face. Her color had not faded a whit. "Would you rather I'd had one of the others undress you?" he asked. "Not that they'd have harmed you in any way, but I thought it best that I look after you."

He *couldn't* have allowed anyone else to take care of her.

She turned her hand in his and linked their fingers together. "Thank you," she murmured. "For everything you've already done."

Unwilling to release her quite yet, he raised her hand and pressed a kiss to her wrist. "I truly did try to undress you with my eyes closed," he told her, chuckling. He lowered their hands, still joined, to her lap. "However, I soon realized that working by feel was likely to get me into more trouble than by watching what I was doing."

The feel of her flesh beneath his hands during the

simple act of searching for the lacing of her gown had sent his imagination soaring—and his senses reeling.

As if he hadn't already felt like the most rapacious beast in nature. How could he feel desire and compassion for her at the same time? It couldn't be right for the man to ache for the woman at the same time the knight wanted to look after the injured young noblewoman.

Yet both were how he'd felt.

How he still felt.

'Twas most confusing—but far beyond his scope to understand.

In any event, he would be better served to deal with the here and now.

"You needn't worry that I saw anything. 'Twas very dark in the shelter, and I did all I could to maintain your privacy."

"I trust you, Padrig." She glanced over at Rafe, who continued to studiously ignore them, before shifting her gaze to Padrig's.

Her flush had faded. Nonetheless, her amber eyes glowed with a tempting fire. "'Tis foolish, is it not?" she added, pitching her voice low so it would not carry. "To feel uncomfortable at the notion that you undressed me, when I all but invited you to do so later on."

"The difference, Alys, is that you were awake later on, and aware of what we were doing." He leaned closer, held her gaze, felt his body heat up. "Truth to tell, milady, if you were going to be undressing me, I'd prefer to be awake for the experience."

"Sir Padrig," Rafe called, jolting him out of the spell Alys seemed to cast over him. "The day's getting away from us, milord. You might as well cut that knot loose with your dagger."

Padrig looked behind him. Rafe had moved closer; Peter, who had come back outside and gone to the horses, hobbled nearby.

Rafe glanced meaningfully toward the other man before pointing to his own arm. "Do it now," he mouthed.

Regretfully Padrig slipped his hand free of Alys's and rose. "We cannot put this off any longer."

"I know," she told him. She smiled, her face surprisingly calm. "Don't worry about me. Just do what you must. I trust you, Padrig. Let's be done with this."

"Aye." He drew his dagger from the sheath on his belt and sliced through the knot.

Alys reached up and placed her hand over his. "Before we do anything more, did you still want me to tell you about my father's holdings here? Perhaps something I remember will sound similar to what you saw this morning." She glanced away, her lips thinning, her body tense. "In case I'm in no state to think clearly later."

"All right." He didn't know if she'd recognize any of the details he'd noted, but he sat next to her and briefly described what they'd seen when they'd explored the surrounding area.

She recognized some of what he told her and swiftly narrowed down their location to the locale of Winterbrooke Manor, a minor keep and village under her father's dominion.

He hoped she was correct. If so, even though they'd have to travel very slowly, they could get there before sundown.

"Thank you for your help, milady." Taking her hand, he brought it to his lips. "Now—'tis time to take care of you."

He'd been vaguely aware of Rafe sending Peter back

to the shelter. He'd rejoined them as Alys had finished her description of Winterbrooke Manor and its environs.

"How are you going to get this thing off over her arm?" Rafe asked now, pointing to Alys's dress. "Mayhap you should leave it on?"

"Nay, it will be in the way," Padrig replied. "'Tis difficult to get a good grip as it is, without—"

"Enough!" Rafe said, shuddering.

"You got my other gown off, and this one on," Alys pointed out.

"You'd swooned," Padrig said. "Nothing seemed to rouse you! I ended up cutting off the gown you were wearing. I'd the devil of a time wriggling you into this one. I'm amazed you didn't awaken then."

"You may cut up this one, as well, if 'tis easier." Alys grabbed a handful of the loose sleeve and held it out. "Or slice this part open. Then I could wear it again. Mayhap you could just take off the sleeve, so you can get to my arm?" She gazed up at him hopefully. "Since I'm awake now, I'd really rather you didn't wrench me about any more than necessary," she added dryly.

"I'll see what I can do." Working carefully, Padrig poked the wickedly sharp knifepoint into the top of the sleeve and began to ease the fabric away from the dress.

Now that the moment had arrived, Alys felt as though she had become one huge ache. Her pulse thumped through her entire body with every beat of her heart. She couldn't even bear to watch as Padrig worked on removing her sleeve, for so slight a movement as that action generated felt exaggerated, as though her arm were ready to explode from the merest touch.

She'd grown accustomed to the pain since last night, but now her stomach roiled with it.

She looked away and met Rafe's sympathetic gaze. "If I scream, would you cover my mouth for me till I stop?" she asked him. Though she hoped she'd more courage than that, she couldn't be certain.

Mayhap she was simply a coward who had yet to be put to the test.

"If 'tis your wish, milady." Rafe knelt beside her and took her hand in his. "But I very much doubt 'twill be necessary."

"There," Padrig said, satisfaction lacing his voice. He dangled her sleeve in front of her and dropped it into her lap. "No undressing required, with eyes open or closed."

Everything moved swiftly after that, when it felt as though the past day—since the storm came upon them—had lasted a week, at least.

Was it only yesterday morn that she'd awoken in their camp, found Padrig bathing in the pool, begun to realize the strength of the powerful attraction drawing them toward each other?

So much had happened in that brief time. So much had changed.

As she let Padrig shift her into place, braced herself against Rafe's strong body with his arms holding her steady and Padrig holding her right arm in a firm clasp, she realized nothing in her life would ever be the same again.

When she fixed her gaze upon Padrig's deep blue eyes, she was glad of that fact.

Drawing strength from somewhere deep within her, Alys closed her hand tight around Rafe's arm and nodded to Padrig that she was ready.

Chapter Twelve

Never could she have imagined such pain, or such a sense of relief it was over.

Pray God she would forget, quickly, the horrid sound of her shoulder popping as Padrig pushed it back into the socket. The way it felt would likely haunt her for the rest of her life, she had no doubt.

She shuddered still, waves of shaking that made her quake from head to toe.

But she'd not screamed, or swooned or done anything else she'd be ashamed of.

Not this time, anyway.

"You're a brave lass, milady!" Rafe briefly tightened his arms around her before he got up and eased her into Padrig's embrace. "I could not have borne it so well."

"I didn't," Padrig told her as he gathered her close. "Cried like a babe when Lord Connor pushed my arm back into place." Despite Rafe's presence, Padrig buried his face in Alys's hair.

To her surprise, he was trembling as well, though not so much as she. She drew back to look at him. He appeared his usual calm self, save for his eyes. They glowed bright blue in his tanned face, revealing some strong emotion she could not name.

"Thank God 'tis done," he murmured to her. "'Tis a wonder I didn't cry this time, as well." He gave a wry laugh. "I think I'd rather have been in your position, sweeting. Though I knew what I had to do, 'twas damned hard to make myself do it."

He pulled away, stroking his hand over her hair in a fleeting caress before rising to his feet.

Alys remained where she was, for she'd not a bit of strength left within her. Without the support of Padrig's arms about her, she slumped back on the log, only the tree behind her holding her upright. "I don't think my legs will work," she told him. Her voice sounded strange, slow and muddled, as if she'd drunk too much wine. "Nor will anything else, for that matter."

Her head lolled to the side and she began to slip sideways off the log toward the ground.

Padrig reached out and caught her, letting her slide into his arms. He scooped her up and cradled her to his chest—much as he had last night, she thought, though it might have been naught but a dream she was remembering. Still, it felt so good when he held her—comfortable, necessary, right.

"Thank you for catching me," she mumbled against the side of his neck. "I might have hurt my head if I'd hit the ground. Probably the only part o' me not hurt already." She giggled, the sound seeming to come from a distance. "I believe you could have mended that, too, don't you think?"

She squirmed into a more comfortable position, with her cheek resting against Padrig's bewhiskered face. The dark hair was surprisingly soft. She'd noticed when they'd kissed, now that she thought of it. The feel of it brushing over her skin did something strange and wonderful to her insides.

Smiling, she smoothed her cheek along the firm line of his jaw.

"Alys," Padrig said, his voice soft but sharp. He cupped her head in his hand and held her still. "What are you doing?"

Rafe laughed. He sounded far away, though he looked near enough for her to reach out and touch.

When she tried to do so, however, her arm dropped limply to her side.

Padrig hefted her more securely into his arms and sat down on the log. "Hand me that strip of cloth, would you?" he asked Rafe, pointing to the material he'd used for a sling.

"Going to tie me up, are you?" she asked, not too concerned about the possibility.

Rafe laughed again, and muttered something she didn't hear.

Evidently Padrig heard him, however, for he sent the other man a pointed look that quelled his laughter.

Feeling strangely detached, Alys watched as Padrig wound the linen into an odd configuration and immobilized her right arm against her body. It still hurt, though not nearly as much as it had before.

In truth, she couldn't really tell if she hurt anywhere. A strange numbness had settled over her, softening the edges of her world, making everything a little less harsh.

It appeared she'd lost her ability to worry about much of anything, either. She knew there were others injured worse than she, but she trusted Padrig and Rafe to take care of them as well as they'd tended her.

Some part of her also knew 'twas very wrong of her to cling to Padrig the way she was, knew she shouldn't be watching him with all her lustful thoughts showing in her eyes.

The disapproving side of her was shockingly easy to strike down, to brush away like an annoying fly—leaving the Alys who did as she wished, took what she wanted, cared nothing about whether her behavior was proper or forward...

Only whether it was true and honest...

Padrig gazed down at Alys, nestled so close he could have turned his head and kissed her, and marveled at the sweetness of her expression. With her eyes closed, her face relaxed, she appeared naught but an innocent young woman.

While he didn't doubt she *was* untouched, nevertheless there was little of the innocent in their dealings with each other.

She seemed to be in a deep sleep, not in a swoon. Mayhap her body had finally given in to the shock of the past day and sought refuge in healing slumber. He knew she'd not rested much during the night.

Rafe reached over and gently moved her bound arm to rest atop her chest. "The lass is one surprise after another," he remarked quietly. "We're lucky. Could you imagine if she were a whining, complaining wench? She'd likely have been screaming her head off from the moment the storm hit last night."

"I doubt you'd have let it go on that long," Padrig said dryly. He chuckled. "You'd have found some way to silence her long since."

Rafe's innocent expression sat false upon his swarthy

face. "I'd never lay a hand on a lady!" he protested, eyes wide. He shook his head, his mouth twisting into a devilish grin. "Of course, not every woman *is* a lady…"

Settling Alys more comfortably in his arms, Padrig headed back across the clearing. "I'm certain whatever you did would be for her own good." He smiled at the thought of just what Rafe might do in such a situation.

"It *would* be better than murdering a wench, 'tis true." He fell into step alongside Padrig. "Less likely to get me killed, as well," he added.

His expression suddenly serious, Rafe reached out, caught Padrig by the arm and drew him to a halt, releasing him at once. "I don't know if 'tis fitting for me to say anything about this, milord. 'Twould probably be better for me to keep my mouth shut." He shrugged. "Hell, when have I ever been sensible?"

Certain he didn't want to hear what Rafe had to say, nonetheless Padrig waited for the other man to speak. "Go on," he urged when Rafe hesitated.

Rafe took a deep breath. "Last night I would have said there was nothing between you and the lady, save a natural bit of interest on both your parts."

Padrig met Rafe's gaze evenly. "Aye, you're right. There was nothing."

"This morning 'twould be clear to a blind man that things have changed a great deal." Rafe looked away. "I'm not blind—and neither are the others."

Though his instinct was to end the conversation at once, Padrig knew he needed to hear the rest of it—and he should heed Rafe's advice if he offered any, whatever it might be.

He trusted the man with his life every day. 'Twas just as likely he could trust him in this, as well. He'd served

with Rafe long enough to know his confidence in the
man was well-founded. Rafe's advice was generally
sound, straightforward and to the point.

And mayhap he'd find it easier to heed a different
voice of reason, since he was having so much trouble
listening to his own.

Padrig nodded. "Aye, something's changed." Glancing at Alys, relaxed in his arms, he felt a surge of long-
ing, of confusion, race through him. "Don't bother to
ask me what it is, exactly." He shook his head. "Even if
I had the words, I still couldn't begin to explain what I
don't understand."

"You don't need words to explain lust—and I can tell
ye from sad experience that no one has ever died from
ignoring that particular ailment," Rafe added wryly.
"Just have a care you don't cause this brave lass any
grief. Or embarrassment." His gaze measuring, he observed Padrig and Alys for a moment. "Ye should watch
your step around the others, milord. I'd hate to see either of ye get hurt by such foolishness."

Nodding once, Rafe strode away, leaving Padrig staring after him.

Feeling firmly put in his place, Padrig followed Rafe
back to the shelter. His attention kept wandering to the
woman in his arms, though Rafe's reminder about the others made him consider his recent actions in a new light.

His first responsibility lay with caring for everyone—both the men under his command and those 'twas
his task to protect.

He didn't believe he'd shirked his duty, but he wasn't
certain he'd measured up to his usual high standards,
either.

His assessment of that would have to wait, however, for the day marched on, and they'd much to accomplish before 'twas over.

That in mind, he carried Alys into the shelter and settled her upon her pallet, then went to check on Alys's maid and his men.

It didn't take long to make his evaluation. Peter, Jock and Rafe had done well in caring for everyone, but 'twas the simple truth that their group had been hit hard by the storm's destruction. Few were capable of much more than remaining awake.

Several, though not fit to walk, would be able to ride on their own. However, Marie, as well as several of his men, would have to be led on horseback or be carried with another rider.

Another problem they faced was the lack of enough mounts to suit their needs. If they left behind anything in their baggage that wasn't essential, doubled up on horseback and used the pack horses as mounts, they'd just be able to provide transportation for everyone.

After giving Jock and Peter orders to prepare everyone for the journey and to pack up any useful belongings from the hut, Padrig and Rafe left the shelter to ready the horses. They needed to rework some of the saddles and equipment to cope with the men's injuries and their ability—or lack of it—to stay in the saddle without assistance.

Marie, who appeared to have the worst injuries, would have to be carried by Jock. Since the tall, lean man-at-arms had the most powerful shoulders and arms Padrig had ever seen, he knew they'd find no better way to move the still-unresponsive woman. Jock would hold Marie safe and steady across his saddle no matter what terrain they encountered.

Though Alys had been sleeping when he'd left the shelter, Padrig assumed she'd wake before 'twas time to leave. He had first thought to carry her with him on the journey, but changed his mind after his conversation with Rafe.

Rafe would ride with Lady Alys up before him in the saddle, removing temptation from Padrig's vicinity, yet keeping her out of harm's way. He didn't dare put her on her mare alone. The horses hadn't calmed down much, and would likely be a challenge to control. Alys was an indifferent rider under normal circumstances. With one arm bound to her side, as well as her other injuries, he feared she'd wind up falling off, or carried off on a runaway steed.

Once they'd reworked the equipment and decided on the arrangements for the journey, Padrig and Rafe split up to sort through the baggage and separate out what they would take with them.

The task didn't require all Padrig's attention. The silence gave him a moment to consider all that had occurred since the storm.

It felt as if every move they'd made since dawn had taken an eternity, yet a glance at the sun showed that a surprisingly short amount of time had passed. If not too much went awry once they resumed their trek, they should arrive at Winterbrooke with time to spare before dusk.

Perhaps 'twas lack of sleep that made him feel a looming sense of disaster. Exhaustion dogged his every move, a weighty mantle that sat heavy upon his shoulders until he wanted nothing more than to curl up on the mossy ground near the forest's edge and give in to the blessed oblivion of sleep.

However, he'd more chance of being crowned king than he had of sleeping any time soon.

Needing something to occupy his mind and keep him alert, he let his attention turn to Alys and their situation.

With those thoughts racing through his brain, he'd be wide awake in no time.

He'd not really considered how his behavior might appear to the others. He was in command of the troop sent along to protect Lady Alys on her journey.

He'd always done his best to guard and look after anyone in his charge—yet in truth, he could see that his entire bearing around Alys was very different than his usual demeanor.

'Twas clear to him now that the extraordinary awareness of Alys he felt—both his intense physical reaction to her, as well as the inexplicable emotions she roused—was hampering his judgment and his ability to commit all his attention to his duty.

If he kept to this course, with his mind and body in such turmoil, he feared that in no time at all, he'd be aware of little else in the world but Alys.

He knew this could not go on.

She was a noblewoman on her way to a new chapter of her life, a chapter that, whatever else it held, most definitely would not include him.

Lady Alys was not his to keep, a fact Rafe's simple words brought home to him with a vengeance.

And no doubt vengeance would be his reward, were he to forget that simple fact.

If Padrig caused Alys the slightest harm or hurt, he'd have Rafe to face now…

…and Lord Rannulf to deal with later.

'Twas debatable which would be worse, for while Rafe's response would be direct, and likely painful,

Lord Rannulf's reaction could be both painful now, as well as vastly detrimental to his future.

As a man who made his way in life by his wits, his sword and the delicate web of familial connections, he could not afford to make reckless decisions.

Over the years Padrig had learned one valuable lesson through experience and observation: a man made his own luck. He tried to be deliberate in his actions, to plan as carefully as possible for whatever the future could bring, all the while knowing he'd little control over it—and above all, to hope for the best.

This journey had sent him on a different path than that he'd followed for a long time—the one he'd followed since the journey he'd made to l'Eau Clair from his home in Wales so many years ago.

After that hellish journey he'd first set his feet on the road to knighthood, to self-respect, to overcoming his weaknesses and becoming strong in both body and mind.

He'd do well to return to the course he'd taken up so long ago.

If he paid heed to his own advice, followed the way he'd laid out for himself, he knew he would not go astray.

Why was it, then, that the notion of living the life he'd made for himself made him feel hollow and alone?

Chapter Thirteen

Preparations took longer than Padrig had expected to get everyone ready to travel, mounted and on the road. Still, they managed to set out before midday.

He hoped 'twould be an uneventful journey, but given all they had working against them before they even left, the likelihood of that seemed extremely low.

The logistics of getting everyone situated had been nightmarish. Trying to fit two grown men on a pack-horse, with a saddle made for one, was difficult. When one of those men could barely hold himself upright, or had an arm or leg immobilized in a crude splint, it was damned near impossible.

Marie remained insensible throughout the entire or-deal of settling her in the saddle with Jock. Her body limp, her bruised head lolling against Jock's shoulder, Padrig could not help but wonder how much worse the poor woman's condition would be by the time they ar-rived at Winterbrooke Manor.

If she survived the trip at all.

Lady Alys woke shortly before they left, in a better

state than before she'd nodded off, thankfully. Her
speech sounded normal once again, and it seemed she'd
rested better with her arm back in its proper position,
bound so she couldn't move it.

She was unusually quiet, and gave them no argu-
ment over their arrangements for her. She simply nodded, and let Rafe lead her to her mare.

Her pleasure when she saw Arian and assured herself of the mare's well-being brightened her face for a
moment, the lone spark of joy she showed as they gathered their tattered group in the clearing.

They appeared a sorry lot, battered and bruised, their
injuries ruthlessly revealed in the harsh light of day.

Yet despite their wretched circumstances, several of
his men somehow found the spirit to tease each other
and make light of their situation.

However, the sight of the canvas-wrapped body tied
onto one of the packhorses—Owen, the man who'd
been crushed in the initial fury of the storm—only
added to the weary looks worn by all. Before they set
out, they paused to pray for Owen's soul—and for their
own safe arrival at the haven of Winterbrooke Manor.

Rafe rode Lady Alys's mare, with Lady Alys in the
saddle before him. The horse's lameness had eased
overnight, leading Padrig to believe 'twas not so serious as to keep her from carrying them both.

Alys held herself upright, not depending on Rafe for
support. How long she could keep that up, he'd no idea.
From what he'd learned about Alys in the past day or
so, he wouldn't be surprised if she managed it for the
whole trip.

God knew, she was stubborn enough!

Padrig ended up on foot at the end of the procession,

leading his gelding. The man who rode the horse could remain in the saddle only if they lashed him to it, with his broken leg stretched out in a makeshift cradle of sticks lined with spare clothing. There was no way for anyone else to sit atop the horse. Since the man was in too much pain to control the beast, it made sense for someone to guide him.

They couldn't move any faster than a walk anyway, so it made little difference to Padrig whether he rode or not.

Besides, he was so tired, most likely the only way he would be able to stay awake was to keep moving.

With one last glance at the vast devastation surrounding them, Padrig gave the order to head out, and they were finally on their way.

Alys wriggled in the saddle, trying without much success to restore sensation to her numb backside and legs. Arian's slow, rhythmic stride worked its temptation on her weary body, enticing her to give in to the lure of sleep. It took nigh all her resources not to nod off, to instead remain upright, to not surrender to the urge to slump back against Rafe's body and accept the support he offered.

If Padrig were seated behind her, she'd be much more likely to change her mind. About accepting his support, at any rate.

Nay, she'd have already done so if it were Padrig riding with her, she acknowledged, whether she'd needed any help or not.

She'd have made use of any excuse to touch him, to be in his arms again.

Despite her sheer exhaustion, she had little desire to give in to sleep just yet—and its potential for a nightmarish revisit of last night's terror.

Especially while perched up on horseback. She had enough bruises and pains as it was, without courting still more.

Blinking against the sun's glare, Alys shifted her attention from her body's complaints to her surroundings, hoping they'd serve to stimulate her senses. The day was glorious: warm and sunny, a gentle breeze carrying the birdsong and scents of the forest.

If not for the utter destruction everywhere she looked, and the constant aching of her injuries, 'twould have been a most lovely day.

She and Rafe rode near the front of their ragged column, evidently to take advantage of the fact that she might possibly recognize some landmark, or to note if something about the terrain looked familiar.

In truth, they'd met such devastation along every bit of the way, she could have been on a path she followed every day, and not known it.

Feeling herself begin the slide downward into despair, she shifted her attention instead to the man who sat behind her, guiding her mare and doing his best to protect her from overhanging branches, marauding insects and any other of the myriad hazards of the trail.

That he'd done so in silence she found rather endearing, for she believed that for Rafe, talking was a function of life as much as breathing.

She'd been caught unawares when Rafe, not Padrig, had climbed up behind her after Rafe had settled her into the saddle. She'd felt less surprised a moment later, once she'd seen Padrig take up the reins of his mount, already burdened with one of the injured men, to lead the animal. Horses were in short supply. Someone had to walk, and she couldn't imagine Padrig ask-

ing one of his men to do something he was unwilling
to do himself.

In her estimation, 'twas one of the things that made
him a good leader.

Of course, since Padrig had taken the mount he led
to the rear of their ragtag band, evidently to keep watch
over everything, she seldom caught a glimpse of him.
A few times the road had passed through a somewhat
clear field…and she'd taken advantage of those opportunities to look her fill.

The easy way he moved, with his long-legged stride
carrying him along at a steady pace, ensnared her as
thoroughly as when she'd watched him bathe. Clothed
or naked, Padrig captured her attention.

Rafe nudged her gently on the shoulder, jolting her
back from her reverie. She was extremely grateful he
could not know what thoughts he'd interrupted.

"How are you faring, milady? Do you need anything? Something to drink, or to stop for a moment?"

She shifted slightly in her seat so she could look
back at him. "Nay, I thank you." She glanced ahead at
their motley band as they slowly wended their way
along the winding road, more of a nearly impassable
path, actually, heavily bestrewn with debris from the
storm. "If they can keep up, so can I."

Rafe shook his head, his dark eyes alight with what
looked to be amusement. "They're seasoned soldiers,
milady, well used to surviving all manner of injuries and
dangerous situations."

She deliberately avoided the inference that she was
neither of those things. "You cannot convince me you
are faced with circumstances this extreme every day."

"Not of late, 'tis true—but there have been many

times when we've had to deal with such things, and times yet to come when we shall again. 'Tis a soldier's life, milady," he said simply. "Ask Sir Padrig, or any of these men, what dangers they've confronted in Lord Rannulf's service. I vow any one of us could tell you stories the likes of which a gentle lady such as yourself could never imagine."

"Truly?" His words sparked Alys's curiosity and excited her imagination. Such an opportunity!

Yet one she could not really take advantage of, at least not at the moment.

"Fighting is not all pomp and glory. You might have watched our work on the practice field, but that exercise is simply training to prepare us for battle. It bears little resemblance to what we truly contend with every day. Soldiering isn't about pretty tournaments or fancy shows of swordplay," he added forcefully. "It's about doing whatever we must to stay alive and fight another day."

"There must be some who have journeyed far from the Marches."

"Aye. In this troop alone, we've men who have served in Ireland and Wales, as well as here in England. Back at l'Eau Clair there are even a few battle-hardened ancients who traveled to the Holy Land with King Richard, and two who served under the earl of Pembroke back before Lady Gillian was born."

Those men she'd already met. Their accounts of the Crusades, of journeying Outremer to the hellishly hot lands of Saladin—or in the case of the two who'd been with Pembroke, of fighting and tourneys across France and Normandy—were among the first narratives she'd set down after her arrival at l'Eau Clair.

As one of the younger generation of fighters under Lord Rannulf's command, Rafe represented a new source she could draw upon.

She silently cursed her inability to use her right hand, to make note of what Rafe might say, should she convince him to disclose anything she could use for her chronicles.

"I've heard some of their stories," she told him, greatly understating the case. "Some sounded more fantasy than fact."

"There are a few fellows who embellish a wee bit, 'tis true, but I vow there's more of the truth in their tales than you would imagine. They lived in different times than now, times when ideals like honor and duty had meaning. These days—barring a few exceptions such as Lord Rannulf—you'd be hard-pressed to find many honorable men. There are plenty of 'em among Lord Rannulf's family and friends, and those he commands, but that's not the usual way of it anymore," he added, his voice tinged with bitterness.

What—or who—had caused Rafe to be so mistrustful? She could not mistake the strength of his reaction, for tension was evident in his voice, his face. It nigh vibrated from his body as he sat behind her.

Even as she wondered, a change came over him. He'd been leaning slightly toward her during their low-voiced conversation, but now he straightened. His posture relaxed, and his mouth curled into a smile. "'Twas the greatest honor of my life when Lord Rannulf brought me here, into his service."

A frisson of excitement passed through her, sending her pulse racing and heightening her curiosity.

He seemed a man who liked to talk, someone who

could be depended upon to make even a simple tale exciting.

And from what she sensed, he'd many a story to tell.

If she could only manage to remember what he told her until she was able to wield a pen once again, 'twas possible she might gain a great deal of information to add substance to her work.

She sought to stifle her eagerness. Doubtless he'd believe her a most bloodthirsty maid as it was, once she began to ask him for more details.

It would be best, she decided, if she could ease into her questioning, so he would not notice the depth of her interest.

She realized as well that she could use this as an opportunity to learn more about Padrig. Rafe seemed to know a great deal about his commander. He certainly hadn't appeared shy this morn about sharing what he knew.

Rafe himself had given her the perfect opening to begin her questioning. He wished to talk.

And she certainly wanted to hear what he had to say.

"Whom had you served before?" she asked. "It was not at l'Eau Clair, then?"

"I suppose you could say I've always been in the FitzCliffords' service, for I was born at Birkland, a small property in Nottinghamshire owned by Lord Rannulf's father. I was employed there in one way or another since I was a small lad. Eventually I became a man-at-arms, part of the garrison charged to defend the place. By then, the man who held Birkland for Lord Rannulf was Sir Richard Belleville." He made a disparaging sound. "Though Belleville may be of noble birth, in truth he's naught but a lying, thieving knave."

"What did he do?" Alys asked impatiently. "Why do you hate him so much?" She wriggled round so she could see Rafe's face more fully. "How did you come to leave Birkland and travel to l'Eau Clair?"

"By the saints, but you're a curious maid!" He watched her for a short time, his scrutiny polite, but obviously intent upon measuring her in some manner.

Finally his lips quirked up in a faint smile and he shook his head. Perhaps he wasn't sure what to make of her. Mayhap she'd not been so easy to read as he'd anticipated she'd be.

Good! It gave her an odd sense of satisfaction to take people by surprise, to keep them wondering precisely who she was, and what she might do.

Though in truth, she wasn't certain she surprised anyone all that often.

"Do you always ask so many questions?" he asked.

She took a moment to compose herself, so she'd not let her eagerness show. "'Tis but a pleasant way to pass the time," she told him in an even voice. "On a journey such as this where we cannot travel very swiftly, conversation serves to speed the way—or to make it seem so, at any rate."

She peered up at his expression from beneath her lashes, trying to judge whether he believed her. 'Twas hard to tell. "Don't you find it so?" she added sweetly.

He sent her a stern glance that looked odd upon his usually jovial countenance. "Do *you* find using such womanly tricks to befuddle a man to be effective, milady?" He held up his arm to keep a branch from knocking against her. "I'm assuming that's your reason for doing it. Or perhaps I'm wrong, and you've another reason entirely?" he asked, his tone provocative, his eyebrows raised in inquiry.

Whatever did he mean? Did he believe she'd been *flirting* with him?

A tide of mortification rose to heat her face. In spite of the discomfort, she forced herself to meet Rafe's considering gaze.

She'd never thought of her actions in that way. She didn't set out to "befuddle"—nor to entice, she thought indignantly. 'Twas more an attempt to distract the other person from discovering her true purpose, to put him at ease while still achieving her own goals.

Dear God, that sounded nigh as terrible as being regarded as a tease!

Now that she considered her behavior, however, she could see how it might appear. In the past she'd employed such wiles almost exclusively on the old knights she'd spoken with in the barracks. They'd treated her with respect, and seemed flattered by her interest in their tales.

Using those same tactics on a man nearer her age might be construed in a completely different manner.

Rafe continued to watch her, his expression unreadable.

She suspected her wiles had no effect upon him. That fact, combined with her ever-present curiosity, emboldened her to ask him, "What reason do you think I have?"

That startled him out of his complacency, she noted with satisfaction, for his tanned face reddened a bit and his expression grew cautious.

"What do you mean?" he asked.

Laughing, Alys settled herself more firmly in the saddle and leaned closer to him. "Come, Rafe," she placed her hand on his arm, "you cannot accuse me in such a fashion, and then pretend you don't understand what I'm talking about."

He shifted from cautious to hunted in a heartbeat. His gaze dropped from her face to her hand, the color riding upon his cheeks darkened.

Rafe seemed, amazingly, at a loss for words.

The sense of feminine power flowing through her at that moment felt enormous. She'd never realized she had the capacity to produce that kind of effect on a man.

However, she'd prefer to make use of her charms on another man, not Rafe.

She took pity on him, moving her hand from his arm. "I'm not saying 'twas the case, mind you—but you thought I was trying to entice you, didn't you?" Watching his eyes widen in reaction, she added eagerly, "Did it work?"

Chapter Fourteen

Alys was vastly relieved when Rafe gave a dry laugh and shook his head. "Nay, lass. Though the fault lies with me, not you."

"Oh, good," she said. While she was glad 'twas so, she was also curious as to the reason. "Why not? Not that I was actually *trying* to—"

"I believe you, lass," he reassured her. "I didn't truly consider ye'd be trying that on *me,* anyway. But I couldn't resist teasing you. If you could have seen your face, milady… I could tell exactly when you understood what I was saying by the look of horror that crossed your face."

Alys felt a flush rise to her cheeks once more, knowing her feelings had been so obvious. When he began to laugh at her, she poked him in the ribs.

"I doubt 'twas *that* funny," she protested—until the memory of Rafe's earlier expression, when she'd placed her hand on his arm, made her chuckle, as well. "I supposed it was," she conceded. "As was yours. Come, admit I frightened you."

"For a moment," he agreed. "You do know how to startle a man, Lady Alys."

They rode along in silence for a moment. Alys could feel the weight of Rafe's gaze upon her face, but she remained quiet, unsure what to say.

Rafe tugged on the reins to guide Arian around an uprooted tree. "I didn't mean to strike you mute, you know. Nor to make you uncomfortable." He halted the mare in the middle of the path. "Would you rather I get someone else to ride with you?"

"Not at all," she said. "'Tis not you making me quiet. It's just that now I find myself with a bit to consider. I'd never thought of myself as someone who might lead a man to think things I didn't mean."

Before he could reply, someone behind them shouted, "Is everything all right? Have you found the road we seek?"

"Nay," Rafe shouted back. "Just paused for a moment." He turned round enough to peer behind them. "Sir Padrig, shall we stop soon?"

"We've plenty of distance left to travel," came the reply. "Let's keep going for a while longer."

Rafe nudged Arian into motion. "What were we talking about?" he asked. He nodded. "Ah, yes. Are ye the kind o' woman who would lead on a man?" Amusement filled his gaze. "I wouldn't say you are, milady. Not unless you meant to be, anyway."

Uncomfortable with where considering *that* notion took her, Alys glanced up and scanned the area. They'd been riding for some time. They ought to have reached the road to Winterbrooke Manor by now.

Of course, for all she knew, there might be more than

one road leading to the place—in which case she'd be of no help whatsoever, she thought wryly.

She might as well continue her conversation with Rafe, she decided. At least then, she'd keep herself from wallowing in melancholy.

She brought a smile to her lips. "Then tell me, what is the fault that lies with you, not me?"

"You're much too noble for me, milady, if ye know what I mean." He shrugged. "I know better than to aim so high. I vowed long ago that with women, I'd never get myself caught up in a situation I couldn't control." He turned his head away from her, but she heard him mutter, "Unlike some I could name."

"No offense to you, but I'm glad my wiles—whether that was that I intended or no—didn't work on you," Alys told him. "I'm having a difficult enough time as it is, contemplating the fact that I might be behaving in that fashion. Do you think I have been, without realizing it?" she asked, giving voice to her concern.

"What I think, milady, is that I shouldn't have teased ye about this in the first place." Rafe's tone, the look in his eyes, held reassurance. "You've done nothing wrong at all, and I apologize for making ye believe you had."

He closed his hand about her shoulder and turned her to face forward in the saddle. "Now then, focus those pretty eyes of yours and let's see if you can find something you recognize."

Padrig plodded along in the wake of the troop, grateful that no one had fallen from their mount, and that everyone, so far as he could tell, had come to no further harm from the rigors of the journey.

As he'd expected, it had been no hardship to keep

pace with the others while on foot. The terrain was rough in places, made doubly so by the effects of the storm's wrath. The magnitude of devastation, and the size of the area affected, was unimaginable. Downed trees, blasted by lightning, lay in splintered lengths all around them. Other trees and bushes had been uprooted by the wind, their branches ripped free and tossed about willy-nilly.

'Twas similar to what had occurred on the road they'd been following when the storm struck. Despite the rising warmth of the day, the sight sent a chill down Padrig's spine. God or the saints—someone up above—must surely have been watching over them, for it was truly a miracle they'd not been hit harder than they had.

His eyes took note of his surroundings, but his mind seemed to prefer other matters. Unfortunately trudging through the forest gave his mind too much opportunity to mull over things he shouldn't be thinking about.

Too many chances to stare ahead at the woman he knew he could not have.

She was in good hands with Rafe—but must they lean so near each other to talk?

What could they be discussing that involved touching, that made them smile and gaze into each other's eyes in such a way?

Was the reason Rafe had warned him away from Alys because Rafe wanted her for himself?

Padrig halted in his tracks, taken aback by the possibility.

His gelding gave him a nudge in the back, jolting him out of his bewilderment. Turning to check on his charge, Padrig handed John a flask of water, absently answered the man's question, though he scarce knew what the question had been, and adjusted several of the ropes securing John atop the horse.

All the while, he kept hearing Rafe's voice echoing in his head. Telling him that Alys wasn't for the likes of him, that he should have a care how he behaved with her around the others.

What of Rafe, the wily bastard?

Rafe's birth was even lower than his own, so far as Padrig knew. And the man had not won his spurs yet, either.

A simple knighthood did not a true nobleman make, but the honor certainly brought him closer to that position.

Padrig's heartbeat raced, his pulse sounding loud in his ears. His hand closed snug about the hilt of his sword. He was battle-ready...

Yet who was he to fight?

His second in command? 'Twould be a difficult thing, to tell Lord Rannulf he'd attacked Rafe because he'd suddenly turned into a jealous fool.

Should he battle himself? Aye, mayhap he did need a sword taken to him.

For being an idiot.

The dull thud of his pulse slowed. Rational thought replaced hot-blooded jealousy.

By Christ's bones, but he was a fool!

He shook his head at his own idiocy and forced himself to pay heed to his surroundings. They'd been traveling for some time now. They ought to be within the borders of Winterbrooke Manor's demesne by now.

He'd not noticed any signs of settlement, but anything much less than the keep itself could likely be hidden beneath the chaos. Anything as small as a shepherd's hut or the road to a remote farm could be nearby, and they'd never find it under these conditions.

If Alys had noted anything familiar, surely she'd have told him.

If she was paying attention to the area, not the man sitting so close behind her…

Disgusted with himself and his mindless jealousy, Padrig handed over the gelding's reins to the man ahead of him and wended his way around the plodding horses until he caught up to Rafe and Alys.

"Sir Padrig," Rafe called as Padrig drew near. "We were just now about to call for you." He halted the mare, moving her to the side of the trail so the others could continue past.

Alys smiled down at Padrig as he joined them by the edge of the rough path.

That simple action sent warmth throughout him, made his heartbeat stutter, then speed up.

Silently berating himself for a fool, he ruthlessly ordered his disobedient body to behave.

Yet he found himself smiling up at Alys in return.

"How fare you, milady?" he asked quietly, resting his hand on the mare's tangled mane and twining his fingers in the coarse hair. He barely kept himself from reaching instead for Alys's hand, resting so enticingly near on the mare's withers.

"I am better than I expected to be, milord, thanks to your help." She touched the cloth that immobilized her arm. "You are a skilled chirurgeon. With this binding in place, I cannot move my arm by mistake, and I scarce feel the pull on my shoulder."

"You may make light of it, Lady Alys, but I know 'tis painful." He scanned her face, noted the way she held herself in the saddle, as he tried to judge precisely how much she did hurt.

Quite a lot, if he used the tension that fairly radiated from her body as a guide.

Her expression grave, she watched the slow procession of the injured past them. "'Tis not so much I cannot bear it," she told him. "Compared to the others, my case is not so bad."

He nodded. He well knew the guilt that could strike after a tragedy. Sorrow for those worse off than yourself...

Combined with everlasting gratitude that it wasn't you.

She had a soldier's outlook, a practicality that should stand her in good stead in the days to come.

"I would have told you if Lady Alys needed to rest, Sir Padrig," Rafe said abruptly. "You can trust me to keep a close watch over her."

"I'd not have had you ride with her otherwise," Padrig replied, his tone equally short.

Padrig glared at Rafe, who met the look with a similar one of his own.

Mayhap he'd not been so far off the mark with his earlier notions, Padrig mused. Rafe seemed as wound up as he felt himself, when he had no reason to be.

Unless he'd an interest in Alys, as well.

"I don't know what your problem with each other might be," she mused, glancing from Rafe to Padrig, a stern expression on her face. "Whatever it is, we shall have no more of it." Alys continued to stare at Padrig, her amber eyes darkened to a tawny gold, the look in them speculative.

He held her gaze and felt his irritation begin to fade away.

"Aye, milady," he said. "We'll behave, if 'tis your wish."

"It would hardly serve us well if you don't," she told him, her voice tart. "Besides, we've more important business for the nonce than waiting while you two take out your aggravations upon each other."

She turned slightly in the saddle. "*That* is what I noticed." She pointed toward an oddly-shaped rock formation that loomed up through the wreckage of the forest. "I wish I could remember what they called it—'tis Welsh. I believe it means the Devil's Lair."

"*Ffau gan 'r diafol?*" Padrig offered. He'd heard of the sprawling rock outcropping, rumored to be riddled with caves and shafts that led deep into the earth.

Or to hell itself—hence its name.

"Aye. 'Tis a lovely sounding name, despite its meaning. To me, everything sounds beautiful in Welsh. Even the most foul curses would, I imagine." Alys gifted Padrig with a winsome smile. "Thank you, milord. Most likely I would have mangled the saying of it even had I remembered what it was."

Jesu, he thought wryly, if that was her reaction when she heard his native tongue, he'd have to speak it round her more often.

Or not. He *had* vowed to keep her at a distance.

Damnation! He felt his foul mood rushing back with a vengeance.

"'Twas not so visible before, when the trees grew all around," Alys said. "We rode quite close when we were hunting deep within the woods beyond the keep. Game is plentiful here. Sir Cedric, who holds Winterbrooke for my father, told us most everyone hereabouts is too frightened of the place to go near it, so they've done naught to clear away the trees or to plant the fields nearby."

Padrig looked around at the ruins of the forest. "They might change their minds now. There's years' worth of easy pickings here for the woodsmen."

"They will still be afraid," Alys pointed out. "It appears the place got its name from all the strange mishaps that have occurred here as long as anyone can recall. This damage will only make their fears more real."

Needing to look away, to see anything but the temptation Alys represented—save perhaps Rafe's satisfied expression as he continued to sit so close to Alys, raising a questioning brow when he met Padrig's gaze—he instead glanced up the road.

The others had moved quite a ways ahead while they'd been stopped here, he realized—and 'twas not as though they'd been traveling quickly.

He'd be glad to move on. Perhaps with some distance between them, he wouldn't be so tempted by Alys.

Or so troubled by Rafe.

"I'm sure I'd find this most fascinating some other time, milady." Only with great effort did he manage to temper his voice from the snarl welling inside him to a more moderate tone. He took a step back from the mare and settled his sword belt more comfortably at his waist. "However, I would be more interested to hear whether you can tell us how much farther we must travel to reach the keep."

She glanced up at the sun, climbing closer to its zenith in the clear summer sky. "We cannot be more than an hour from Winterbrooke. Mayhap less." Her lips curved into a smile. "I believe if we continue along this route, 'twill take us straight to the postern gate at the rear of the curtain wall. We'll be within the manor before dinnertime."

Chapter Fifteen

Padrig's expression, so dark and forbidding but a moment earlier, changed in an instant. He grinned, his teeth bright against the dark beginnings of a beard covering his chin and jaw, his eyes flashing blue fire.

She breathed deep in reaction, even as she returned his smile.

One hand on his sword hilt, he sketched a bow. "Thank you, milady. 'Tis precisely what I wished to know."

He turned and headed off at a jog to catch up to the others.

After he'd gone a few paces, however, he halted and spun to face them. "Come along, you laggards," he called. "Just imagine—hot food, hot baths, clean clothes..." he coaxed, his expression more carefree than Alys had ever seen it. "You don't want to be the last ones through the gates, do you?"

Not awaiting a response, he set off along the road once again.

Alys shook her head as if to free it from some strange enchantment. She turned to Rafe, opened her mouth to speak, and found she didn't know what to say.

A most unusual reaction for her, under any circumstances.

Rafe had leaned over to adjust something on the saddle. He sat up, looked at her face, and groaned. "Jesu save us, you're as bad as he!"

Though she could feel her face heat, she raised her chin and held his gaze. "Whatever do you mean?" she demanded.

"You're a pair of reckless fools." His movements abrupt, he picked up the reins and urged Arian into motion. "This path you're headed down is madness! You're a lady, nobly born and bred. He's a landless knight who owes his service—his very position in life—to another's whim. What do you think I meant?" he asked, his tone as brusque as his movements.

"We've done nothing—" she protested.

He cut her off with a look. "Doesn't matter what you've done or haven't done," he growled. "That's none o' *my* business, at any rate." He lowered his voice as they caught up to the others and took a position at the end of the line.

When she would have turned away from him completely, he caught her by the arm and held her there. "It's where the two o' you are headed that has me worried, Lady Alys—for both o' ye."

Tears welled in her eyes, but she blinked them away before they could fall. "I thank you for your concern, Rafe." She wasn't able to keep her emotions out of her voice, however, which sounded·odd even to her ears.

"Here, lass, I never meant to make you weep," Rafe said quietly. He glanced ahead at Padrig, then back at her. "He took it little better when I spoke to him this morn."

"You spoke to Padrig about me?" she asked, all the while knowing 'twould be better if she let this entire subject fade away.

Rafe hesitated, then, perhaps realizing he'd already admitted as much, nodded. "Warned him o' the foolhardiness of where it seemed he was heading. Told him he'd do your reputation no good if he kept lookin' at you the way he was." He shrugged, then continued, "You know what I'm sayin' without my having to explain it all to you, just as he did."

Now she truly had no idea what to say. Not that she could have forced a word to pass through the tightness in her throat.

To hear another say what she already knew deep in her heart only served to compound the pain of it.

"'Tis the way o' the world, lass," Rafe said wryly. "Ye might as well get used to it."

To Alys, the remainder of the journey passed in a blur. Rafe had, blessedly, kept silent once he'd had his say, perhaps realizing he could do no more than he'd already done.

Perhaps he'd known if he'd continued to speak of it, she'd have done more than blink her eyes free of tears and listen in relative silence.

She could not have said even now if her reaction would have progressed to outright weeping, or whether she'd have instead erupted into a seething, snarling ball of anger, lashing out at everyone and everything.

She *was* angry with herself for tossing aside, in her thoughts, at least, her dreams of joining the abbey. One heated glance at Padrig, one touch of her lips to his, and she'd been ready to abandon the future she'd planned and hoped for for years.

And for what? Padrig had made her no promises. They'd scarce discussed much of anything at all, the few times they'd been together. Rafe was correct, that any contact beyond the most basic between her and Padrig would be looked at askance, questioned and frowned upon—if not worse.

Their worlds might touch repeatedly, overlapping along the seams of their day-to-day existence—yet no one would expect either of them to become an intimate part of the other's life.

She'd do well to remind herself, as often as it took, of the hopes she'd nurtured. To write was an essential part of her being. She knew of no other way to attain that goal other than what she'd hopefully set in motion.

Straightening her spine, she also firmed her resolve. If her parents would not send her to the abbey, she'd follow whatever path *she* chose.

She fixed her gaze upon Padrig's loose-limbed stride, the strength and grace of his movements despite the armor he wore.

She smiled with pleasure at the sight. Aye, she would most definitely take the path she desired.

The top of the small watchtower standing guard over the rear approach to Winterbrooke Manor stuck up above the distant tree line, the crude stone ramparts a stark gray against the vivid green of the trees.

Alys noted the sight with a sigh of relief. She didn't know how much longer she could manage to hold herself upright in the saddle. Rafe had lent her his support, and she'd finally accepted it, leaning back against his armor-clad chest and permitting him to hold her about the waist, but even with his help, she was nigh drooping in Rafe's loose clasp.

She glanced ahead at the rest of their party. Everyone seemed to move with the sluggishness only true exhaustion could bring. They'd all reached the end of their reserves.

This close to the keep, less storm damage was visible, mayhap because most of the trees and brush had already been cleared away for some distance all around the outside of the curtain wall to add a measure of defense.

As they drew nearer, she could see that the gate was closed and there were guards clearly visible on the low rampart above it. Her father would be pleased by Sir Cedric's vigilance. The responsibility of commanding any Marcher holding this close to the Welsh border could be a daunting task. Sir Cedric was evidently up to the test.

The guards called down a challenge as their party reached the gate. Once Sir Padrig identified himself, pointing out their need for assistance, and that he'd their lord's own daughter with him, as well, the gate swung ponderously open.

Several men-at-arms appeared in the opening, motioning for the first riders to come in. Padrig moved to allow them space to do so, then made his way to where Rafe and Alys, still mounted on Arian, hung back and waited for the others to enter first.

"Hopefully they will be able to care for everyone," he said as he paused beside the mare. "It's been a grueling journey. Any respite will be most welcome."

Rafe shifted around and slid down, groaning. "I've grown spoiled. Can't ride bareback without getting a fierce pain in my ars—" He coughed. "Beg pardon, milady. Didn't mean to offend."

"You didn't," she said, shaking her head. Rafe seemed to always be entertaining—merely by being himself.

Alys's back suddenly cramped without the support Rafe had provided. Gasping, she flexed her shoulders to ease the spasm, and instead set loose a sharp, throbbing pain in her right shoulder.

Padrig reached up for her at once, grasping her about the waist. "Let me help you down, milady," he said as he easily lifted her from the saddle.

When he set her on her feet, she was able to stand by leaning heavily against him.

Her legs felt as though they might simply fold up beneath her. If not for the fact that Padrig kept his arm firmly around her waist to steady her, she'd likely have crumpled to the ground.

"Give yourself a moment for the feeling to return to your legs," he cautioned. "We can wait a bit longer to get inside."

She continued to lean into him, letting him bear some of her weight for a moment. The cramp faded, leaving behind more of an ache than before and making her glad he hadn't let go of her yet.

For any number of reasons, only one of which that she still needed his help to stand.

Since she'd been given the opportunity, she allowed herself the guilty pleasure of savoring his strength wrapped around her, of feeling the warmth of his body seep into her where they touched, of enveloping herself in his scent.

"Everyone's made it inside," Rafe said, jolting Alys's attention from Padrig to the world around them. "Should we go in now as well, or will you be needing to rest a moment longer, milady?"

"Nay, I can manage, with Sir Padrig's help," Alys said. "Shall we?"

With Rafe leading Arian and Padrig still lending Alys his support, they slowly headed for the gate.

They were almost halfway there when Padrig paused. His eyes intent, he scanned the wall, his gaze coming to rest on the gate. He shook his head. "Something doesn't feel right," he muttered. "Though I cannot determine what it is."

Rafe passed the reins from his right hand to his left and glanced uneasily around them. "'Tis very quiet, but this *is* the rear gate. Mayhap 'tis the lack of noise from the village, the fact that there's no one around, that makes it seem so strange."

"Mayhap." Padrig loosened his hold on Alys slightly, as if testing her ability to stand on her own.

She stepped away from him, noticed her legs shook, and grabbed hold of his arm to steady herself. "A thought just occurred to me. Shouldn't Sir Cedric have come by now, to see how we fare?" she asked.

"'Tis possible," Padrig agreed. "Though not all castellans would necessarily be so polite."

Their disquiet had spread. She could feel it now, too—an odd sense of something not quite right. "You told the guards I was here, I heard you. They ought to have informed him at once. For myself, I care not for such ceremony, but Sir Cedric's not the kind of man who would dare offend my father in any way." She met Padrig's gaze and drew no comfort from the fact that his eyes had paled to a frosty shade of blue. A shudder passed through her and she tightened her grip on his arm. "He'd certainly not risk Father's wrath by slighting me."

Padrig reached down, took Alys's hand in his and, after giving it a reassuring squeeze, closed her fingers about his heavy leather belt. "To keep my hands free," he told her quietly. He slid his arm lightly about her waist as though he continued to hold her up.

"I can walk on my own," she whispered fiercely.

She made to let go altogether, but he wouldn't let her. "Nay, Alys—let it seem you still require my help. If I need you to let go, I'll tell you."

He turned to Rafe. "Come, we cannot linger here forever." He added more loudly, "If we don't bestir ourselves, there will be nothing left for us to eat."

They'd scarce taken two steps closer to the gates when the silence was broke by a ruckus just on the other side of the wall.

"Sir Padrig," Peter shouted. "Don't come in, 'tis a trap!"

Padrig caught Alys by the wrist, tugged her hand loose of his belt and, drawing his sword in one hand and his dagger in the other, spun away from her and raced toward the portal.

Rafe dropped Arian's reins and took off hard on his heels, the two men covering the distance to the wall in but a few long strides.

The two guards who'd stood waiting in the passageway ran to the gates, each grabbed one of the heavy wooden doors, and began to tug them closed.

Alys caught Arian by the bridle and held the mare steady as she watched.

Padrig on the right, Rafe on the left, they hurtled into the guards, weapons slashing furiously as they pressed their attack.

Several more men rushed out to join the fray, till all Alys could see was a chaotic melee of flashing steel and flailing limbs. Everyone seemed to be shouting, as were the men who appeared along the wall.

She couldn't understand a word they were saying, but she knew they were speaking Welsh.

By the saints, the Welsh had taken Winterbrooke!

How dare they, she fumed, letting go of Arian. She gave the mare a slap on the rump, knowing that otherwise, the horse was like to follow close on her heels. Arian didn't go far, but at least she was less likely to get in the way.

Left hand fumbling at her belt, Alys finally got hold of her eating knife and slid it from its sheath. 'Twas not much, as weapons went, but she could hardly stand by and do nothing while Padrig and Rafe were so outnumbered.

Her knees felt a little unsteady, her stomach roiled, but she pushed herself into motion and began to walk as swiftly as she could toward the fray. Before she reached it, however, the men who'd rushed out to fight abruptly broke away and raced back through the gates.

She halted, waiting to see what would happen next.

Before Padrig and Rafe could stop them or follow them through, they'd jerked the tall doors shut. The loud thud of the bar being dropped into position on the other side sounded loud as thunder in the sudden silence.

Rafe ran up and kicked the massive door, yelping with pain and earning a reproving look from Padrig.

Padrig said something to Rafe. They turned to go. They had nearly made it back to Alys when several archers, bows already drawn, appeared just behind them, up on the wall.

"Archers! Run!" she screamed, turning to do so herself without waiting to see if they obeyed her.

'Twas near impossible to run with one arm bound

tight to her body, but stark fear was a great motivator. She got to Arian just as the first volley of arrows hit, the soft, strange thumping of the arrows sinking into the ground all around them frightening the mare as the clash of steel had not.

Arian ran toward the distant trees. Alys, terrified to provide a target by remaining on her feet, flopped face first onto the grass.

She stayed there, sprawled uncomfortably atop her right arm and muttering vengeful prayers, until she felt Padrig drop down beside her.

"Are you all right?" he asked urgently. His hands were shaking, she noted absently, when he eased her onto her back and adjusted the binding on her arm. "Where are you hurt?"

"I'm unharmed." She tried to sit up, but at the whirring sound of another flight of arrows, Padrig pressed her down into the grass and covered her protectively with his body.

Incensed that he'd protect her over himself, she tried to push him off her, but she was no match for him in size or strength.

He captured her left hand in his and pinned it to the ground beside her, using his lower body to anchor her legs. "What are you doing?" he demanded. "Do you want to be shot?"

"Nay—nor do I want *us* to be!" she snapped. Anger poured out of her in waves, consuming her with the necessity to protect Padrig, to somehow get them out of this hellish mess. *"Get off me."*

More arrows flew. They thumped into the ground all around them, making her blink, her skin writhing with the need to escape them.

"Padrig," Rafe called urgently from close by. Suddenly Padrig's body jerked twice, then collapsed atop hers.

She could barely breathe. Turning her head, she could see why. Rafe had been shot, too, and had landed at least partially on Padrig. His arm hung slack over Padrig's shoulder, dragging on the grass near her head.

She was pinned beneath two men, neither was moving, and more arrows were flying their way.

How in God's name was she to get them out of this?

Chapter Sixteen

Howls and whoops of unmistakable approval, or so it sounded to her, filled the air as the three of them lay pressed to the ground. Though Alys didn't know what, precisely, the Welsh were saying, their meaning was clear enough.

Sorrow and anger fought for dominance within her. Anger won out. She'd no time to give in to sorrow now. For the first time in her life, she understood the meaning of blood lust, for it truly felt as if her blood boiled with rage and the desire for vengeance.

Oh, to be a man, a warrior, able to rise up and avenge Padrig and Rafe!

The shouting continued, the words flowing over her in a noisome cloud that clung to her and gave her strength.

She wished she spoke Welsh, to return the enemy's insults in kind.

A surge of energy flowing through her, Alys loosened her hand from Padrig's grasp and pushed at his body, trying to wriggle out from beneath him.

His grasp? Wouldn't his fingers have relaxed if he were dead?

Her heart racing, her mouth dry with the fear she was wrong, she caught hold of Padrig's shoulder and shook him. "Wake up!" she screamed. "Padrig!"

He suddenly drew in a gasping breath. His eyes popped open as suddenly as they had closed. "Rafe," he called, his voice little more than a croak of sound.

Mary be praised, he was alive!

"Rafe," she echoed urgently. Filling her lungs with as much air as she could, she tried again, more loudly. "Rafe?"

The other man didn't answer, or move at all that she could tell.

Alys reached up past Padrig's begrimed face and poked at Rafe's arm. He remained unresponsive. His arm, when she tried to move it, simply flopped back down.

"I'm not sure he's alive," she said weakly, short of breath from the men's weight. "Does it feel to you as if he's breathing?" she asked Padrig.

He shook his head. "I'm not certain. He seems very still."

She caught hold of Rafe's wrist, but his mail sleeve was in the way and she could not get at his skin. "I cannot tell if his heart is beating, either."

Padrig flexed his arms and carefully levered himself up off Alys, turning as he got to his knees to seize hold of Rafe. He held him up and shifted him to the grass on his stomach, careful not to jar the arrows sticking out of his back.

Gasping, Alys glanced up at Padrig as soon as he moved away from her. Her heartbeat quickened with fear when she saw the feathered shaft protruding from his mail-covered shoulder. "You've been shot!"

"Aye." Angling his body to protect Rafe, he paid the arrow in his back no heed whatsoever.

Rafe had been struck twice in the back. Perhaps 'twas worse than that, but she couldn't see much from her position on the ground. Padrig bent low over him, checking for a pulse at his throat.

"He's still alive," he said without looking up.

"Thank God," she whispered, crossing herself.

Wondering if she could be of any help, she propped herself up on her elbow and struggled to raise herself off the ground.

"Stay down," Padrig hissed. He glanced up from tending to Rafe, his expression wild. "Unless you want to end up like this, as well."

Rolling to her side, she gazed past him. The archers were still on the rampart, but their shouting had died down and they'd lowered their weapons. That likely didn't mean anything save that they'd ceased firing at them for the nonce. That could change in a heartbeat.

"They've stopped shooting," she told him. "And shouting, whatever it was they were saying."

"I could tell you, but 'tis not fit for you to hear," he said darkly.

"I didn't think they were complimenting us," she shot back in the same tone. She scanned the area, searching for any sign that the Welsh were elsewhere, but saw naught else. The sight of them spread out along the wall, ready and waiting for who knew what, sent a chill racing down her spine. "They're just standing there, watching us."

"Let them watch, the devious bastards," he snarled. "They can watch while we get up and walk away."

Turning to her, he helped her to sit up, his hands gentle despite his fierce expression. "Are you all right?" he asked. He sounded less frantic now, though an intense blue fire smoldered in his eyes. "I didn't hurt you when I leapt upon you? Or when Rafe landed atop us both?"

She noticed he continued to use his body to shield Rafe—and her. That fact infuriated her! "I'm fine," she told him brusquely. The full skirts of her gown had tangled round her legs. She kicked them loose and, tugging the fabric out of her way, rolled to her knees.

"Will they come out after us?" she asked him, casting an uneasy glance back at the men on the wall.

"Who can say? Doesn't look like it, but I don't intend to stay here to find out."

After casting a swift look over his shoulder at Winterbrooke, he held out his hand to help her up.

Wishing she could ignore his offer of assistance, but knowing she wasn't likely to stand without it, Alys placed her hand in his and allowed him to pull her to her feet. As soon as she was upright, however, she jerked her hand free and bent down to peer at Rafe.

How could they get him away from here? She looked around for Arian, but saw no sign of the mare. Though if she could find her—

"What are you waiting for? Go," Padrig commanded. He bent. Wincing, he hoisted Rafe over his uninjured shoulder and rose.

Catching up her skirts in her left hand, Alys hurried away from Winterbrooke without a backward glance.

Although the flesh of her back crawled with every step she took, as if she could actually feel the weight of the enemy's gaze upon her.

Padrig, despite his injury and the extra burden of Rafe's motionless body, swiftly passed her. "Come on, move faster," he told her, his voice urgent. "Now we're

up—" the whirring hiss of a fresh volley of arrows filled
the air once more "—they'll try for us again."

Alys lengthened her stride, her feet flying over the
uneven ground at what felt like breakneck speed. She
expected to trip and fall on her face at any moment, for
it took all her concentration to keep from pitching over
sideways to the ground.

Panting, she glared at Padrig's back. If they survived
this, she vowed she'd tie down *his* arm and force him
to race through an open field while her father's best
bowman used him for target practice!

An eternity later, it seemed, they ran far enough beyond the archer's range that the few arrows that reached
them dropped harmlessly to the ground. They kept running anyway, until they reached the protection of a large
cluster of trees.

Ducking beneath the branches of a tall fir, Padrig
stopped. Breathing heavily, he closed his eyes, braced
himself against the thick trunk and lowered Rafe to the
ground. Straightening, he opened his eyes and met her
gaze. "God only knows what harm I just did to him," he
said, dropping to his knees alongside Rafe.

"Or what harm you did to yourself," she pointed out
dryly as she knelt beside them. She reached out and
touched Padrig's back near the arrow. He flinched and
jerked away. "Will you let me tend this?"

"Later." Moving swiftly, he rose and strode off into
the trees. Other than the occasional snap of twigs underfoot, she didn't hear him again until he emerged
from the brush near where he'd gone in.

"No one here but us," he informed her. "Though
that'll change before long, I'd imagine. We've not much
time to do what needs to be done."

He knelt by Rafe's side. Closing his hand around the two arrow shafts sticking out of Rafe's back, he snapped them off, leaving only a short bit of the wood visible. Rafe moaned, but didn't do much more than twitch. "We cannot stay here, 'tis too close to the keep."

"Where can we go?"

In a swift move, he drew his dagger and then reached toward her, startling a gasp from her. She threw herself back away from him before she could stop herself, her heart pounding wildly.

He tossed the knife on the ground between them and held his hand out to her. "Alys!"

She thumped down on her backside and drew in a deep breath.

What was wrong with her? She knew he'd never harm her!

"I only wanted a bit of cloth from the hem of your gown," he told her, his voice calm, holding out his hand to her as if he were soothing a frightened animal. "Sweeting, 'tis all right."

She took his hand, let him move to sit beside her. Once there, he pulled her close for a moment, pressing his face into her hair. "I'm sorry," she mumbled into his surcoat. "I'm not used to this."

"You've had no reason to be, thank God," Padrig said. "Would that you'd no reason now, either."

She drew back so she could see into his eyes. "Does it ever get easier, having someone try to kill you?" she asked with a weak laugh. "I feel ready to jump out of my own skin."

"You get used to it, after a fashion." He set her back from him, took up his knife and reached for her hem.

His look questioning, he held the knife poised over the bedraggled linen.

At her nod, he used the wickedly sharp blade to chop off a long strip of fabric, then cut it into three pieces. Two he folded into heavy pads, the third he split into two long strips, which he tied together. 'Twas clear from the swift efficiency of his movements that he'd performed this task before. "Either that, or you're killed because you're careless."

Returning to Rafe's side, he placed the pads over the wounds and began to wind the bandages around Rafe's torso. "Or mayhap because the one you fight is better at it than you are."

Pausing with the linen strip wrapped halfway round, he glanced up at her and added, "Or perhaps because 'tis simply your day to die."

Alys looked down at Rafe's motionless body and felt her anger rise again. "'Tis not his day to die," she said fiercely. She knelt opposite Padrig and reached for the end of the bandage. Handing it over, Padrig lifted up Rafe so she could slide the linen under him. "Nor is it ours," she said as she awkwardly tugged the two ends of the strip together one-handed.

By the Virgin, 'twas impossible to do anything trussed up like a Christmas goose!

Nigh growling her frustration, she turned her attention instead to the band of material immobilizing her arm. Her fingers fumbled with the knot, but she could not loosen it. "Help me with this, will you?"

He caught her hand in his and tugged it away. "What are you doing?" he demanded.

"I cannot do anything like this." She jerked free of him and grabbed the knot, pulling on it to no avail.

"Here's something to use your dagger on," she told him. "Cut this loose so I may help you."

"I will not." His tone as terse as hers, he ignored her demand and, tugging on the ends of Rafe's bandage, bound them in a snug knot. "'Twould hurt like the devil, and I doubt you'd be able to use your arm anyway."

By the rood, men could be such dolts!

"How do you expect me to break off that arrow in your shoulder, if I only have one hand to do it with?" she asked.

"I don't," he said shortly.

"Am I to chew it off with my teeth then?"

"You've a sharp enough tongue, Alys!" He rolled his eyes and sighed. "Mayhap you could use that."

Finding his words unworthy of a response, she ignored them. "You cannot do it yourself—"

"It wouldn't be the first time," he said wearily. "It's painful, but I'll live. 'Tis true I'll need your help once we've time to deal with it, but I'll not have you harm yourself to give it. That's my final word," he added when she opened her mouth to speak again.

She could see no way to help him, not in her present state. Her mind working furiously, she watched as Padrig turned away to look back at Winterbrooke.

She'd not get a better opportunity to do something. She'd shoved her knife into her belt earlier, when the first volley of arrows had begun and they'd had to run. Moving swiftly now, she freed the knife and, holding it awkwardly in her left hand, sawed at the knot Padrig had refused to cut.

The last threads gave with a snap. Her arm dropped to her lap, numb. She wished her shoulder had lost sensation, too. Unfortunately, it hurt.

Far more than she'd imagined it would.

Alys sucked in a deep breath and tried to move the fingers of her right hand. They wriggled, the movement barely noticeable, and more pain shot through her back and arm.

A hard hand closed about her wrist, stopping her. "You damned idiot!" Muttering a steady stream of curses and making no apology for them, Padrig grabbed the piece of binding and, moving her arm gently until it rested at an angle, wound the fabric into a sling and slipped her elbow into it.

"There. Now you can use your hand, if you're careful about it." He took her knife from her and replaced it in its sheath at her waist before handing her his much larger dagger. "If you've a mind to start chopping at the damned arrow, you'd best use a decent blade." He turned his back to her.

She looked from the dagger to Padrig's back and felt her stomach twist. There was no way she could do this without causing him pain.

"What should I do?"

"Just hold the shaft still, and use the knife to lop the arrow off as near my hauberk as you can," he told her. "Be quick about it, for I believe we'll have Welsh company soon if we linger here much longer."

"You'll have to sit lower," she told him. As soon as he moved and brought his shoulder to within her reach, she tried using her right hand to hold the arrow shaft steady, but she hadn't the strength for it. Nigh growling with frustration, she instead shifted the knife to that hand and, fighting back a moan of pain, closed her fingers about the thick hilt.

"Are you ready?" she asked Padrig, her voice scarcely audible to her over the fast, heavy thudding of her heart. Though she'd not done anything yet, her stomach whirled uneasily.

"Aye."

She grasped the arrow tight in her left hand and raised the knife. As soon as she pressed the blade to the shaft, however, her fingers opened and the dagger fell to the ground.

Muttering words she'd never have permitted past her lips under other circumstances, Alys picked up the knife with her left hand.

"What's wrong?" Padrig looked back at her, saw the tears streaming down her cheeks and the way her right hand rested uselessly in her lap. "By the rood! Alys, why didn't you tell me 'twas so bad?"

He turned and took her right hand in his. "Squeeze my fingers, as hard as you can," he ordered.

She tried to do as he asked, but could barely tighten her grip on his hand at all.

"You'll not be able to do anything with that hand quite yet," he observed. He brought her hand to his lips and pressed a kiss to her palm before gently lowering it to her lap. "Let me see if I can reach the arrow. If I can, I'll hold it myself while you cut the shaft."

If she'd thought her stomach felt bad before, 'twas nothing compared to the way it churned now. How could she hack at the arrow with her left hand, while Padrig himself assisted her?

He twisted his arm at what looked a most uncomfortable angle, but managed to grasp the shaft. "Come on, sweeting. I doubt I can stay like this for long," he said, his voice sounding strained.

Alys took hold of the dagger with both hands, hoping she'd be better able to guide her movements that way. If Padrig could endure this, so could she withstand the pain radiating down her right arm.

"Now." She focused all her attention upon her task, trying to saw through the shaft with as few strokes of the blade as possible.

Padrig sucked in a breath when she began to cut, but otherwise betrayed no discomfort. His grip remained tight, so that when the wood gave way, his arm dropped heavily to his side. He leaned forward, his weight resting on his bent arm. "Thank you, milady." Amazingly, his voice remained strong and even.

Alys slumped down and laid her cheek against the coarsely woven surcoat covering Padrig's back. She muttered a prayer of thanks before forcing herself away from his warmth. She still needed to pad the wound and bandage it as they had Rafe's.

'Twas an easy matter to do so with Padrig sitting there helping her.

They'd no sooner knotted the binding when a rustling sound from the bushes behind them startled them.

Alys still had Padrig's knife. Holding it clutched at the ready, she whirled on her knees.

Crawling out from the thick underbrush, his dark eyes huge as he stared at her, was the filthiest child she'd ever seen.

Alys shrieked. The child did, as well.

Padrig turned and lunged for the boy, grabbing him by the front of his tunic and dragging him forward.

The lad's eyes rolled back in his head and he toppled over in a dead faint.

Chapter Seventeen

Padrig scooped the child up off the ground and gently propped him against a nearby tree. "Where in God's name did he spring from?" he asked. He straightened out the boy's legs and smoothed his tousled mop of dark hair away from his filthy face. The child didn't stir at all, save for the shallow rise and fall of his chest.

He looked to be about seven, Padrig thought, for he was about the same size as the lads who came to l'Eau Clair to be fostered. His clothes were as dirty as his skin, and Lord knew he smelled none too fresh, but he didn't appear to have gone hungry.

Padrig glanced at Alys, about to ask her if the lad had said anything, and instead leapt to his feet to catch hold of her.

She'd jolted up from her knees when the boy came out of the bushes. Now she stood next to him, her body swaying precariously, her amber eyes providing the only color in her pale face. She looked ready to keel over right next to the boy.

Padrig lunged for her and caught her up in his arms.

"Ah, sweeting, what shall I do with you?" he muttered to himself.

"You could set me down and let me see to that poor child," she said, her voice tart. Despite her bravado, however, her body trembled as she drew in an unsteady breath.

"You're shaking," he pointed out. "At least let me hold you until you've had a chance to calm down."

She shoved weakly at his chest. "Put me down! You've an arrow in your back. You shouldn't be carting people about." When he ignored her words and continued to clasp her in his arms, she cupped his jaw in her hand and stared into his eyes. "Padrig, please."

He could not mistake her sincerity, for her eyes glowed with it. Nor could he look away from her intense gaze. "Alys—" He closed his eyes, then turned his head and pressed a kiss to her hand.

"Save your strength for moving Rafe," she told him when he opened his eyes. "He needs it more than I."

As if he needed a reminder! "I'll be fine, Alys." He set her on her feet, but kept his arm supportively about her waist.

"As shall I." She stroked her hand over his cheek, her touch soothing, before she stepped away and turned to the child. "We need to get out of here at once," she said, looking over her shoulder as though expecting to see Welsh archers leap from the bushes. "Since I doubt you could carry a grown man and this lad both, we must get one of them to awaken." She peered closer at the boy, then glanced at Rafe. "I believe the child to be the more likely of the two to do so."

"Aye, milady. If you'll see to the boy, I'll finish tending to Rafe." He took a step back from her before he gave in to the compulsion to pull her close once more. "Although I fear there's little more we can do for him here."

He could not spare the time to indulge his curiosity about the child, but he trusted Alys to take care of him. Padrig took Alys by the hand and helped her to kneel by the lad before returning to Rafe.

He checked the bandages on Rafe's back. Blood seeped at a slow but steady rate from beneath the linen padding they'd placed over the wounds, he noted with concern. No doubt 'twould continue to do so until he removed the arrows and stitched the holes closed.

That procedure, however, would have to wait. For now, all he could do was ensure Rafe didn't bleed to death bit by bit in the interim.

He replaced the dressings and took a moment to give Rafe a swift examination, looking him over for any other wounds that needed tending.

A strange sense of urgency had been plaguing Padrig since just before they'd arrived at Winterbrooke Manor. He'd ignored it then, but 'twas clear now there'd been reason to worry. He didn't know who the enemy was, how and why they'd ended up in control here, or why he'd felt something was wrong in the first place, but he'd do well not to discount his instincts again.

He felt that same sensation thrumming through him still, warning him to take Alys and Rafe, and now this poor child, and get them away from this place as swiftly as they could manage to do so.

He should have known, he berated himself, should have realized something was wrong.

Was that not part of being a good leader, knowing how to read the signs that all was not as it should be?

Instead, because of his carelessness, he'd sent his

people into danger. Mayhap even to their deaths, either outright at the hands of the Welsh in command of the keep, or for those already hurt, through lack of attention to their injuries.

What could he expect for them, having entered all unknowing into a dangerous situation—to be tossed into a cell or the dungeon and left to rot?

Simple lack of care would likely be all it would take to send the worst injured to their deaths.

He doubted any of his men would have permitted themselves to be taken captive without a fight, and most of them were in no condition to fight a child of ten, let alone an armed warrior.

Having checked over Rafe from head to toe and found no further wounds, Padrig glanced at Alys, who looked busy with the now-awake child. They were talking, both appearing intent upon the conversation.

Leaving her to it, Padrig sank down to sit on the ground and closed his eyes, giving in, momentarily, to the pain in his shoulder—but more than that, the devastating sense of failure that threatened to overwhelm him.

'Twas no use taking himself to task any further, however, for he could do naught to change the past.

All he could hope was to make things right in the future…and that no one else would die because of his mistakes.

But for now, 'twas time to leave.

Breathing deeply, he sought that dark and quiet place within himself where determination and equanimity dwelled in equal measure.

The procedure worked, thankfully, as it often had in the past when he'd been overset by his inability to breathe. 'Twas not in his nature to panic, but neither was it to indulge his emotions, or his discomfort, for long. He settled himself quickly, regaining his composure. Saying a silent prayer for the help they surely needed, he opened his eyes.

And found Alys sitting before him, watching him with an intensity he found most disquieting.

He'd no time, however, to do more than fix the memory of her expression into his mind for later examination. He feared if he took the smallest step toward discovering what she meant by it, they'd once again fall into a situation they'd no business exploring.

And this was most definitely not the time or place.

He stood, reaching down to help her to her feet.

"Are you all right?" she asked, keeping hold of his hand when he would have moved away.

He nodded, and she let him go. "What of the boy?" He moved to the lad's side and knelt near him. Alys gathered her skirts in her hand and sank down beside him with a surprising grace, considering her hurts.

Like any good soldier, she'd already begun to adapt to her limitations. Her resilience amazed him.

The child watched Padrig, his face pale beneath the dirt, his dark eyes wary.

"Dickon, this is Sir Padrig ap Huw. He is a knight in Lord Rannulf FitzClifford's service, and my protector on this journey. Like you, he is very strong and very brave." Dickon's gaze shifted from Padrig to Alys once she said that. She reached out and brushed the lad's hair from his face, gifting him with a reassuring smile. "If you would tell Sir Padrig what you told me, I'm certain he will want to help."

His expression solemn, Dickon sat up a bit straighter against the tree. "Lord Rannulf came here to Winterbrooke once." His voice started out weak, but grew steadier with every word. "I got close enough to 'im that I could see the carving on his sword. He asked *me* to hold his horse for 'im," he added with an emphatic nod, his face glowing with pride.

"Lord Rannulf is a good man," Padrig said. "If he trusted you with his horse, and since Lady Alys also vouches for you, that's more than enough recommendation for me." He leaned closer to Dickon and lowered his voice to speak with him man-to-man. "What news have you to tell me, Dickon?"

The child glanced past Padrig for a moment, looking toward Winterbrooke Manor. When he shifted his gaze back to them, his expression had hardened with a determination Padrig didn't expect to see in one so young. "Aye, milord, I'll tell you what's happened here." He met Padrig's eyes straight on, his gaze steady and true. Padrig could see he need not doubt the truth of the boy's tale.

"Go on, lad," Padrig prompted when Dickon hesitated. "No matter what you have to say, neither Lady Alys nor I will hold it against you."

Alys laid her hand on the boy's arm. "'Tis all right. You may tell Sir Padrig anything," she added. The look she sent Padrig made him believe she meant the words. "He needs to know what has happened here, so he may make it right again."

'Twas gratifying, almost frightening, to be the recipient of such sweeping faith. Padrig wasn't certain he deserved it, or even if Alys truly meant it, but if her confidence in him would prod Dickon along, he'd accept it gladly.

"Aye, milady. Do ye mind if I stand up now?" Alys

shook her head. Dickon stood and paced away from them and back several times as though gathering his thoughts, then paused, facing them. "The Welsh've been after us for months, piddlin' little raiding parties stealing our animals from out in the hills, or ruinin' the crops in the fields. Anything to lure the garrison out o' Winterbrooke, my father says." Tears welled in Dickon's eyes, but he blinked them away. "They never come near the village for the longest time, though, nor attacked the keep. They'd go after the farms far away from here, or steal sheep from the flocks way up in the hills. Naught to cause anyone any real harm, 'cept for the worry about us goin' hungry this winter." He stared down at the ground, then glanced up. "Thought mayhap they was hungry, too."

"How and when did they get inside the keep?" Padrig asked quietly.

Dickon's hands clenched at his sides. "They come down from the hills like a huge herd of beasts." His voice trembled. "Many on horseback, more'n half o' them, mayhap. I never seen so many soldiers before, not even when your father came here, milady," he added. "They swept through the village afore Sir Cedric could muster his men and get outside the walls. Everyone tried to reach the keep, but a lot o' 'em didn't make it." Tears ran unhindered down Dickon's dirty cheeks, leaving a pale tracery of lines in their wake. "I think my family made it, but I'm not certain. I've not seen any sign o' them out here."

"Is there anyone left hereabouts who could help us?" Padrig asked. Surely others besides the child had survived!

Dickon shook his head. "Nay, milord, not a one." His

eyes filled with tears once again, but he stood bravely and went on. "If you'd come to Winterbrooke from the other road, you'd never have traveled past the village, for the stench alone would've told the tale. The streets are filled with bodies," he said, choking back a sob. "I tried to bury 'em at first, but there were so many—"

Alys gathered Dickon close. He clung to her, and she held him while he cried. She met Padrig's gaze, her eyes wet with unshed tears, and whispered, "Give him a moment, milord."

How could he not? he thought, nodding.

Christ save the child, and bless the poor souls who'd fallen, Padrig thought, making the sign of the cross.

The lad was a tough one, no doubt about that!

He turned away, pacing the small confines of the area, pausing to stare out at the walls of Winterbrooke Manor. Once again, they were empty save a few guards, but how long might that last?

What were they planning to do next? That the attackers would come after them sooner or later, certainly once they realized they'd not yet gained possession of Lord Roger's daughter, he could not doubt.

"Padrig," Alys called. "Dickon is ready to tell you more."

He joined them, taking Alys by the arm and drawing her down to sit once he saw how pale she'd become. When she made to protest, he shook his head and told her quietly, "Rest now, milady, for 'tis like to be the last chance you'll have for a long while."

He settled beside her and motioned for Dickon to sit with them.

"Dickon, I know you've much yet to tell us, but right now, 'tis more important that we move Lady Alys and

Rafe—" he pointed to the still-unconscious man "—away from here. We need to go for help, and we need a way to escape this place without being followed. Do you know of any way we can do that?"

The boy's eyes were alight with eagerness by the time Padrig finished speaking. "Aye, milord. I know a place where the Welsh'd never think to look." He moved closer to them and lowered his voice, as though the wily Welsh were just outside the stand of trees. "I've been hiding there myself, and they've never caught me yet!"

He hated to dampen the boy's enthusiasm, but Dickon evidently didn't understand what he meant. "We're not in need of a place to hide, lad. We need a way to safely leave this place and go for help."

Dickon nodded. "'Tis one and the same, milord! I've stayed here 'cause I didn't know how to go anyplace else, but there's passages we could follow that'd carry us for nigh a league away from here."

"What do you mean?" Padrig asked, confused.

"'Tis the Lair, milord," Dickon said.

"Ffau gan 'r diafol?"

"Aye, milord, though I'll not use that heathen tongue to call it so. The Devil's Lair, that's how we can get away."

Alys remained seated, her back nigh twitching with impatience to be gone from this place while they still could leave, while Padrig and Dickon swiftly hammered out the details of how to convey Rafe to the Devil's Lair. She didn't look forward to the trek herself, given her present awkwardness of movement. As it was, walking was a challenge under the circumstances. Climbing a massive rock outcropping one-handed would be nearly impossible.

In addition, she didn't like heights. Merely looking out the windows of a tower or standing on a narrow wall walk had the power to make her head spin and her stomach roil. Jesu, how was she to manage this climb, when she was already listing drunkenly to the side before she even began?

Yet climb she would, one way or another. The alternative, to be captured by the Welsh, scarce bore thinking of. They might treat her decently, if they hoped for a rich ransom from her father, but what if they did not? Not all men were honorable in normal, day-to-day life. When it came to war, or raiding, or whatever their current situation was, she could not expect that the Welsh invaders of her father's keep would consider her anything other than a spoil of war.

What little she knew of them from Dickon didn't inspire her with any hope in that regard.

That they might treat Padrig, Rafe and Dickon far worse than herself, she'd little doubt.

They'd no other choice but to leave this place. She'd not had a chance to discuss with Padrig what they'd do once they got away, but it made sense to her to retrace their route and return to l'Eau Clair. There were few villages between here and there, and nothing larger that she was aware of.

They had truly fetched up in the wilderness, with scant resources upon which to depend except themselves.

And Dickon.

The poor child had been on his own here for nigh a week. He'd taken refuge in the rocky hills during the attack. Once the Welsh had left the village and taken up residence in Winterbrooke, he'd crept back down to look for survivors and to forage for supplies.

There'd been plenty of food and clothing available, though he'd been careful to only take things from his parents' home. Evidently the raiders hadn't been interested in looting, not from poor village folk, at any rate.

All the people Dickon had found, however, were dead, cut down while they tried to defend themselves. Some had knelt and begged for their lives, or the lives of their children, and been murdered there in the streets.

Dickon had seen and heard enough before he ran off to show him these invaders possessed no mercy. Indeed, to his mind they'd gloried in their brutality.

Alys drew in a deep breath and let it out slowly, seeking to calm her troubled soul. 'Twas difficult for her to imagine such pitiless actions, though she knew 'twas the way of war.

For all she knew, Padrig, Rafe, her own father and brother—perhaps any man would behave thus during the heat of battle.

Yet somehow she sensed that could not be true, not to the extent of cruelty displayed here.

From things she'd heard as she sought information for her chronicles, battle lust could sap the very ability to reason from some men, cause them to act in ways that would horrify them under normal circumstances.

Indeed, she knew herself to be capable of great fury without thought of the consequences. In defense of her family or friends, of her own honor, to protect a child... She couldn't truthfully say just how far she would be willing to go.

However, she believed herself incapable of wanton violence for its own sake, of robbing and killing for the sport of it. She believed the men she knew incapable of it, as well.

Though perhaps that was simply a delusion she permitted herself, to keep from seeing their true faces.

While she'd not been paying attention to what Padrig and Dickon were saying, the sound of their voices murmuring had lent a pleasant background for her unsettling thoughts. The sound had stopped; she glanced up and found that while she'd been distracted by her thoughts, Dickon and Padrig had been busy.

Biting back a moan as her aching body protested movement, Alys got to her feet and went to see what they had done.

Using Rafe's tunic and Padrig's cloak, along with several sturdy branches, they had rigged up a litter for Rafe. He lay facedown, tied to the framework with wide strips of cloth.

It looked hellishly uncomfortable for him, and would doubtless be difficult for Padrig to move.

Not to mention…well, she *would* point out the flaw she could see with this plan.

Though unfortunately, she hadn't a better one to suggest in its place.

Padrig finished tying the last knot and stood, shifting his sword belt back into place. "I'm not certain how well it will work, for 'tis flimsier than I like, but I don't know how else to move him while he's like this. He scarcely made a sound when we shifted him about to get him on the frame. His eyelids didn't so much as flicker, though we must have hurt him."

"Won't we leave a trail if we drag this over the ground?" she asked, watching Padrig's face as she brought up her concern. "How will we keep the Welsh from following us? They're bound to move much faster than we can. They may catch up to us before we can get very far away."

"Rafe was right, milady, you are a clever lass." Padrig grinned, the look in his eyes sending heat flowing through her in a completely inappropriate way.

She'd expected him to be upset by what she'd said. His approval confused her, though she'd happily accept compliments from him, especially when they were accompanied by such a look....

"What do you mean?" she demanded.

He reached out and tapped her on the cheek with his finger, his mouth still quirked in a smile. "I mean that you're right. 'Twould be folly to drag this over the ground for any distance." He waved at Dickon, who stood on the other side of the litter, holding a strong, leafy bough in his hands like a broom. "Thanks to Dickon, we needn't go far before we can travel beneath the earth. As long as he can wipe away the trail we leave from here, I doubt anyone will find us where we're going."

"And where might that be?" Alys asked warily, though she was afraid she already knew.

Dickon fairly danced with excitement, his smile a slash of white in his filthy face. "Didn't ye wonder how I got here earlier, milady? You didn't see me comin' and I surprised ye, didn't I?"

"Aye, you did," she admitted. He'd nearly made her heart stop beating!

"That's 'cause I popped out o' the ground like a rabbit," he told her. "Come on, I'll show you where I came from."

Chapter Eighteen

Alys found herself turning to peer back over her shoulder at Winterbrooke Manor as they slowly made their way through the trees toward the hidden entrance to the Devil's Lair. The keep looked quiet, its gray stone gleaming in the afternoon sun.

'Twas naught but a foul deception, as so much in life appeared to be.

Why hadn't anyone come after them yet? She refused to believe the Welsh would simply leave them be.

There was not a sign of the short battle that had raged earlier at the gates, but the image remained etched in her mind's eye.

She would not rest, she vowed, until they'd found a way to free the people of Winterbrooke, if there were any left, and those of their own party who had been lured within those shimmering walls.

'Twas not a long trek, as Dickon had said, but the hard-packed track they traveled was rough going, passing over jagged stones and through a heavy undergrowth of brush and small trees.

Once Dickon had set Padrig, towing the litter behind him, upon the path, the lad fell into line behind Alys. He used his makeshift broom with great diligence, whisking away any tracks the litter made, and making certain they hadn't left a trail of bent or broken branches in their wake.

Padrig had the more difficult task, for it looked to Alys as though he was practically carrying the litter. Whether that was because it didn't move easily, or because he was trying to keep from jolting Rafe along the uneven ground, she couldn't tell, but a steady stream of sweat trickled down his face and neck, and his tanned face grew rosy with exertion.

He had to be in pain, as well. The bandage she'd placed over the arrowhead in his shoulder kept her from seeing whether the wound had begun to bleed from his exertions. Even if it had not, it had to hurt like the devil to be carrying a piece of metal embedded in his flesh.

There was naught more she could do about it for now. She'd be better served to focus upon putting one foot in front of the other. Weariness dogged her every step, making her movements awkward and her feet clumsy.

She could not imagine how Padrig kept going. He'd had no rest at all that she knew of. He'd walked here from their encampment while she rode, had fought hard against several foes. Now, injured, he must haul along a tall, well-muscled man, working as though he were a packhorse. She had no idea how he did it all, but she was very grateful for everything he'd done.

Lord Rannulf could not have chosen a better leader for her guard than Padrig.

And so she'd tell him, should they survive to see him again.

They were moving so slowly, she had no problem keeping up, but she feared that would change once they reached the tunnel. According to Dickon, 'twas but one entrance to a vast maze of passageways that ran underground, like a huge honeycomb beneath the entire area. Most of the tunnels Dickon knew about led into the heart of the Devil's Lair. From there, several traveled quite a distance from the outcropping itself.

Dickon was a smart lad. He'd set up a series of snares and alarms within the passageways, so he'd always know if anyone had got in, or was coming in. Once they were inside the Lair, they'd likely be as safe as if they were in their own fortification.

'Twould be a blessing, indeed, to lose the constant sensation of being hunted she'd felt since the first barrage of arrows from Winterbrooke.

The notion of passing under the ground like a mole did not lend itself to her, but even less did she like the idea of capture by the Welsh. She'd grit her teeth and crawl through hell itself if necessary, if 'twould lead them safely away.

"Here we are, Sir Padrig," Dickon said quietly. He leaned his broom against a tree and edged past Alys, joining Padrig as the knight lowered the litter to the ground.

They stood at the foot of a grass-and-bush-covered dirt mound. Boulders lay scattered over its surface, most big enough to hide a man, but none so large as to provide cover for two.

Alys saw nothing to hint at the fact that there was an entrance to anything here. Save for the fact that the mound was hidden from the keep by a stand of tall trees, there wasn't anything notable about it at all.

"It's down in here," Dickon said. "I'll go take care of the snares." He ran past them, wriggled into a pile of large, flat stones jutting out of the hillside and disappeared.

Alys and Padrig moved toward the pile more slowly, Padrig shaking his head and Alys trying to stifle her disappointment.

"Damnation! I doubt he meant to mislead us," Padrig said. "But he cannot have understood what we needed, either."

"Mayhap if we take Rafe off the litter, and the three of us try to move him—"

"Milady, Sir Padrig, come along." Dickon popped up out of the rocks, gesturing impatiently to them. "We need to get going before 'tis dark, else we won't be able to see to go get to the torches."

"Torches?" Alys asked.

"This part of the tunnel is too low to carry a torch, but there's a bit o' light comes through it, enough so we can see where we're goin'." He scampered toward them, pausing to look up and gauge the sun's position. "But we must hurry."

Padrig climbed to the rocks and clambered over them, suddenly disappearing into them as swiftly as Dickon had done earlier. After a moment he stuck his head back out, a smile brightening his face. "The lad's right, milady. We will fit within, even Rafe on the litter." He levered himself from between the boulders. "'Twill be a bit of a challenge to get him in here, but after that, there's room aplenty."

"Will you need help getting Rafe down there?"

"Aye. But mayhap Dickon will be able to do it." He came to stand beside her. "I don't believe you should try this, Alys. 'Twas difficult enough for you to wield a knife." He took her hand in his and once again tested her ability to grasp his fingers. Her grip was still weak, of course, no matter that she'd squeezed as hard as she could. Shaking his head, he said, "Nay, I fear 'twould damage your shoulder more. You could keep watch for us, love, if you would. Let us know if anyone's coming. I don't know how long it'll take to move Rafe down there."

She ignored what he'd called her. Did he think to charm her into his way of thinking? She caught him by the arm when he would have walked away. "What of *your* shoulder, milord? How can you ignore it so easily? Does it not hurt?"

"Aye, it does hurt, when I let myself think of it." He leaned closer to her, so his warm breath feathered her cheek. She held her breath lest she do something foolish—try to leap into his arms, mayhap.

She did meet his gaze, however, a mistake she realized at once. His eyes glowed dark blue, their intensity threatening to tempt her to further madness.

"The trick is to not think of it," he murmured. "I try to fix my mind on something else as a distraction instead."

"What could possibly divert your attention from this?" she asked once she found her voice, gently touching the bandage where it wound round his torso.

He captured her hand in his and laid it over his heart, holding it pressed there beneath his own. "You, Alys. Thoughts of you could distract me from just about anything."

Had she felt the way his heart had raced beneath her hand? he wondered as he carefully dragged the litter up the side of the mound. Had she realized the truth hidden in his words?

He *did* realize. What frightened him even more than what she might think of his boldness was the fact that he'd meant every word of it.

Had she noticed how endearments fell so easily from his lips, as though he'd the right to say them? In truth, he shouldn't be calling her "Alys," let alone "sweeting" or "love."

Yet he found it difficult to think of her in any other way.

He hauled Rafe the last few yards to the entrance to the tunnel. Dickon had gone down into the tunnel to make certain the way was clear for Rafe's litter.

Since he had to wait for the lad, Padrig checked that Rafe was all right, as much as he could be under the circumstances, anyway.

This prolonged swoon was odd for the injuries he'd sustained. Could he have hit his head, or been struck in the head while he was fighting? That, at least, might explain why he'd yet to awaken at all. Two arrows lodged in his back was not a good thing, but he ought to have come to his senses by now.

After assuring himself he'd done all that he could for Rafe for the moment, Padrig looked down the hill to make certain Alys had followed him. She moved cautiously up the hillside, her attention alternating between where she put her feet, and glancing behind her to make certain no one was following.

He'd noticed she had trouble moving with her arm bound, not to mention she had to be bruised and sore from the accident last night.

Lord Rannulf would not be best pleased, when next he saw Lady Alys. Padrig had been charged with her care, with seeing her delivered safely to her father at Lord Henry Walsingham's keep in the northern Marches.

At this point, he'd be happy if he could return her to l'Eau Clair without further mishap.

He settled on the pile of stones to wait for Alys, wondering, as he had when they first set out on this journey, whether he had been delivering Alys to her future husband. The notion had not set well with him *before* he'd come to know her.

Now 'twas likely to drive him mad.

Despite the relatively short duration of their relationship, he *did* feel he'd begun to know the real Alys. They'd experienced a great deal together in a brief time, more than many people shared in years.

He wanted to share more, to share everything, with her.

In reality, they'd share nothing beyond the remainder of this journey. Lord Rannulf would never permit him to accompany her again.

Were the occasion to arise. Which it very well might not.

He'd most likely demand an accounting from Padrig, as well, as would Alys's father, no doubt.

Once Lord Roger learned of all the hazards his daughter had endured, he'd be likely to come for her himself.

Or mayhap, Padrig thought, torturing himself more, her father would send her future husband to escort her home. He could think of no other reason for Alys to be going directly to Lord Henry's keep but that they were to be married.

The thought of her wed to Lord Henry, who was a notoriously vicious sot, disgusted Padrig beyond words.

'Twas rumored his late wife's death had been sudden, unexpected and difficult to explain.

Could he permit Alys to meet that same fate?

She reached him, slightly out of breath from the climb, and perched beside him on the sun-warmed rocks. "'Tis a most lovely day, is it not, milord?" she asked, her voice and face both alight with amusement. "The sun is shining like a blessing upon us."

Her hair blew in the faint breeze, trailing across his neck and arm. He caught the errant tresses in his hand and kept hold of them, his fingers twining in the silky strands. "Aye, 'tis lovely indeed," he agreed. However, 'twas her face he gazed upon, not the sky. The scratches and bruises scattered over her skin, the smudge of dirt on her cheek, did little to detract from her beauty. "We've little to smile about, milady, yet something has brought a smile to your lips."

A tinge of rosy color tinted her face, but she didn't look away. "So far as we know, no one is after us for the nonce, no trees are falling atop our heads, and we're alive. Is that not reason to smile, after the days we've had?"

He tugged lightly on her hair and shifted closer to her, until their arms were touching and he could see the flecks of gold mixed with light brown in her eyes. "'Tis the woman beside me who makes me smile," he whispered, lowering his head till their mouths were but a breath apart. "And that is true no matter—"

"Milady!" Dickon's voice, echoing slightly, sounded from right below them. Alys leapt to her feet as though she'd sat on a live coal. Padrig took his time getting to his feet, reminding himself all the while that Dickon was a fine lad who would show them the way out of their current predicament.

No good would come of snarling his frustration like a wounded boar and frightening the boy.

Though he'd wager 'twould take something unusual to alarm Dickon, after all he'd seen of late.

Dickon popped his head up out of the rocks. "'Tis fine, milord. A clear path for us all." He turned and pulled himself up out of the hole. "'Tis just this part that's hard, but once we're in the passage, 'twill take no time at all to get to the Lair."

Padrig cast one last look down the hill. No Welsh came after them. Alys was right, 'twas a beautiful day, after all.

He picked up the edge of the litter, then set it down. "Milady, let's get you in first, shall we?"

Dickon had been correct. Once they got into the tunnel, it had been surprisingly easy to traverse the relatively smooth passageway. The low ceiling made it necessary to move at more of a half-crouch rather than walking. Only Dickon could stand upright.

Despite the limitations, they were able to move more swiftly than Padrig had anticipated. 'Twas a pleasant surprise, to have something go better than expected, instead of worse. He could only hope their good fortune continued.

Within a short time they reached a small chamber, a junction point where several tunnels met and branched off. The ceiling was higher here, permitting Alys and Padrig to stand upright with room to spare. They took advantage of the opportunity to rest while Dickon raced ahead to unhook the snares, his voice echoing eerily off the damp stone walls as he explained where each branch led.

He returned with a pair of torches and a small brazier of coals. "I brought these from the village first off," he explained. He placed the brazier carefully on the floor. "'Tis so wet here in some places, I couldn't strike a spark to light a fire."

He kindled the torches and handed one to Alys, who gave it back to him. "I'll trip on my gown if I try to walk and carry this, as well," she told him. She gathered her full skirts and tucked them up into her belt so they'd be out of the way. Her left hand free, she took the torch and stepped back to let Padrig, dragging the litter, move between her and Dickon.

Padrig could tell that the tunnel was gradually sloping upward, making it more work to drag Rafe behind him. His chest felt tight, the sensation of invisible bands pulled taut about his ribs familiar, though it had been years now since he'd felt it. 'Twas not exertion making it hard to breathe, but the malady from his childhood.

Mayhap once they got out of here the symptoms would ease. The air was stale and dank so far below ground. He'd had trouble with that when he was a lad.

At least, thank God, 'twas nothing worse than tightness in his lungs. If he were going to go off into a full-blown spell, as he'd done so often in his youth, he'd already be on the ground gasping for air like a stranded fish.

He concentrated on filling his lungs slowly and completely with each breath, and sought within himself for serenity. If he stayed relaxed, did not give in to panic, all would be well. Lady Gillian had taught him that, had helped him learn to live his life despite his malady, rather than letting it steal his life from him.

His mind focused on each breath, he kept plodding along in Dickon's wake, hoping that soon they'd reach the boy's camp deep within the Devil's Lair.

He'd no way to know how long they traveled beneath the earth. Eventually the passageway widened and he could smell a pine-scented breeze instead of the dank, musty air of the tunnels. A last, steep stretch taxed his already-screaming muscles before they emerged from the passage into a large, shadowed chamber.

He stopped and filled his lungs with the blessedly fresh air, drinking it in as though 'twere a refreshing draught after traversing a desert.

Stars glowed through a narrow opening high above them in the ceiling of the vast room. Though it felt as if the night should be over, he could see from the position of the stars and moon that the sun had set only a short while earlier.

Padrig lowered the litter to the ground and stood, reaching his arms high and flexing his back. He repeated the movement despite the shards of pain radiating out from the arrow in his shoulder. The muscles in his back and neck were so cramped from the awkward position he'd been in, he felt as though he'd never stand straight again.

Alys jammed the torch into the ground nearby and, groaning, sat down close to it. "I shall *never* complain about a lady's chores again," she said forcefully. "Nor about my back aching when I've been bent over a table writing for too long."

Her words caught Padrig's attention, especially the last thing she'd said.

Writing?

Why would a young noblewoman be doing so much writing her back would hurt?

Now was not the time to explore that path, but he'd every intention of asking her about it later.

Meanwhile, they'd work to do. Most unpleasant work. With a bit of luck, Alys would be able to help him, for he didn't know anything about how to sew, nor did he carry needle and thread with him. He hoped she did. Otherwise, he'd not be able to do much for Rafe until he'd had a chance to raid the village for supplies.

Dickon moved about on the opposite side of the chamber, lighting several torches and starting a fire. "I've food and fresh water, milady, if you've the strength to come over here." He scampered to Alys's side. "Here, I'll help you," he offered. He bowed low, prompting a laugh from Alys, and reached down to assist her to her feet.

She let the boy lead her round the fire to a pile of blankets near the wall. "I thank you, Dickon. 'Tis just what I need."

Padrig knelt beside the litter and touched Rafe's cheek. 'Twas cool, thankfully. The man had troubles enough already. All they needed was for him to become feverish, as well.

Padrig lifted up the litter, hopefully for the last time, and dragged it round the fire to Dickon's camp. "Have you room for us by the fire?" he asked. "I must do some cutting, and I'll need as much light as we can muster."

"Are you going to cut into Rafe?" Dickon asked, his voice full of awe, as well as a lad's eagerness for gore, from the sound of it.

"Aye." Padrig set down the litter and, kneeling, went to work untying the bindings that held Rafe to the frame. "He's two arrows in his back that must come out. I'm hoping Lady Alys will help me with the stitching," he added, purposely not looking at her when he said it.

He didn't know how she'd react to his suggestion, but mayhap if he behaved as though 'twas natural for her to do it, she'd simply agree. "I'm afraid learning such a task is not part of a knight's training."

Alys made a sound somewhere between a laugh and a snort. Padrig glanced up at her then, and caught her wry expression. "Considering how often you slice each other up, perhaps it ought to be."

He smiled. "But milady, how else might a lowly knight garner a noble lady's attention?"

She laughed again, more lightheartedly this time. "You're telling me that knights go forth in battle and get cut up merely for the privilege of being sewn back together by a lady?" She gathered her hair from where it lay loose about her shoulders and swept it back, then looked him full in the face.

The smile she cast his way now held far more than lighthearted amusement. He nigh forgot to breathe at the passion in her eyes, the promises she made with that not-so-simple glance.

By God, when had Alys become a sorceress? He shook his head slightly, though it did naught to break the spell she'd cast over him.

The look she sent him nigh scorched him with its heat. He held her gaze, feeling his body respond to hers in a manner so inappropriate, he ought to be embarrassed.

Yet he felt not a whit of shame. Instead he reveled in her attention, yearned to collect on the promises she made with but a glance.

Thank God Dickon was busy on the other side of the fire, where the dancing flames hid them from view!

Somewhere in his addled brain, he realized he ought to say something, but he was scarcely able to form words. "Why else?" he mumbled.

He'd sounded a complete dolt. His competitive spirit

roused, he forced his mind clear, his attention focused completely upon Alys. "Why else," he said again, "do ladies send men into battle wearing their favors?"

Her smile grew. "I'd think there might be easier ways for a knight to gain a lady's favor."

You have no idea, milady, what lengths I'd go to, to gain yours.

"Might there indeed, milady?" he asked, finally connecting his tongue to his brain. "Would you care to instruct this simple knight?"

Her eyes widened and her expression changed, grew serious for a fleeting moment. Had he surprised her? The notion pleased him.

Alys smiled again and raised her chin slightly, as though challenging him.

To do what, he hardly dared imagine.

"I would be honored, Sir Padrig," she said. "Whenever you wish."

What had he just agreed to?

Somehow he dragged his gaze from hers, not caring that he'd looked away first. If he had not done so, he feared he'd have lost his will completely with but a few moments more of Alys's enticing stare.

They'd more important things to take care of for now, he reminded himself.

Imagining—and *instructing*—would have to wait.

But not for much longer.

Chapter Nineteen

Alys leaned back against the rough stone wall and struggled to cool her overheated mind.

And body.

What had she been thinking, to stare at Padrig as she had?

To offer…what had she offered, exactly? Whatever it was, she'd discover it later, that she vowed.

To smile at him as though she was ready to tear his clothes off?

Mayhap 'twas because she *had* been thinking of his naked body that she'd lost sight of proper behavior. By the rood, the man could tempt a saint!

And she, Alys was realizing more and more, had very little that was saintly about her.

Nay, she was but a woman, with all a woman's wants and needs. With desires she hadn't known existed before she and Padrig entered each other's sphere.

Desires she believed Padrig shared.

Should she ignore those feelings, shove them deep

within the darkest recesses of her mind where they could not tempt her into indulging them?

She bit back a bitter laugh. There *was* no place she could bury the sensations, and the emotions, Padrig made her feel. They were too strong, too compelling, too much a part of her very being for her to ignore.

She hadn't the strength of will to do so.

She had wanted to live her life fully, to experience it for herself, rather than through the recollections of others.

There would never be a better opportunity than here and now, away from their day-to-day lives and the stifling constraints of society.

She suppressed a moan and lifted her hair from her neck to let the cool breeze pour over her skin. She knew precisely what thoughts had been passing through her brain when she'd sent him that look, started that conversation...

...made promises she had every intention of keeping.

As she'd walked along behind Padrig through the seemingly endless series of tunnels, she'd sought to keep her mind occupied with something other than their situation. Her concern for Rafe, and for the others trapped within Winterbrooke. Her fears that the Welsh would come after them soon and take them captive as well...it all whirled round and round in her head in a noisome stew, sapping her strength from within even as exhaustion and pain battered her from without.

Her choices for distraction were few, and only one possessed the power to completely remove from her mind almost any other thoughts at all.

She'd fixed her fascinated gaze upon Padrig's back, from head to toe, she recalled with a giggle, and discovered 'twas not difficult at all to remember precisely how that same view appeared without the concealment of mail, surcoat, leggings and boots.

In her mind's eye she savored the memory of Padrig standing in the pool, streams of water sluicing over the lean musculature of his back.

She wondered again about the strange, dark markings he bore on his shoulder, the same shoulder where he now carried a Welsh arrow.

By the time they arrived in the cavern, her thoughts had carried her to a far different place than this. She'd been back at the pool with Padrig, nestled in his arms on the shore. Even the harsh bite of the reality surrounding them could not completely drive away the lingering effects of her fantasy.

Slightly cooler now that Padrig was no longer returning her own heated gaze, she watched as he carried Rafe to a pallet of blankets placed by the fire and, with Dickon's help, prepared to remove the arrows from the poor man's back.

She doubted 'twas normal for a man of Rafe's size and strength to have fallen into so deep a swoon from injuries such as those he'd sustained. He'd scarce twitched since he'd been shot down and fell atop them. Hours had to have passed since then, hours when he'd been dragged about like a load of baggage, bumped and prodded, nigh stood on his head so they could maneuver the litter through the narrow entrance to the tunnel.

Yet through it all, he'd not awakened, nor so much as moaned. He'd made no reaction to anything they'd done to him or for him. If not for the fact that he still breathed, that his heart maintained a strong and steady beat, she'd have believed him dead.

A part of her hoped he'd remain as unresponsive

when they got him out of his mail shirt and cut into his back, but she knew that could only be a bad sign.

She could not wish Rafe to be worse off, even if that made their task easier.

Padrig's low-voiced cursing caught her attention. He and Dickon were trying, without much success, from the look of it, to remove Rafe's mail.

"Could you use another hand?" she asked, rising to her knees, then getting to her feet for a better look at what they were doing. "I've only the one, but it might come in useful."

Padrig eased Rafe down onto the pallet on his side. "If you feel you can do it, aye," he said, wiping sweat from his brow with his forearm and sitting back on his heels. "If you could keep his head up off the ground while we slide this off—" he lifted the hem of the mail shirt "—'twould be a help. Mayhap if we rest his head on your lap?"

With a bit of maneuvering, they got Rafe's mail shirt up around his shoulders, eased it over the shortened arrow shafts, then wriggled it over his head.

Rafe chose that moment to come to his senses most spectacularly, flailing about in confusion and cursing the Welsh as though he were still fighting them.

Alys, her legs pinned beneath the weight of his head and torso, could do little save speak to him in a soothing voice and attempt to stroke his face to calm him. Evidently her ministrations caught his attention, for he abruptly stopped thrashing around.

Instead, in a swift move he captured Alys's hand and brought it to his lips, while nestling his head in her lap in a very intimate manner.

"Rafe!" she cried, her voice little more than a squeak

as she attempted to scramble back away from him. At this point she didn't care if he dropped face first onto the hard ground. "Stop at once!" She jerked her hand free and used it to shove at him, trying with scant effect to push him away from her.

Padrig caught hold of him by the back of his shirt and hauled him up and off. "Rafe, enough!" he shouted, lowering the injured man onto the blankets.

Rafe flopped down onto the pallet. He slowly turned his head toward Alys, stared at her, eyes widening, and groaned. "Tell me that was a dream," he mumbled, rolling onto his side and squeezing his eyes shut.

"More like a nightmare," Padrig said dryly.

Rafe opened his eyes and peered at Alys so swiftly, she almost missed it. "Did I really do—"

"Aye, I'm afraid you really did." Padrig placed a hand on Rafe's uninjured shoulder. "Welcome back to the world of the living, my friend. We've been worried about you."

Alys shifted onto her knees and leaned closer to Rafe. "I've been so concerned, I'm willing to forgive you your…" She waved her hand about, uncertain what to call what Rafe had been doing. "As long as you swear to me you'll *never* do it again," she added in a rush.

"I swear—" he held up his right hand "—I'll never do that to *you* again, milady." His hand dropped to rest upon his chest and he closed his eyes.

'Twas interesting that he'd only vowed to leave her alone, Alys noted with a laugh as she settled back on the hard ground, putting a generous amount of space between Rafe and herself.

Evidently there was nothing seriously wrong with his head, if he was capable of changing her wording to suit his fancy.

Rafe and Padrig carried on a low-voiced conversation now, too quiet for her to overhear. She watched them closely, but could not tell what they discussed. Details of their situation, mayhap, or an explanation for Rafe of how they came to be here. Whatever it was, it left both men looking worn and frustrated once they were finished talking.

When Padrig went to search through the supplies Dickon had piled along the wall, Rafe turned his head toward her and called her name. Concerned, she moved closer to his pallet. His color was somewhat better than it had been earlier, but his skin remained pale, his color ashen. To her eyes, he was in a great deal of pain, though no doubt he'd deny it.

"Can I get you something?" she asked. "Padrig will be back shortly with ale—"

"I don't need ale," he said. He shook his head and patted the wooden flask he wore on his belt. "Got my friend here." His voice sounded stronger with every word, thankfully. 'Twas such a relief to hear him speak at all. She'd still not recovered from seeing him after he'd been shot down.

He'd appeared dead, and in all honesty, had not looked too much different until he'd awakened.

Moving slowly, he patted a spot next to him. "You could keep me company, if you would, while I wait for Sir Padrig to return with his torture devices."

"Of course." She settled alongside his pallet. "Are you certain there's naught I can do for you?" she asked.

"You could tell me where you found the boy." He glanced round the cavern. "And how we came to be here. Wherever this is," he added.

"Actually Dickon found us," she told him, settling in

to tell him the story. She wished she could hold her pen so she could make note of it all as she told it to Rafe, while 'twas fresh in her memory. "Dickon found this place, as well," she told him, bring the tale to a close as Padrig returned.

The time for stories was over, unless Padrig wanted her to tell Rafe some fantastical tale to distract him.

Padrig had brought supplies from Dickon's cache, wrapped in a small bundle he spread out alongside Rafe's pallet. Dickon piled wood on the fire and lighted several more torches in preparation for their undertaking, standing them in a rough circle nearby. Soon the end of the chamber glowed with light, and Padrig declared it time to begin.

Alys hoped she'd never again have reason or need to put anyone else through the procedure that followed.

Padrig offered Rafe a stick to bite down on, which Rafe refused with a string of amazingly creative insults that had them all chuckling in spite of the gruesome task ahead.

She, Dickon and Padrig together barely had the knowledge they needed to remove the arrowheads without doing Rafe further injury. Even had they known precisely what to do, none of them had much skill to do it, unfortunately.

Poor Rafe! He bore their rough surgery stoically, remaining motionless as Padrig used the tip of his dagger to dig out—she could think of no other description for it—the two arrowheads. Quite possibly the reason Rafe was able to stay so still was because he feared what they might inadvertently do to him otherwise.

Sweat poured from them all before they were through, Rafe most of all. His dark hair was nigh dripping by the time Padrig was finished, and she had not yet begun to inflict her own painful task upon him.

Padrig bade her pay close attention, for later she would have to remove the arrow embedded in his back. She prayed 'twas shallowly lodged there. She'd have to use her left hand, and she'd neither the strength nor the dexterity to do much of anything with it.

If her hand had not been so weak and shaky, she'd have been able to do a better, and much faster, job stitching the wounds closed. As it was, she'd nigh been in tears before she was done, with Rafe in worse shape, though he remained still and silent throughout the entire procedure. She'd wished he would swoon again, for just a little while, till she was finished torturing the poor man, but he remained alert until the end.

He did make her cry then, when he thanked them for their care of him.

She just hoped he was as appreciative once he saw the scars he was certain to bear from their evening's work.

She settled back against the cavern wall a little ways away from Rafe's pallet, giving them privacy while Padrig helped Rafe with, as Rafe put it, "men's business."

Still reeling from her attempt at surgery, her mind immediately returned to her earlier, feeble attempt to wield Padrig's knife to cut the arrow shaft. It had been a dismal failure. Could she manage to do better the next time?

She would have to, she told herself firmly. 'Twas another aspect of living her own life—to face the challenges that appeared in her path, meet them head on and deal with them.

'Twas time—past time—that Lady Alys Delamare learn how to contend with both the good *and* the bad.

'Twas time to grow up.

* * *

To Alys's amazement, they'd got Rafe stitched up and settled on his pallet by the fire fairly quickly. In a day that had seemed to last forever, it felt strange for anything to move swiftly.

Rafe accepted their awkward ministrations with good humor. Having slept so deeply and long earlier, he offered to stay awake through the night to tend the fire.

Dickon fell asleep very shortly after they'd finished with Rafe, curled up at the foot of Rafe's pallet. Padrig spoke quietly with Rafe again, then searched through the cache of supplies Dickon had stored in the cavern. He found several blankets and made a bed for Dickon near Rafe's. Settling the boy there, Padrig then brought food for the rest of them.

Despite not having eaten much all day, Alys hadn't thought she'd want anything after their recent, bloody activities. However, once Padrig placed a chunk of cheese and an apple in her hands, she'd realized she was hungry after all.

He'd tapped into a small keg of ale as well, a welcome change from the mineral-laden water they'd been drinking since they'd entered the tunnels.

All too soon Padrig cleared away the remnants of their meal and gathered together the supplies they'd used to tend Rafe's wounds. However, he didn't suggest they attend to his shoulder next. 'Twas a relief to her, not to have to face that trial right away, but in truth she'd just as soon get it over with.

Considering Padrig had been moving around half the day with an arrowhead embedded in his back, she'd have thought *he'd* like to have it dealt with as soon as possible.

Instead he wrapped the supplies in a blanket and

tucked them under his arm. Then, taking one of the lighted torches from near the entrance to the chamber, he headed down a passageway that ran deep into the hillside from the other side of the cavern.

Padrig shifted the loose bundle to a more secure position under his arm and held the torch in front of him. Dickon had told him he couldn't miss the chamber he sought, as long as he remained in the largest passageway. Once away from the main cavern, however, the darkness was unyielding and a torch was necessary. Even in full day, no light would penetrate here.

Of course, that meant no one would see a fire here, either. He'd been concerned the brightness and smoke of the torches and fire in the other chamber would be visible from outside. There was a sizeable opening high in the ceiling, but Dickon assured him he'd been lighting fires there every night, with no one the wiser.

Most likely 'twould only be visible to someone climbing atop the outcropping. Since that was unlikely, especially in the dark of night, they ought to be safe from discovery.

The smaller chamber where he was headed would be the perfect place to bring Alys. They'd have privacy, whether for talking, or for other, more interesting pastimes.

In addition, the surprising feature of this particular cave—a small, warm water pool—would likely appeal to Alys. She could bathe, and soak away some of her aches and pains.

The woman had been battered and dragged about under terrible circumstances, shot at and forced to do bloody work, all with nary a complaint.

Tomorrow he intended to leave here and trek back through the forest to l'Eau Clair, on foot, as swiftly as he could manage. 'Twas the closest place he could go for help. He'd rather leave her here, as he might do with Dickon and Rafe depending on the latter's condition on the morrow, but he doubted she'd stay.

She'd become incredibly independent of late. Mayhap she'd always been that way and no one had noticed, but from what he'd observed, Alys would do whatever she wanted now. Given how upset she was that the rest of their party were trapped in Winterbrooke, he didn't trust her to remain here, hidden in safety, until he returned with help.

He came to the end of the passageway. Dickon was correct. He couldn't have missed this place.

The lad had piled dry brush and wood in a makeshift fire pit, ready to be set alight should the urge strike him to take a bath. Strange behavior from a lad who looked as though he'd not been near water in a year at least, but Padrig could only be grateful for Dickon's forethought.

He rearranged the fuel a little and used the torch to light it. By the time he brought Alys here, it should be a cozy blaze.

He carried the torch near the pool next. The water looked clear, and hadn't the foul smell such springs sometimes did, thank God.

Wouldn't it be wonderful to wash away the stink and dirt of the past few days?

The potential it presented for seduction had captured his notice, as well. 'Twas certainly large enough for two, he noted with a grin, should Alys be inclined to share.

Their brief time together at the pond earlier in the journey, before everything went awry, stood out in his memory as a particularly arousing experience.

And that had been when the water was chilly, they scarcely knew each other and they could have been discovered by his men or her maid at any moment!

What would it be like, to have the opportunity to share this warm, private place with Alys now that they knew each other better?

His body stirred at the possibilities that came effortlessly to mind....

If he was willing to risk his future, perhaps even his life, by becoming Alys's lover.

He knew she was not for him. Not the way things stood at present, at any rate. He had nothing save his armor, weapons and horses, a paltry hoard of money and his position with the FitzCliffords. He could not offer Alys a home or a noble name, and his ties to the FitzCliffords were tenuous, to say the least. If he angered Lord Rannulf or Lord Connor, he could lose that advantage, as well.

What her father might do to the man who stole his daughter's innocence, he didn't know, but he doubted 'twould be anything good.

He bit back a humorless laugh. To make Lady Alys a part of his world presented just the sort of challenge he liked, the kind where the outcome looked bleak, but where with determination, he could triumph.

He'd faced down such trials all his life, with more successes than failures.

In an admittedly short time, Alys had become an essential part of his life. For something this important, he'd not permit himself to fail.

She'd noticed Dickon talking to Padrig and pointing down the tunnel soon after they'd arrived here, but hadn't heard what the boy had said about it.

Alys glanced over at Rafe, who'd been quiet since they'd tended his back. 'Twas a wonder he was still awake, after all he'd been through. The past several days had been grueling. Most likely he was exhausted and in pain.

Silence from Rafe was so unusual, however, it made her uncomfortable.

"Where is Padrig going?" she asked, simply to start a conversation.

"What?" Grimacing, he shifted on the pallet to face her.

"I asked where Padrig was going." She moved closer to Rafe, so he wouldn't have to keep craning his neck to see her.

At least he was looking at her. Evidently he'd recovered from his shock over waking in her lap, she thought wryly.

"Answering nature's call, I imagine," he replied offhandedly. "He'll be back soon, no doubt." He reached beside him and came up with his precious flask of whiskey in his hand. Uncorking it, he gave it a shake, nodded, and held it out to her. "Care for some, milady? Works wonders against the damp of this place, as well as curing any manner of other problems."

She shook her head. Lifting up slightly from the blankets, he brought the bottle to his lips and took a long drink. Making a sound of satisfaction, he rammed home the cork and settled himself back onto the pallet. "I swear I wouldn't try to make you drink it, or to take anything more than a sip," he assured her, his tone serious for once. "It might help you sleep, you know."

"I cannot rest just yet," she told him. "Once Padrig returns, I'm to take the arrow from his shoulder."

He chuckled. "I'd better save the rest o' this for him, then. I vow he'll need it."

"I pray he doesn't." Though *she* might need a strong drink afterward.

Quiet footsteps echoing in the corridor heralded Padrig's return. He emerged from the dark passageway without the bundle or the torch he'd taken with him when he left.

He approached them, pausing by the fire. "Are you certain you don't mind keeping watch and tending the fire tonight?" he asked Rafe. He gestured toward the pile of dry sticks and branches placed within Rafe's reach. "Dickon set his alarms, and we've plenty of wood here for the fire."

"Nay, I don't mind a bit." Rafe pushed himself upright and, moving gingerly, propped his back against the wall. Snatching a blanket from his pallet, he bundled it up and stuffed it behind his head. "I got enough sleep today to last me for at least the next two."

"Good." Padrig took several unlit torches from a pile near the wall. "You should be all set here, then." Some look that Alys couldn't decipher passed between the two men. Rafe nodded once, and Padrig came to stand before her.

"Good luck," Rafe said, though which one of them he addressed, she could not say. Turning away from them, he stared into the fire.

Padrig extended his hand to Alys. "Are you ready, milady?"

"I am, milord." She laid her palm atop his. His warm, rough fingers closed about hers slowly, as solemnly as a vow.

Her heart beat faster at the passion in his eyes, the faint tremor in his hand as it clasped hers. For her this moment signaled an ending to old ways, and a new beginning she welcomed with open heart and open mind.

What, if anything, it meant to Padrig she would hopefully learn soon.

Smiling up at him, she let him help her to her feet and lead her from the cavern.

Chapter Twenty

Hands clasped, they walked in silence down the corridor. Alys could feel the weight of Padrig's gaze moving over her in the shadowy light spilling into the passageway from somewhere up ahead. She didn't dare look at him, didn't know what to say.

'Twas a surprise to her, considering how easy it had been to be bold with him earlier.

In light of that boldness, he no doubt expected something different from her, as well.

A strange shyness washed through her. 'Twas not that she did not want what she'd hinted at before, but now that the point had arrived to make her imaginings real, she wanted to linger over every moment, savor every detail, create a memory to cherish all her life.

It might well be the only such memory she would ever have.

She wanted it to be wonderful.

She wanted it to last.

The real truth of it, though, was that she didn't truly know what to do next.

Mayhap, the rational part of her mind scolded, 'twould be best if she simply turned round now and went back to the cavern, pretended she'd never wanted this.

Never wanted Padrig, nor a brief chance at a moment of happiness, had never dared to experience a pleasure she knew was a rare prize.

That was a coward's way.

She'd not tread that path any longer. What she did this night could change her future, transform it into it something wonderful. Or to a life she'd hate.

Her parents could disown her, especially if their plans for her included a husband…. One she did not want.

The abbey would certainly not take her once she became damaged goods. However, that knowledge held no power over her any longer. As long as she could think, could feel, could record those thoughts and feelings in some manner, she was a writer. She needn't join the abbey to prove that fact.

Nor could she take a nun's vows under false pretenses. She'd not further endanger her soul with such lies.

She'd do what *she* wanted, take her life into her own hands.

She was willing to take the risk that 'twould not turn out so well, as long as she could have this night.

Her decision made, she tugged on Padrig's hand as they neared the end of the corridor. The light was bright beyond this point, but here they were surrounded by a soft glow, perfect for sharing secrets and making plans.

Perhaps he misunderstood her hesitation, for he turned to face her and, releasing her left hand, carefully brought her right to his lips and kissed her fingers. "You've nothing to fear from me, sweeting," he whispered. "Not ever."

"I'm not afraid of you," she replied. She hadn't expected to hear her voice quiver, to sound so faint. She drew in a deep breath and released it slowly. "Truly, Padrig, I'm not."

He cupped her hand protectively within both of his. "You're trembling."

She leaned closer, brushed her lips across his. "So are you," she murmured, "but I don't think 'tis because you fear me." The realization emboldened her, gave her the courage to lean into him. *Act now, talk later,* her heart told her head.

It did feel so right when they were together. Her heart light, she pressed her mouth more fully against his warm lips.

He returned the caress, then stepped back from her, releasing her right hand and once again twining his fingers with her left. "Come see what Dickon found," he invited. He led her out of the corridor into another cavern, this one much smaller than the first.

He'd been busy in the brief time he'd been away, for there was a small fire flickering by the wall near the entrance, with a blanket spread out near its warmth.

Still holding her hand, he led her past the fire, where he took up two torches, paused to light them, and led her into the shadowed depths of the room. The light spread to the edges of the area, revealing a small pool of water.

Alys moved closer, drawn by the thought of bathing away the last days' dirt.

And, truth be told, sorely tempted by the enticing notion of sharing the small pool with Padrig.

The water was clear, and appeared deep enough to sit in. "'Tis probably cold as an icy mountain spring," she said. "Though it might be worth the chill, simply to be clean."

"Touch it and see," Padrig suggested. Suspicious, she glanced over her shoulder at him. His smile hinted at secrets and promises, making her heartbeat race.

If they got into the water with him smiling like that, she doubted she'd even notice the cold!

Alys leaned down and trailed her hand over the surface.
'Twas warm, almost hot!

She whirled to face him, and found him right behind her. His blue eyes alight with mischief, he caught hold of her hand and brought it to his mouth. He trailed his tongue along one wet finger, then nipped at the tip of it, sending a bolt of heat shooting from her hand straight to her heart.

Sucking in a breath, she dragged her finger over his mouth, savoring the sensual contrast of his soft lips with the very different texture of the soft, dark whiskers around them.

He closed his eyes for a moment. When he opened them, a fiery passion glowed in their depths. "Will you bathe with me, Alys?" Catching hold of her hand, he pressed it to his cheek. "It needn't be anything more than that, if you choose. I'll even leave you to bathe alone if you wish," he offered, then added with a wry laugh, "Though 'twould likely kill me to do so."

"What of your wound?" she asked, caressing his jaw before trailing her hand over to his shoulder. That was a sobering thought, though it did little to cool her ardor. "I must attend to that before anything else."

"I doubt 'tis so deep you'd need to stitch it," he said. "I'll need to remove my hauberk either way. Once it's off, you can see what needs to be done." He reached out and smoothed her hair away from her face. "What say you, milady? Shall I join you, or shall I simply attend you as you bathe?" He smiled. "I warn you now, I expect my injury to have raised me to great heights in your favor. Don't think to cheat me of my due."

"You shall always have my favor," she vowed, meaning every word. "But first, let's see to your injury before we make any other plans."

Padrig had to be content with her promise for now. However, the instant they were through dealing with wounds and injuries, both of theirs, for he'd like to see how Alys fared in that area, as well, the time for caution would be past.

He prayed she'd come to him, join herself with him body and soul.

If she would not, he would honor her decision... though he wasn't sure he'd have the strength to do so with good grace.

Lady Alys Delamare, he feared, held the power to turn him into a howling fool.

At her request he removed the binding on her arm, giving her more freedom of movement. Not that she'd want to use her right arm much. It was going to be painful for many days to come.

In turn, she helped him divest himself of the tools of his profession. Never had removing his sword belt been invested with so much promise as when Alys slowly unbuckled the heavy leather and slid it from his waist. His mail coif he'd worn pushed down about his neck for the last several days; Alys slipped her hand beneath the heavy mesh and soothed his flesh with her touch even as she helped him take it off.

The simplest touch of her hand, the brush of her hair over his skin sent fire and ice flowing through him to settle as an ever-growing passion in his loins.

He couldn't blame his sensitivity to her touch on having been too long without a woman's touch. Though it had been months since he'd last been with a woman, he'd never in his life felt such yearning as this.

It wasn't the fact that Alys was a woman that made him want her, 'twas that she was *the* woman, the only woman with the power to make him ache for passion, for tenderness...for love.

"Almost done," she told him, giving his boot a tug to remove it and tossing it aside with its mate. She reached down and caught the hem of his hauberk in her hand. He bent at the waist to let the weight of the mail pull off the heavy garment. "Careful," she warned, trying unsuccessfully to hold up the area where the arrow had penetrated.

The chopped-off bit of shaft caught in the mail as the hauberk fell off, tugging the arrowhead free of his flesh. "By Christ's bones," he growled as the burning sensation spread across his back and down his arm.

He let the mail drop to the floor, tugged off the padded shirt he wore beneath it and straightened. Alys had already moved behind him. She gasped, and hurried to grab a cloth from the supplies he'd left by the fire.

"'Tis bleeding," she told him. She dabbed at the warm trickle of blood running down his back, following its path with the cloth. "This will hurt, I expect." She pressed the cloth hard over the wound.

He clenched his teeth, but in truth, the worst of the pain was already past. 'Twas a great relief to no longer have the metal poking into his flesh, gouging at him every time the shortened shaft caught in the links of mail.

Her hand on his shoulder, Alys turned him toward the light and stood on tiptoe to examine the cut. "How does it look?" he asked, peering back and trying without success to see her face. "It feels better already."

She pressed the cloth against the wound once more, raised her head to meet his gaze and smiled. "I don't believe I'll be practicing my left-handed stitchery upon you tonight," she told him. "For which you're exceedingly thankful, I'm sure."

"No more than you are, I imagine."

"You've scars enough already," she said, smoothing her hand over a long, thin mark that ran over his other shoulder from his neck to his armpit. Her attention caught by the dark markings near the arrow wound, she traced her finger lightly over the design. "What is this?" she asked. "I've not seen its like before."

He reached for her hand and drew her around so she could see his face. "'Tis an old Celtic tribal marking. I got it while I was in Ireland."

"How was it made?"

He laughed. "You really don't want to know."

She followed the pattern with her fingertip, careful to avoid the wound. "Did it hurt?" She couldn't explain her curiosity about the marking, but she found the contrast of the marking against his tanned skin compelling somehow.

"Let's just say that vast amounts of ale were consumed before, during and after." He tried to peer over his shoulder to look at the wound. "Though I doubt it hurt as much as some of the injuries I've had."

She gazed at the assortment of scars. "Some of them look like they were bad—worse than this one," she added, gently pressing the cloth to the cut.

"Is it bleeding still?" he asked. "You don't need to bandage it, do you?"

"Nay." Relieved, and eager to move on to other, more satisfying things, she slipped her hand free of his and pressed her palm onto his chest, over his heart.

Padrig heard the way her voice trembled a bit, as did her warm hand against his skin. 'Twas clear she had other things on her mind than his tattoo, thank God.

"I'll do it later," she said, her gaze steady and sure. "After we've bathed."

Padrig felt his entire body relax for the first time in days. Some parts of it, at any rate. He cupped her chin in his hand and bent to brush a kiss along her cheekbone. "Have we time for more lessons, do you think?" he murmured. He skimmed his other hand up the middle of her torso, his knuckles brushing lightly over her breast, before pausing to untie the lacing of her gown. He loosened the material, and trailed his fingers over the soft skin of her throat. Pausing where her blood pulsed swiftly at the side of her neck, he bent to nuzzle the delicate spot. "We may need to practice what we've already learned, before we move on to something new."

Her fingers spread out on his chest, her nails pressing lightly into his flesh. "'Twould be best to do so," she agreed. When she tilted her head back, he nudged open the neckline of her gown farther still, until he could trace his mouth over the tender skin he'd revealed.

Her shiver of reaction sent a similar response thrumming through him. Moaning, he gathered her into his arms and held her tight. "Where *did* we leave off this morn?"

Alys moved her hands lightly over his skin, spreading warmth everywhere she touched him, sensitizing his flesh so that even the slight brush of her hair over his arms and chest sent fire flowing through his blood. "I cannot recall where we stopped." She laid her cheek over his heart and laughed. "But I believe we started with you teaching me how lovers kiss."

His heart beat faster. "Show me, Alys," he murmured. He loosened his hold upon her and, cradling her jaw in his hand, bent to gently taste her lips. "Do you remember how?"

She raised her hand to trail her fingertips over his mouth. "How could I forget?"

She'd forgotten nothing. Indeed, her kisses were every bit as overwhelming now. Nay, even more so than they had been before.

She lured Padrig into a sensual web with the mere brush of her lips over his. She'd been an apt pupil, for she'd taken what he'd taught her and elaborated upon it, drawing him to her with an intangible force he'd no will nor desire to resist.

Yet though her caresses might be daring in one so untutored, there was nothing blatant about them. Her touch held an innocence, an honesty and simple pleasure he found enchanting.

Their kisses grew more heated and she clung to him, her body trembling slightly.

While he'd like to believe 'twas solely a reaction to his touch, he feared it could also be the result of a long and exhausting travail.

There was no reason they must remain on their feet, however. Not when there were so many other possibilities to explore.

"Here, love, 'tis time for the next lesson," he whispered. He slipped out of her arms. "Wait here."

Alys stood quietly waiting, watching as he crossed

the chamber, threw more wood on the fire and picked up the blanket.

The weight of her gaze lent speed to his movements. Returning to the pool, he shoved his hauberk and weapons aside and spread out the blanket on the stone floor next to the shimmering water.

He took her by the hand. "Your bower, milady," he said as he helped her to sit on the blanket. He bowed low before her. "Consider me your most humble and loyal servant."

Kneeling beside her, he flipped up the hem of her gown only enough to expose her short boots. "It appears to me that one of us—" he slipped off one boot and set it aside, then reached for the other one "—is vastly overdressed."

"Is that so?" Alys asked lazily, leaning back on her elbow, her gaze fixed upon his face. "What shall you do to remedy that, milord?"

He cradled her bare feet in his hands and began to knead them gently. "I could take off the rest of my clothes," he offered, sending her a teasing grin. He raised one hand to the knotted cord at the waist of his braes, his only remaining garment, and quirked one eyebrow questioningly.

"That would be lovely." Her answering smile dared him to make good his threat. Her gaze, as it swept over him from head to toe, was as a tangible a caress as if she'd stroked that same path with her hands. "Would you like me to help?"

Did she know what it did to him, to share this lighthearted play with her? 'Twas exciting and enticing, of that there was no doubt, yet the fact was, he also simply enjoyed the ease with which they bantered back and forth.

Alys had the power to hold the world at bay, to give him these moments when only they two existed. 'Twas a gift, one he would treasure always.

A gift he hoped he'd be allowed to keep.

"First let me help you, milady." He stretched out alongside her and reached for the lacings of her gown. Since he'd loosened them earlier, 'twas a simple matter to untie them completely. "Shall I?"

Her eyes huge in the flickering torchlight, Alys sat up at his urging and let him undo her belt. When he slipped it from her waist, he noticed how heavy it felt, definitely more so than he'd expect for such a dainty piece.

He removed the embroidered leather pouch from the thin, finely worked leather band and hefted it in his hand. "By the rood, 'tis a wonder you could stand upright. What do you have in here?" he asked dryly. "Rocks?"

"Only one," she murmured. Her face grew pink beneath his puzzled look. He started to loosen the drawstring, but she snatched the pouch from him before he got it open. She jerked at the strings, reached inside and pulled out a jagged stone. "My chastity belt, you called it." Taking his hand, she placed the rock in his palm and closed his fingers about it.

"You kept it?" He didn't bother to hide his amazement.

"You gave it to me," she mumbled, glancing away. 'Twas a piece of rock. It had no value.

Except, apparently, to Alys.

Touched, he reached for the pouch, carefully slid the stone back in and handed it to her. "I am honored," he told her.

Not meeting his gaze, she took the pouch and set it carefully next to the blanket, then sat silently staring down at her lap.

"Do you think we need that rock to serve its original purpose again?" he asked gently.

She shook her head, but the pink tint of her cheeks deepened.

"Alys, if you're uncomfortable about this, I'll bring you back to the cavern." He took her hand and tugged it lightly, but she still refused to look at him. "You know Rafe would protect you from me, if that's what you want. He's quite capable of doing so despite his wounds, I assure you." He tugged on her hand again. "Knowing Rafe, he'd probably enjoy it."

She glanced up at him, slipping her hand free to sweep her hair away from her face. "All I'm uncomfortable about—" she reached out and cradled his cheek in her hand "—is the fact that you're more likely to need something to protect *you* from *me*." She rose up onto her knees and edged closer to him. "Ladies are not supposed to feel these things," she told him earnestly. "Or even if they do, they definitely should not behave this way."

"Behave what way?" he couldn't resist asking. Hope rose in his heart that she wasn't about to leave him quite yet.

"Like a ravenous beast," she muttered, looking away again.

He made her ravenous? He fought back a laugh of sheer joy.

As long as she wasn't talking about food...

"I'd be happy to help satisfy your hunger." 'Twas a challenge to keep an innocent expression on his face, when what he truly wanted was to tumble her onto the blanket and satisfy them both. "What is it, exactly, that you hunger for?"

Her eyes narrowed just before she slipped her hand

into the hair at his nape and gave a sharp tug. "Will you make me say it?" she wailed. Her jaw clenched, she sat back on her heels, her fingers still woven tightly in his hair.

"I will," he said. "You've no reason to be shy with me, Alys. Not about anything at all."

"Very well." Her expression serious, she wriggled closer to him, her breasts brushing against his chest, stopping when their lips were nearly touching. "I want you, Padrig ap Huw, more than I ought to want anything."

Chapter Twenty-One

The words had scarcely left Alys's lips before Padrig wrapped her tightly in his arms and tumbled her down onto the blanket. "I wasn't sure you'd say it," he whispered into her hair. "Hell, I wasn't certain 'twas what you meant."

"If 'twas food I'd wanted, I wouldn't have been shy about asking for it," she pointed out dryly. She nuzzled his chest, savoring the feel of his hair-covered skin tickling her lips. "This is more to my taste."

To her disappointment, he drew back from her, meeting her frown with a shake of his head. "As much as I want you to touch me, sweeting, I doubt I smell too appetizing."

In truth, she found the scent of him—leather, a trace of sandalwood and the sweat of a healthy man—very appealing. Chuckling, she told him, "You smell like a man, not like those perfumed coxcombs my father surrounds himself with." She rested her cheek against his skin. "I like it."

He shook his head. "You're a brave woman to get this close," he said with a smile.

He didn't appear to mind having her cuddled so near, she noted, wriggling closer.

Suddenly he stood and, closing his hands about her waist, lifted her up as though she weighed nothing. She grabbed his brawny arms for balance, marveling at the sleek strength of him as he set her on her feet.

His lean torso was corded with muscle and lightly dusted with soft, dark hair. The skin of his chest and arms was as tanned as his face, no doubt the result of all the training he did out in the sun, garbed in naught but boots and braes.

She'd seen him on the practice field many times, watched and admired him long before they ever met.

The true Padrig, the man she was coming to know, was far more exciting, more interesting, than she could ever have envisioned in her relatively innocent daydreams.

Even her lively imagination wasn't that clever.

Padrig knelt at her feet and, grasping the hem of her gown in one hand, began to lift the material, bit by torturous bit.

Alys watched Padrig's face, noting how his eyes darkened and his breathing quickened, as did hers, as he teased them both.

As more of her legs were exposed, he smoothed his warm, rough hand in the gown's wake, trailing up from foot to calf, knee to thigh. He paused with the fabric hovering just below her hips, running his fingers caressingly along the inside of her thigh. "Shall I continue, milady?" he asked, his voice deeper than usual.

Her heart pounded so loud, 'twas a miracle she could hear him. Her whole being was focused upon Padrig's touch. He knelt so close to her, she could feel his breath on her skin. That, combined with the teasing caress of his callused fingers against her sensitive flesh, made it nigh impossible for her to remain on her feet.

Yet she could not tell him to stop, not now!

Drawing a deep breath, she placed her hands upon his broad shoulders to hold herself steady. "Please, go on," she murmured.

The look he sent her made her glad she'd braced herself. The heated challenge in his eyes sent a tremor of anticipation through her, anticipation that was borne out tenfold when he raised her skirts to her waist and pressed his lips to the quivering flesh of her belly.

"Padrig," she moaned. She tightened her fingers on his shoulders, her nails biting into his smooth skin.

He shoved aside the fabric of her gown and stroked his hands up over her hips. He followed the same path with his mouth, tracing his tongue over her hipbones and up to her navel, then skimming along the curve of her belly.

He pressed a kiss to the sensitive flesh just above the curls at the juncture of her thighs, his hands clasped tight about her waist, her gown crumpled above them.

Kissing her one more time, he eased his hold, moved back a bit and let her gown drop down over his arms. "Let's get into the pool," he said, his voice rough. He tried to slip his arms from under her skirts and got the fabric tangled round them. Laughing, he gathered the material in both hands and swept it up her body, pausing only to ease the sleeve he'd cut carefully over her right arm.

He left her wearing her linen shift, made of cloth so sheer her nipples showed through it. "You cannot trust me to do this right," he said with a laugh. "I'm too easily distracted by you."

He led her to the water, slid his hands into the wide neckline of her shift and slipped it off her shoulders, letting it slither down her body to pool at her feet. She stepped out of it and closer to Padrig, reaching for the tie at the waist of his braes.

He stopped her from going further, catching her hand in his and shifting it to his chest. "If you only touch me above the waist, love, I *might* be able to control myself," he told her, chuckling. "If you do otherwise, I fear *I'll* turn into a ravening beast." He bent his head and pressed a kiss to her knuckles. "Right now, 'tis my most ardent wish to become acquainted with yours."

If he kept up with what he'd started, her "beast" just might surprise him with the depth of her passion. It took more control than she knew she had within her to stand passively before him while he worked his magic upon her oh-so-willing body.

His touch held a combination of reverence and urgency, making her entire being hum with pleasure barely suppressed. He scattered kisses over her face, her neck and throat, all the while holding his hands clasped loosely around her waist.

Her hair hung nearly to her hips, the disheveled mass veiling her breasts. Padrig slowly skimmed his mouth down over her throat and along her collarbone, nudging aside the tangled tresses and sending shivers of reaction skittering down her spine to settle deep within her belly. All the while, his fingertips drifted over her ribs in a tantalizing caress, but he never moved his hands from about her middle.

In no time she was ready to scream with frustration. The more he touched her, the more bold her desire became, until she was ready to grab his hands and move them to where she ached most to be touched.

She restrained herself from doing so, barely, by reminding herself that anticipation, as well as desire, could be savored.

Perhaps 'twas time to make *him* experience a bit of anticipation, as well.

Smiling, she brought both hands to rest upon his chest and began to stroke them lightly over the firm muscles banding his torso. Her fingers drew teasing patterns, following the thin line of dark hair down his stomach, moving ever-closer to his waist, then darting up to twine in the mass of curls covering his nipples.

He sucked in his stomach, which made her smile, and grabbed her hands to still them, which did not.

She wriggled her fingers, eliciting a stern look. He raised her hands from his chest and twined his fingers with hers. "You may touch me, but I may not do the same to you?" she asked. "Is that fair? My hands never strayed past your waist."

"They did enough mischief where they were," he ground out. He rested his forehead against hers and closed his eyes for a moment. She tried to free her hands, but he held them in a firm grip and would not release her.

When he opened his eyes, they glowed with an unexpected humor. He let go of her hands and, grinning, untied his braes and stepped out of them. Before she had a chance to enjoy the sight, he scooped her up in his arms, stepped over the edge of the pool, and sat down, immersing them both in the warm water.

Alys shrieked, then clamped her mouth shut as the water closed over her head. She popped up, sputtering and swiping frantically at the lengths of wet hair trailing over her face and tangled round her arms. "Have you gone mad?" she demanded.

Padrig snaked out his arm and hauled her into his lap, crushing his mouth to hers as she'd wished he would do earlier. She stopped squirming at once and returned the kiss full measure.

Gasping, she pulled away from him just far enough to see his face. "No more games," she said, voice shaking. "I vow you'll drive *me* mad with them."

"No more," he agreed. He gathered her hair away from her face and neck. Wrapping it about his fist, he tilted her head back slightly and stared into her eyes. "Is this what you wanted, Alys?" He dipped his head and trailed his mouth down her throat to the tops of her breasts and back again, the rasp of his whiskers on her tender skin blazing a trail of heat in their path. "The two of us together, like this?"

A bolt of heat tore through her at the look in his eyes. Darkened to a deep indigo, they captivated her with their intensity.

"Aye, 'tis what I want," she agreed.

"I've made you no promises," he said. "We've spoken no vows—"

She caught hold of his face between her hands. "No more words, Padrig." Smiling, she brought her mouth to his for a kiss that laid bare her desire. "Let our bodies speak instead."

His mind a passion-hazed blur, Padrig sank into Alys's kiss, did as she'd ordered and let his body show her all the feelings he'd no words to express.

The unusual mixture of bold sensuality and enchanting sweetness that was Alys fired his passion far beyond his experience. Now that she could let her hands wander wherever she wished, she let them linger on his neck, chest and stomach. She teased him nigh beyond endurance, dipping her fingertips just below the water—just below his waist—to tempt and tease so near to his aching manhood.

Her flesh was warm and soft, slick with water, made for his touch. She twisted round in his lap to face him and stole his breath away. Her breasts glistened in the flickering torch light, beads of water trickling down her creamy flesh to disappear into the pool.

He bent his head and pressed a kiss to the shoulder he'd had to manhandle earlier in the day, lingering there as he savored the expression on Alys's face.

Passion glowed in her eyes as she watched him, their amber depths alight with desire. And mischief. She shifted delicately upon his lap, the movement brushing her hip against his aching flesh.

Temptation was a game two could play, he reminded himself silently. She might not want words, but he could let his actions speak for him instead.

He kissed her slowly, using tongue and teeth to savor her taste. Once her eyelids drifted shut, he gently cupped her breasts in his hands, his fingers plucking at her nipples in rhythm with his kisses.

Her eyes opened wide and she moaned against his lips, breaking away to gasp for breath. "Dear God, what are you doing to me?" she asked, her voice shaking and weak.

"Savoring you." He bumped his nose against hers, smoothed his hands up her arms and shoulders to frame her face. "Cherishing you." Her gaze met his, the heat in her eyes softening to a golden glow. "Loving you," he murmured, pressing a kiss to the soft spot below her ear.

"Love me now," she whispered. "Let me love you." Her expression solemn, she covered his hands with hers and swept them back along the path they'd followed, settling on her breasts. "Make me yours."

"Gladly, sweeting." His heart thundered in his chest as, hands braced upon his shoulders, she shifted in his lap to straddle his legs. "Easy, love. There's no hurry," he said with a low laugh. "Let's take our time. I don't want to hurt you."

He clasped her about the waist and slid her back a bit, then slipped one hand slowly along her leg from foot to thigh. This time he let his hand wander higher, let his fingers linger on the soft petals of her femininity.

He swallowed her gasp of surprise with an unhurried kiss, his tongue dueling with hers at a leisurely pace despite her efforts to make him move more swiftly.

It took all his control not to do just that, to give in to his body's demand that he take her now, make her his without further delay.

He refused to be rushed, however, by Alys or by his own unrelenting desire for her. He wanted her poised on the precipice of satisfaction before they joined their bodies, so that when they did, she would have no other thought in her mind but of the pleasure they created together.

Evidently realizing he would not give in, Alys set about to tempt him as he had been teasing her. Slanting her mouth on his, she deepened their kiss, using tongue and teeth, as he had taught her, he reminded himself, to build the tension between them higher still.

As he continued to caress her intimately, she brought

her own hands into play. Smoothing her fingers lightly down the middle of his torso, she didn't stop at his waist, but boldly slid her hand lower.

She paused with her open hand cupped loosely about his manhood, almost touching him. Her fingers flexed, stirring the water about him in a subtle caress. His hips flexed in reaction, seeking her touch, but she moved her hand away slightly, keeping him from what he sought.

She tore her mouth free of his and, gasping, raised her other hand to cradle his jaw. "Look at me, Padrig," she said, the unruffled demand in her voice at odds with the tension spiraling round them.

His breathing uneven, he met her gaze. Her face was flushed, her body trembled and her eyes blazed with a golden fire.

"You are mine, as I am yours." She closed her fingers about him and slipped forward on his legs until his manhood was just touching the haven it sought.

He covered her hand with his. "Aye, Alys." Their gazes joined, he slipped into the warmth of her body. *"Always."*

Her gaze fixed upon his, Alys moaned at the feel of Padrig sliding into her. She couldn't have looked away at that moment, for he held her captivated as much by what she saw reflected in his eyes as what his body made her feel. 'Twas anticipation, intense pleasure and an irresistible sense of claiming and being claimed, all swirled together into a maelstrom that threatened to overwhelm her.

She clung to his upper arms, savoring the flex of his muscles beneath her fingers, enjoying the sensation of barely restrained power emanating from him.

"Almost there, love," he murmured. Clasping his hands about her waist, he drew her down upon his body as his hips shifted upward until they were truly joined.

She'd expected 'twould hurt more, but the twinge of pain swiftly faded as Padrig helped her to move upon him, with him. She felt as though her heart might burst from her chest, it pounded so swiftly, and 'twas all she could do to breathe.

She felt compelled to move faster, to hurtle toward the bright glow of pleasure she sensed glimmering just beyond her reach, but Padrig would not allow her to hasten the pace of their loving.

She leaned down to kiss him, echoing his leisurely pace with the unhurried slide of her tongue along his, the duel of their mouths building on the excitement of their bodies moving together.

Despite the urge to let her eyes drift closed, she kept them open as they kissed, her gaze on Padrig's face. The tension gripping his body was reflected there, his features drawn taut with passion, a flush riding high along his cheekbones, his gaze heated, intense.

Her own desire grew apace, making her frantic for more—of what, she wasn't certain, but she could sense 'twas almost within her grasp.

Short of breath, she eased her mouth from his, breathing deeply.

Padrig gave her but a moment to catch her breath. In a swift movement, he shifted her hands to his shoulders. Wrapping one arm about her back, he raised the other to burrow his fingers into her hair. Cupping her head in his hand, he deepened the kiss, his body driving into hers in a quickening rhythm.

The elusive pinnacle she sought suddenly loomed before her with frightening intensity. Her nails biting into Padrig's shoulders, she tried to ease away from him, but he would have none of it. He broke off the kiss, held her still with arms that trembled. "Nay, love." He leaned down and stroked his tongue over one nipple, sending a lightning bolt of fire streaking through her. "Almost there, Alys," he gasped. "Come with me. Be mine."

When she lowered herself upon him and began to move again, the yearning in his expression hurled her body beyond her control.

Her heart pounding wildly, her mind awhirl, Alys stared into Padrig's eyes and gave herself into his keeping, body and soul.

Pleasure overwhelmed her, sending her into a realm where she was aware of nothing but Padrig and what he made her feel. Her body curled round him, she held tight to him as he joined her in ecstasy.

Chapter Twenty-Two

Alys returned to her senses slowly, aware of little beyond what she could see and hear without raising her head from Padrig's chest. Her world had shrunk to Padrig's face, the sound of his heart beating steadily beneath her ear, the warm smooth feel of the water shifting over her sensitized flesh.

Padrig remained joined with her, his hands shifting in a soothing caress over her back and neck. He'd slumped back against the edge of the pool. He wore her draped over him, her body sprawled atop him like a blanket.

She'd strength enough to press her lips to the side of his neck, nuzzling against the prickly whiskers with her cheek before nipping lightly at his throat.

"I wanted to do that before," she said with a quiet laugh, not quite certain she wanted him to hear.

He drew his head back so he could see her face, which felt as though it had gone scarlet as soon as the words had left her mouth. "You should have," he said. He grinned, his eyes merry. "I'd not have minded."

"I'll remember that," she warned him, emboldened by his reaction. She raised herself up on his chest, looking at his face, his expression with eyes newly opened by passion.

The mere sight of him had always had the power to stir her, but now when she looked at him, she saw so much more than a strong, handsome knight. Padrig could be serious, tender, amusing...

He quirked an eyebrow at her as she continued her scrutiny. "Have I grown an extra nose?" he asked. "Or a third eye, perchance?"

"That would be different." Most likely he looked no different to anyone but herself, she realized, 'twas just that she viewed him now with a lover's awareness. She stroked her palm over his cheek, trailed her fingers across his full lips, marveling yet again at their softness. "But no, you've not grown any extra appendages."

"That's good," he said, chuckling. "It's all I can do to keep up with the ones I've got." He cupped his hands about her backside and pressed her more firmly against him. Her breath caught as she felt his manhood begin to swell within her. "Some need more attention than others," he added. Catching her lower lip in his teeth, then soothing the spot with his tongue, he straightened, drawing her up with him. "Very demanding." He kissed her, his arms wrapping around her firmly. In a deft move, he withdrew from her and flipped them about so that 'twas she who sat propped against the rim of the pool.

Breaking off the kiss, he knelt beside her. "Unfortunately we'd better get out of here if we don't want to be lame tomorrow," he said. "The warmth is good for aches and pains, but wrapping ourselves into knots, no matter that it feels wonderful at the time—" he grinned "—will not serve us well later on."

He gathered her hair in his hands and squeezed the water from it. "We've no soap, milady, but I could still help you bathe," he offered.

'Twas a tempting notion, yet she knew where that would lead. "If you want us to get out of this water any-time soon, 'twould be best if we wash ourselves," she told him regretfully. She smiled mischievously. "Be-sides, we ought to be well rinsed by now, we moved about so much in the water."

"You make a fine washerwoman," he said. "Very thor-ough." Unmindful of his nudity, he climbed from the pool and reached down to assist her. "Much more beautiful than any laundress I've ever encountered." He lifted her easily from the water. "So very lovely," he added, gath-ering her into his arms and cradling her against his body.

Scarcely allowing her to pause for breath, Padrig kissed Alys, at the same time carrying her to the blan-ket he'd left ready near the now-dwindling fire. He eased her down onto it and stretched out alongside her.

She felt freer now to explore his body, to be more bold in her caresses. It gave her such a feeling of power, to make this strong man tremble from her kisses, to have him want her as she wanted him.

She'd thought his body wondrous when she'd seen him by the pond, streaming water and glistening in the early morning sun.

That was but an introduction, however, compared to this. He lay on his back on the blanket, his head propped on one arm, one leg bent at the knee. Shimmering drop-lets of water clung to his skin and hair, while the strength of his muscular body was limned by firelight.

Alys knelt beside him, not as comfortable in her nudity as he appeared to be with his. Yet she'd no intention of hiding herself away in the enveloping layers of her clothes, not while there was the possibility she and Padrig would make love again this night. However, she'd not yet become so bold as to sprawl before him in all her glory, either.

Letting her hair fall forward to veil her body seemed a reasonable compromise.

She ran her hands from Padrig's face to his feet, slowly touching him everywhere in between, until he caught her hands in his and tugged her down beside him. Rolling her beneath him, he proceeded to share with her the next lesson in lovemaking.

Afterward she lay snuggled to Padrig's side, her body sated with loving, her heart humming with the joy he'd given her, and prayed that they be given the chance to be together beyond this night.

A tear leaked from the corner of her eye and rolled slowly across her cheek.

For if they could not, now that she knew what she might have had, she'd just condemned herself to a most lonely life indeed.

Padrig woke with a start, uncertain for a moment where he was. He blinked, bringing the dimly lit cavern into focus, feeling the soft warmth of the woman nestled to his side.

The fire had burned down to coals, and all but one torch had died. It must be nearly dawn now, time, unfortunately, to bring this interlude to an end and return to the harsh reality of the world beyond these caverns.

Memories came rushing into his mind. Of Alys,

naked in the pool with him, her warm and welcoming body joined with his in pleasure. Later, holding her after they'd loved again, feeling the weight of her silent tears trickling onto his chest and being too cowardly to ask why she cried.

He could think of too many reasons for her to be upset, and not nearly enough why they might have been tears of joy.

They should have talked after they'd made love, or more likely, they ought to have done so before. There were so many things they'd never discussed, important details of their lives that they had surely affected by their actions.

How could they pick up their lives as though nothing had changed?

He knew he could not. Mayhap nothing would change outwardly, though that seemed unlikely, but the man he was inside would be different for having known Alys, for having loved her.

He closed his eyes at the impact of the word. Aye, he'd loved her—physically made love to her, *with* her— but he greatly feared 'twas more than a simple physical attraction that drew him to her.

In the past when he'd wanted a woman, the desire to be with her had always disappeared once they'd coupled.

With Alys, the more time he spent in her presence, the more he shared with her, knew her in every sense of the word, the more he wanted of all of it.

If he'd not been holding her in his arms now, feeling the comfort, the sanity, she brought him, with the way this journey had fallen to pieces he'd have been ready to go out to pound someone into the ground.

He closed his eyes, then opened them to stare down at her lovely face.

Jesu, what had he done?

He'd taken what wasn't meant for him to have, forged ties he had no way to maintain, made unspoken promises he could not honor.

To his shame, he didn't regret a moment of it.

For himself, he didn't care.

His only regret would be if he caused Alys pain.

Padrig had lain there as long as he dared, watching Alys as she slept, but he knew it must nearly be sunup, and they could not linger here once there was light enough to travel.

She slept deeply, the past days' exhaustion taking its toll, no doubt. Deciding to let her rest until 'twas almost time to leave, he slipped out of her arms, stirred the fire to life and dressed.

He felt battered and weary from head to toe. Two nights with little rest, and plenty of activity in between, had a way of draining the life out of a man, he thought wryly.

Nonetheless, he'd not have traded the night with Alys for a few hours' sleep under any circumstances.

He carefully tugged the blanket round her and crept from the cavern without touching her, not daring to so much as kiss her cheek lest he be tempted to abandon what little sense he had left, and stay with her. Ignoring his duty, however, was so foreign to him that he could not take a chance. Better to remove himself from temptation, and get to work putting things right.

Judging from what he could see of the sky, there was still a while left before dawn. Despite the hour, however, Dickon was already up and wide awake when Padrig entered the large cavern. Rafe and the boy sat by the fire, Dickon chattering away between bites of an apple while

Rafe, sitting propped against the wall, appeared ready to stuff the fruit into the lad's mouth to silence him.

The boy hopped up, a smile upon his lips when Padrig crossed the chamber to them. "Where were you, milord? Was Lady Alys able to fix your back for you? Where is she? Rafe said—"

Padrig cut off his questions by the simple expedient of covering the boy's mouth with his hand until he stopped talking. "Are you always so lively in the morn?" he asked, moving away his hand and laughing. "Rafe's had not a wink of sleep, if I know him." Rafe, his face drawn with pain, shook his head wearily. "Perhaps we should move away from the fire, give him some quiet. After all, he kept watch over you all night."

He led the boy toward the far end of the chamber, where Dickon had stored the things he'd filched from the village. "My back is fine, I thank you."

"Did milady have to sew—"

"Dickon," Padrig said sharply. "Don't speak so loudly, if you please," he added, lowering his voice. "Lady Alys was asleep when I looked in on her last. Perhaps she can rest a bit longer."

As he'd expected, mentioning that Lady Alys needed something was enough to capture Dickon's attention. "Of course, milord. Do you want something to eat? There's food by the fire."

"I'll get some in a bit," he replied. "In the meantime, would you look through your supplies, see what you've got for food we can take with us on a journey?"

Dickon opened his mouth to speak again, but Padrig cut him off with a look. "I need to talk with Rafe, then I'll come help you."

Leaving the lad to his task, Padrig picked up two

mugs and the small keg of ale they'd tapped the night before and went back to the fire. He sat down near Rafe's pallet, poured the ale and handed a cup to his second in command.

"A quiet night?" he asked.

Rafe nodded, then drained the mug in two long swallows. Padrig took it back, refilled it and returned it before broaching the subject he'd come to speak to Rafe about.

"How fare you this morn? Are you able to get up and move about? Are your wounds paining you?"

"By Christ, you ask as many questions as the boy," Rafe muttered. He closed his eyes as though gathering his strength. When he opened them, 'twas clear that he was holding himself together by sheer force of will. His eyes were clouded with weariness and pain, and he slumped against the wall as though it were all that held him upright.

Padrig topped off his own ale, brought the cup to his lips, then lowered it untouched. "I beg your pardon," he said quietly. "I've so much on my mind, it races ahead of me. 'Tis no excuse." He drank, guiltily aware that while he had spent the most intense, exciting night of his life in the company of a beautiful woman, Rafe had stood watch out here.

Weary, in pain, alone but for a sleeping child.

Somehow it had made sense to Padrig when Rafe had suggested he stand watch, but in retrospect, Padrig felt he should have made a different decision.

Rafe shook his head. "'Tis nothing. It's only that I'm so damned frustrated. We've work to do, and I cannot be counted on to do it." He dragged his sword across his knees and toyed with the worn loop attached to the hilt, his gaze focused on his hands. "When I get up to piss,

I stumble about like a drunken sailor. After resting all night, 'twas all I could manage just now to tend to business and get back here without gettin' down on my hands and knees and crawling like a babe," he added with disgust. "Fat lot of help I'll be if—" he ripped a frayed piece of leather from the loop and cast it aside "—when we have to fight again."

"There's not much we can do at the moment in any case," Padrig pointed out.

"'Tis still bloody aggravating," Rafe muttered.

"Could you have been knocked in the head when we were fighting?"

"There's no lump on my head, and I don't remember it happening." Rafe glanced up at Padrig, his lips twisted into a mocking smile. "Though if I had been, I wouldn't recall it, would I? 'Twould explain why I was out o' my wits for so long, though." He snorted. "'Course, there's some would say I never had my wits about me anyway. Still can't imagine how I slept through you hauling my arse through this place."

Padrig sipped his ale. "I'd have been pleased if you'd woken up." He rubbed his shoulder above where the arrow had hit him. "That litter is not the best way to move an unconscious man, especially in this terrain. 'Tis a wonder you didn't rap your head on something when I was dragging you about."

Rafe set aside his sword and handed Padrig a couple of apples and a chunk of cheese wrapped in a cloth. "The lad's a hard worker," he remarked. "Came to check on me, see if I needed anything as soon as he woke." He glanced up at the sky, where the stars were fading. "And 'tis not yet daylight."

Padrig used his knife to slice off a chunk of the

cheese, stabbing it with the point of the blade and holding it out for Rafe to take. "He'll be good help for you while I'm gone," he said offhandedly as he lopped off a slice for himself. "Should you need it."

Rafe's dark eyes burned with frustration, but his expression was resigned. He nodded. "I ought to go with you, milord, but I know I'd slow you down, especially on foot. Mayhap once my brain's working better, Dickon and I could spy out the situation at the keep, see if we can learn anything useful for when you return. You're going to l'Eau Clair for help, are you not?"

"Aye," Padrig said. "'Tis closest, and Lord Rannulf's there, with plenty of men to mount an attack on Winterbrooke should that be necessary." He bit into an apple so hard, juice spurted out all over his chin. Swiping it away with the back of his hand, he added wearily, "And I'm certain it will be."

"Most likely." Rafe took a bite of cheese and chewed, focusing his attention on the fire. "What of your lady?" he asked, shifting his gaze back to Padrig. "Will you leave her here with us?"

The sound of loose stones crunching underfoot caught their attention. Padrig looked up and discovered Alys standing on the other side of the fire, watching them. "He shall not leave *her* anywhere," she said, swiftly making her way round the fire pit and stopping in front of him. "I'm going with you. There's naught you can do to stop me, Padrig, so don't even bother to try."

Chapter Twenty-Three

Alys glanced from Padrig to Rafe and back again. She clearly hadn't surprised either man.

Rafe's expression held a tinge of amusement. Indeed, she'd wager he was trying not to laugh.

Padrig's reaction was more difficult to decipher. She gazed down at his face, trying to judge dispassionately, without allowing her feelings for him to taint her assessment.

Admiration mixed with a bit of resignation, perhaps?

He watched her as though uncertain what she might do or say next, that much she *was* sure of.

She reached for the apple he'd been eating. He gave it up without comment. She watched his face as she brought the fruit to her lips and nibbled at the edge where he'd bitten into it. The flavor burst upon her tongue, the sweet juice beading on her lips. She licked the moisture away, smiled, and handed the apple back to him.

He took it from her absently, his gaze never leaving hers. Her heart beat hard in her chest at the desire darkening his eyes to indigo. She'd teased him apurpose, curious to know whether the night past had been enough to sate his desire, or as in her case, had merely whetted his appetite.

She found the results of her test most pleasing.

And arousing, which she'd not expected since they weren't alone. She kept smiling, all the while praying her legs wouldn't give out on her. She took a calming breath and stepped past Padrig toward the open space between the two men. "Is there time for me to eat more than that before we go?" she asked, hoping her audacity would hold out long enough for her to sit down and compose herself.

"Dear God, but I hope so," Rafe muttered, looking offended when Padrig glared at him.

Alys, meanwhile, wanted to slink back to the other cavern. She hadn't considered how her actions would appear to Rafe.

'Twas a different matter entirely, to tease her lover in private. Her boldness with Padrig surprised *her,* for he brought out a side of her she hadn't known existed.

She glanced up through her lashes and found Padrig was watching her. He caught her gaze, his mouth curving into a teasing smile, then brought the apple to his lips and took a bite.

Rafe made a rude noise and turned to look the other way. "I'm glad I'll not be making the journey with the two of you," he said dryly. "'Tis too much for a man alone to bear."

Alys's face felt so hot, 'twas surely blazing red. Leaping up from her seat, she wended her way past Rafe's pallet and moved to the other side of the fire.

They'd not be able to see her face past the fire, she

hoped. Glancing up at the sky, she could see 'twas brighter than when she'd entered the cavern but a few moments ago. They would be leaving soon.

Then, thank goodness, she and Padrig would have other things on their minds than what they'd done the night before.

They'd barely left the passageway from the Devil's Lair and entered the forest before Padrig shouldered the pack he was carrying and caught Alys by the hand to slow her headlong stride over the uneven rocks. In the misty light of the dawning day, 'twas difficult to see where they put their feet. "I know we're in a hurry to be gone from here, love, but you'll wind up bouncing down the hill on your backside if you're not careful."

She jerked her hand free and, gathering her skirts out of the way, got two steps away from him before he grabbed the back of her gown and tugged her round to face him. "Alys, what's wrong?" He captured her chin in his hand and gently forced her to look up at him. "Did you want to stay with Rafe and Dickon after all?"

That notion sent a shudder of humiliation through her. "Absolutely not," she told him, shaking her head. "I couldn't wait to leave."

He let go of her gown and reached up to smooth his hand over her hair. "So I saw," he said with a rueful laugh. "I just don't understand why."

She shifted her gaze, staring over Padrig's shoulder as the rising sun revealed a large, dense thicket below them. "You heard Rafe. I'm sure you know what he thought," she whispered. "What I did there by the fire…I'm embarrassed."

Padrig sighed. "Rafe thinks I'm a fortunate man," he

said. "Truly. He told me so before we left. He believes you are charming and honest. 'A rarity among women,' he said."

She didn't bother trying to hide her scorn over that obvious falsehood. "'Tis not how a noble lady ought to behave."

"Not in public, mayhap," he conceded. "But in private—" He grinned suddenly. "Milady, you may be playful as you like with me, any time you wish. If 'twill preserve your modesty to save your boldness for when we're alone, I'll not complain." He bent and kissed her, hard and fast, then released her before she could respond in kind. "As long as you don't hide it away completely."

Breathless from his kiss, she stared at him. "Do you think, once we get back, we'll ever be alone together again?"

He touched her cheek. "If you wish it, sweeting, we shall."

She noticed sudden movement from the corner of her eye, something large and dark in the thicket on the slope below Padrig. "Hide, quickly!" she cried, grabbing the front of his surcoat and tugging him down with her.

Padrig wrapped his arms about her, cushioning her with his body as they hit the hard ground. He rolled them so he could peer down the hill, yet shield her at the same time. "What did you see?" he whispered, fumbling to free his dagger from the sheath on his belt.

"I don't know." Craning her neck, she tried to look over him, but all she could see was the tangle of branches atop the thicket just below them.

However, the greenery was shifting wildly, as though some large beast were crashing through.

"I don't think it's a person," she added. "From what

little I saw, 'tis large and dark." Something was poking her in the side. She reached beneath her and shifted her belt until her embroidered pouch was safely out of the way. "Could it be a bear?"

"I hope not!" Padrig rolled clear of their tangled clothes and limbs and knelt, still screening her with his body. "I hear something," he murmured. "But 'tis no bear." He drew his sword from its scabbard, the deadly blade hissing quietly as it slid free, and rose to a low crouch. "Stay here," he ordered.

Hoping Alys would obey him, Padrig raced down the hill toward the thicket, a blade held tight in each hand. As he reached the edge of the trees, a horse shot out and dashed past him, squealing frantically, a large boar hot on its heels.

The horse kept running straight toward Alys, but the boar halted abruptly and turned to face Padrig. Head shifting as it caught his scent, wickedly curved tusks gleaming in the morning sun, it dug at the loose dirt and stone with its hooves and let out a fearsome sound.

"Padrig!" Alys cried.

He could tell the moment the boar's beady eyes focused on him. Now he needed to keep them directed his way.

If Alys caught its attention, however, it could just as easily be her the beast went after next. "Stay still and be quiet," he told her without turning to look at her. Instead he shifted sideways, so she wouldn't be in the animal's line of sight.

He'd rather not waste time dealing with the creature, but knew the chance of it ignoring them was nonexistent now that it had caught their scent. "You're mine," he muttered to the beast, drawing in a deep breath.

And then he charged toward it as fast as he could move.

The added impetus of running downhill let him leap onto the animal, crashing into it with such force that they tumbled together into the underbrush at the edge of the trees. He tossed aside his sword as he leapt, for 'twas of little use in these circumstances.

Padrig somehow managed to wrap his arm about the boar's neck, narrowly avoiding a slash across the face from the razor-sharp tusks. Gripping his dagger tight as they pitched backwards, he thrust it into the flailing beast's chest and rammed it up into the heart.

Blood gushed everywhere, hot and stinking, yet still the animal squirmed in his hold. Finally the flow of blood slowed and the beast went lax in his arms. Breathless, Padrig slumped back against the ground, the ungainly body draped over him.

Suddenly his sword blade came into his line of vision. Tilting his head back, he followed the blade up, to the foolhardy wench gripping the hilt tight in both hands, and felt his blood go as hot as that of the beast he'd just killed.

Shoving the carcass off him, he stumbled to his feet, his dagger still clutched in his hand. "What are you doing?" he demanded, barely retaining enough sense to keep his voice pitched low when what he really wanted was to roar the words at her like a weapon. "I told you to stay—"

"What if you'd needed help?" she tossed back. Her arms shook, making the sword blade waver, but she held it at the ready. "Rafe's not here to watch your back. Someone had to do it, and I'm the only one here."

Still gasping, he took the sword from her and rammed it into the scabbard. "Don't *ever* do that again," he growled.

As soon as her hands were empty she flung herself into his arms, heedless of the pig blood spattered over him from head to toe.

"I was so afraid!" She held him tight for a moment, then stepped back far enough to look at him. "Is any of this abattoir from you?" she asked urgently.

"It could just as likely be from you." He pointed to the front and sleeves of her gown. The green cloth was splotched with darker patches of blood where she'd been pressed against him. "But no, none of it's mine."

He bent and wiped his dripping dagger on the grass, scouring away the blood before he slipped it into its sheath.

Alys went to stand over the boar, nudging it with her boot, before glancing over her shoulder at Padrig. "You could have been killed," she said quietly.

"I wasn't." He stood beside her and reached up to wipe a smear of blood from her cheek. "We're both alive to live another day, Alys."

He leaned down and rolled the boar into the bushes, scraping away the worst of the blood-soaked grass with a stick and tossing it into the trees. "I doubt anyone from Winterbrooke will venture this way," he said. "But in case I'm wrong…"

Alys watched him work in silence, then took his hand and turned him to face back the way they'd come. Their packs lay abandoned upon the rocky ground, the contents scattered about.

And standing just above them, reins tied to a spindly tree, stood Alys's mare.

"'Twas Arian who almost ran you down," she said, smiling and starting up the hill. Padrig walked by her side, his attention on the liveliness of her expression. 'Twas something he'd seen all too seldom of late.

She'd had so little to be happy about.

"I'm doubly glad the boar did not get her, for she's a fine horse," she said once they reached the mare. Her hands gentle, she stroked Arian's tangled mane. "I was certain she'd be too frightened to let me catch her, but she stopped running as soon as she saw me. Poor lady, she's had such a terrible journey since we left l'Eau Clair."

Padrig swiftly examined the mare. Other than several scrapes on her withers and rump, and a rip in the saddle, she and her accoutrements appeared to be in good shape. Excellent shape, when he considered what she might have endured since she ran off yesterday.

He straightened from tightening the girth and paused to rub Arian's ears, hopefulness settling in his heart. "She might have had a terrible journey here, but she's going to ensure that we have a much faster journey back." He grinned. "Even riding double, it should take us no more than two days to return to l'Eau Clair."

Smiling in return, Alys headed for their scattered supplies. "Come help me, then, milord," she said, gathering everything up in her arms. "The sooner we leave, the sooner we'll be back to help the others."

Pausing only to scrub the worst of the blood from their clothes and Padrig's armor, they set off for l'Eau Clair before the sun had climbed much higher in the sky. They'd a long journey ahead of them, one he'd like to complete as swiftly as possible. Every day they were on the road was another day their people trapped in Winterbrooke Manor would suffer in captivity.

They couldn't push Arian to any great speed, but the mare was hardy and fleet of foot, and she made the journey less arduous for Alys. Padrig alternated leading the mare with riding her, but he refused to allow Alys out of the saddle except when they stopped to rest the horse.

They made the trip back to l'Eau Clair dogged by a sense of urgency; Padrig and Alys both so tense they scarcely spoke a word to each other till they stopped to eat and rest at midday. For Padrig's part, revisiting the area where they'd suffered the storm's wrath was difficult.

Judging by Alys's wan face and pain-filled eyes, she'd rather be anywhere else but there.

He led them through the destruction as quickly as possible. By the time the sun was high overhead, they'd passed through the worst of it.

The mare was flagging, as was he, when they paused near a stream. He lifted Alys from the saddle and settled her upon the grass-covered bank of it before loosening the saddle girth and leading Arian to the water to drink.

Once he'd tended the horse and hobbled her nearby to graze, he returned to Alys's side bearing food and a mug of cool water. He found her curled up on the soft turf, her hair spread about her and her eyes closed.

'Twas a pleasure to see her so relaxed, the tension gone from her face, a tinge of color riding along her cheeks. Mayhap she felt the weight of his scrutiny, for he'd not been there long when she slowly opened her eyes.

She met his gaze and smiled. "Come here, milord, and take your ease," she invited, sitting up and holding out her hand to him.

He set down the food and drink and joined her. "'Tis a shame we cannot stay here long," he told her regretfully. "It's a beautiful place."

Alys placed her hands on his shoulders and drew him down on the grass, his head upon her lap. She smoothed her cool hands along his brow, stroked them over the aching muscles of his neck. If he'd been a cat, he would have purred his pleasure at her touch. "Mayhap we could return someday, when we've the time to linger here."

Catching one of her hands in his, he pressed her palm against his neck and shifted so he could look up at her face. "Do you believe we shall ever have the chance to be together once we return to l'Eau Clair?" His heart thudding hard in his chest, he added, "Do you want us to be together?"

"Aye." Her hand trembled beneath his. "More than I thought it possible to want anything." She shook her head. "I don't understand how this has happened so swiftly! 'Twas only a few days ago that I was fairly happy to be headed home, grateful that my parents were finally going to allow me join the abbey, that I could devote my life to my writing—"

"A nun?" He sat up and swung round to face her, her hand still clasped tight within his. "You were to be a nun?"

He couldn't wrap his mind around that notion no matter how he looked at it!

Her face flushed. "Aye, a nun," she said firmly. She tugged to free her hand, but he refused to release her. "You needn't look as though you're about to laugh, damn you. I know I've given you reason to think me a willing wench, no doubt, but I've never—"

"Alys." He gathered her into his arms and buried his face in her hair. "'Tis my guess that the only man you've been *willing* with is me." He burrowed his fingers into her mass of hair and drew it gently away from her face. "The only reason you make me laugh is the pleasure I take in your company." He brushed kisses along each cheekbone, then settled his lips briefly upon hers. "You *did* surprise me. A lifetime spent in an abbey is not what I would have expected for your future."

"'Twas a place where I could write unhindered," she said simply. "'Tis what I do, you know. Write down tales of valor, the stories of the people I meet. My years at l'Eau Clair have been a treasure trove. I'd never imagined meeting so many people with such interesting lives!"

There was no mistaking Alys's excitement about writing, though he believed it didn't bother her too much to have given up on the notion of joining the Church.

Learning of her writing made clear to him why she so often had been distracted and aloof, or been thought to be. He'd seen her thus himself earlier in their journey, before the world around her became so intense. From what he'd observed, she possessed the ability to focus very deeply upon something only she could see or hear, so that she truly appeared to be lost in her own world.

But…why had she said she was going home to join an abbey?

"Alys, you knew I was not taking you to your father's keep, didn't you?" he asked, watching her face carefully. "I heard nothing about an abbey, either."

"Where were we going, then?" she asked, her voice laced with wariness. "My parents had sent for me. To go home, I would swear." She eyed him cautiously, suspiciously. "Where were you to deliver me?"

"Into your parents' hands," he confirmed. "But not at any of your father's estates."

Her face grew pale. "Where?" she demanded, her hands clenched into fists by her sides.

He covered her hands with his and held them tight.

"To Lord Henry Walsingham," he said simply. "I was never told 'twas the case, but it was my impression you were to be his bride."

Chapter Twenty-Four

If Padrig had drawn his dagger and stabbed her through the heart, he could not have shocked her more.

Indeed, it took a moment for her pulse to resume its measured beat, for the unspeakable notion to wend its way from heart to head and send a wave of disgust slashing though her.

"How fortunate for me that I am now tainted goods." Alys could not guess where she found the strength to say the words, when inside she felt as though she were crumpling to pieces. 'Twas all she could manage to draw breath into her lungs. "Do you believe that fact might change their plans?"

Her own parents would give her to that ale-swilling, wife-killing swine?

"How much did it take, I wonder, for my parents to agree? How much land did Walsingham offer, how much gold? How many men to fight in my father's stupid little wars?" she demanded bitterly.

"Alys." Padrig tried to pull her into his arms, but she resisted him.

"Nay, I want no comfort now, not even from you." She held her hand to his face for a moment, however, and hoped he'd understand. She needed to give her hurt full rein while she sought to come to terms with the fact that her parents had evidently sold her for whatever advantage they could get.

He nodded and lowered his hands, staying close but not touching her. Closing her eyes, she sat back on her heels, her hair streaming wildly around her, and let her growing sense of betrayal transform her pain into rage. "What is my life worth?" she cried.

That was what it amounted to, in her estimation—her parents would gain whatever it was they wanted this time, and Lord Henry would get another wife to abuse and kill, if he chose to do so.

If he'd already done it once, 'twas bound to be easier for him the next time. How long would it have been, before she drove him to take her life, as well?

"I should have known, should have realized 'twas just a matter of time before they got round to me," she said bitterly. "My brother and sister both—" She looked up and met Padrig's steady gaze. "When the time came for each of them to marry, they were sold to whomever could give my parents the most power and prestige, the most land to increase their holdings."

"'Tis the way of the world, love," he pointed out quietly. "Happens all the time."

"But in both instances, they chose mates for their children that you'd not give a dog to." A tear leaked from the corner of her eye; she swiped it away angrily, sniffed, and went on. "Terrible people, Padrig, from terrible families." She fisted her hands by her sides and gave a bitter laugh. "Of course, you could say my family, my parents, at any rate, are horrible, as well. 'Tis nothing but the truth."

She rose to swiftly pace back and forth along the edge of the stream, pausing to stare out at the lively cascade. The sound of water flowing over rocks, the glimmer of sun shimmering on the wet, moss-covered banks soothed her soul. Padrig came to stand behind her, closing his hands gently over her shoulders and lending her his strength.

Finally her overwhelming anger and hurt eased, leaving in its wake a steely determination.

This time, her parents would not win. She would refuse to marry Lord Henry, or anyone else her parents might suggest.

Somehow she would make a life for herself, a life of *her* choosing.

She turned and caught hold of Padrig's hands. "If I choose to defy my parents, refuse to allow them to dictate my fate, would you help me?" She stroked his be-whiskered cheek, watching him, trying to gauge what he felt in his eyes.

Though she couldn't read his gaze nor his expression, she wouldn't let that deter her from her goal. His continued silence, however, made her wonder just what it was he might hesitate to say.

Letting her hand slide from his face, she took a step back. "I understand if you don't wish to be involved," she said evenly. "'Tis not your battle to fight, and entangling yourself with me against my father might cost you everything you have."

Padrig shook his head as though waking from a deep sleep and closed the distance between them. "We've not known each other long," he said, his voice low and deep.

"Nor, despite last night, do we know each other well—" he buried his hand in her hair "—yet."

She smiled at that, her lips trembling despite her efforts to still them, her eyes filling with tears.

His gaze blazing a dark-blue fire, he carefully tipped her head up and kissed her with a gentleness that stole her heart. The tears she hadn't shed in anger, Padrig's tenderness sent trailing down her cheeks now.

When he eased his mouth from hers, he angled his head back just enough that their gazes could meet. "But know this, milady." He combed his fingers through her hair, brought his hand to rest atop hers on his shoulder. *"You are mine.* I know it here, in my heart." He entwined his fingers with hers and slid her hand to rest upon his chest. "There is nothing I would not do for you, Alys. You have only to ask."

His declaration was one more shock on top of a veritable mountain of them. Her legs went weak and she crumpled to the grass.

Padrig dropped down beside her and pulled her into his lap when she tried to sit up. Her head swam, and her entire body felt shaky. "Are you all right?" he asked urgently. "What's wrong?"

She laughed weakly. "You've never swept a woman off her feet, milord?"

"Never." He shifted so her head rested upon his shoulder. "Did I frighten you?" he asked quietly. "'Twas not my intention."

Feeling stronger now, she met his worried gaze and shook her head. "You surprised me, 'tis all. I hoped for your help, but I wasn't expecting your heart," she told him. Her own heart thundering wildly, she added, "You've mine as well, you know."

He kissed her, hard, his arms wrapped tight about her, then set her off his lap. "The good Lord ought to grant me a boon for my strength of will," he muttered when she sent him a questioning look. "Instead of undressing you and making you mine this instant, I'm going to see you fed and then we're heading off before I get us into any more trouble." The intense look accompanying his statement made her knees go weak all over again. "You make it difficult for a man to remember his duty, Alys."

He picked up the food he'd brought her earlier and set it in her lap, then pressed the mug of water to her lips until she drank it all. "You've not really eaten today, nor much yesterday, either," he reminded her. "Likely that's why you collapsed just now. Eat something while I get Arian ready to go."

Alys took some cheese and an apple and set the rest aside. She crumbled a bit of cheese off the wedge and popped it into her mouth as she watched him secure the saddle and adjust the bundles tied to the back of it. Taking the extra food and the mug from her, he tied them up in a cloth.

"You know, I still believe 'twas what you said that made my legs give way, not lack of food," she said, not quite teasing. "'Twas most romantic." Lord knew, the mere memory of his words, of the way he'd looked at her, had the power to make her heart race.

He made a face at her. Laughing, she got up and offered him the last bite of cheese. "You'd best be ready to catch me the next time you gift me with such stirring words," she said as he took the food and began to chew. "Or mayhap if you speak to me in Welsh," she mused. "Aye, that would likely do it, as well."

He burst out laughing.

"What?"

"You mean I could say anything to you in Welsh, and you would think it lovely? Or romantic?"

She thought for a moment. "Aye, as long as it sounded beautiful." She grinned. "Of course, you realize you can only say things that *are* lovely and romantic. How pretty you think I am." She sent him a teasing glance. "Or mayhap how I make you feel—though that would be better in words I can understand."

"Give me a moment, sweeting. Once we're on our way, I'll speak Welsh to you as much as you like."

She paused to rinse her hands in the stream, reluctant to leave this beautiful place, but they'd far to go before nightfall and could not linger here.

Padrig boosted her up to sit sideways in the saddle and swung into place behind her. He guided Arian onto the road, looped the reins about his arm and turned his attention to Alys.

He framed her face with his hands and whispered, *"Ach lovely fel 'r morn."*

The way he said the words, the way he looked at her made her breathing quicken and her skin flush.

She'd never forgive him if the words he said didn't match his intent expression. Suppressing a shiver of reaction, she said, "I'm trusting you didn't just call me a horse's backside, or something more disgusting."

He chuckled, skating his mouth over her brow and cheekbones. *"Cei 'm asgre, 'm anwylyd."*

She slipped her hand up into his hair and drew his mouth closer to hers. "Tell me what you said, milord," she whispered against his lips. She caught his lower lip in her teeth, nipping gently. "Unless you want me to get rough with you."

"Is that supposed to discourage me?" His body shook with suppressed laughter. "I'm more likely to misbehave," he warned her, his smile teasing. "To discover what you have in mind."

Trying not to laugh herself, she sent him a stern look. "And if I promise to make good on my threat whether you tell me or not?"

"Well, then, *'m asgre,* I shall tell you whatever you wish to know."

He gathered her hair in his hands, burying his fingers in the tousled curls. "You are as lovely as the morn." Alys drew her breath in sharply, for she could not mistake the sincerity in his eyes, his voice, his touch.

He kissed her cheeks. "You have my heart, my darling." He nuzzled her throat. "You see, love, not an insult among them."

Alys watched Padrig's face, gazed deep into his eyes, and knew herself for a coward. He had opened his heart to her, much more openly than she had to him. He knew the words to melt her heart, words she'd never heard used save for in tales of love and valor.

And at l'Eau Clair, she realized. Lord Rannulf and Lady Gillian shared their love and respect for each other openly, there for anyone to see.

Be bold, Alys, she reminded herself yet again. *If Padrig is as pleased to hear you express your feelings as you are to hear of his, 'tis worth the risk.*

She pulled him closer, bumped her nose lightly against his, and asked, "How do I say 'I love you' in Welsh, milord?" She drew back and stared into his eyes. "Because I do."

Suddenly breathless, Padrig returned Alys's intent gaze. *"Cara 'ch,"* he whispered.

She repeated the words, which had just as much effect upon him in one language as the other.

He gathered her close in his arms and kissed her, pouring every bit of what he felt into the caress.

The mare, evidently aware of their complete inattention, chose that moment to stray to the side of the road and walk beneath a low tree. Padrig barely noticed in time to prevent them from being slapped by the branches; as it was, they ended up with leaves in their faces and hair before Padrig dismounted and led the wanderer back to the middle of the road.

"Think she's trying to tell us something?" Alys asked, plucking more leaves from her hair.

He laughed. "Probably reminding us there's a time and place for our behavior—and this isn't it."

Padrig led Arian at a brisk walk until the road widened and he'd given his unruly body something to do besides trying to get beneath Alys's skirts. If he could get them to l'Eau Clair without touching Alys again 'twould be best, but since they needed to get there quickly, he'd simply have to learn to master his impulses where she was concerned.

They covered an amazing distance considering their limitations. By the time it had become too dark to travel safely—nigh too dark to see at all—he estimated that, barring any additional complications, they'd make it to l'Eau Clair before sunset the next day.

Alys slumped against him in the saddle, sound asleep. The mare had borne her burden well, though he'd noticed her pace had slowed till she was barely moving unless he urged her to it.

As soon as they got to a likely place to stop, he lifted

Alys from the saddle, settled her on a blanket and made camp for the night.

Both man and horse were too tired to eat. Arian nodded off as soon as he unsaddled her. As for himself, he greatly feared if he made himself comfortable, he'd sleep like the dead for the next two or three days. If he stayed a little cold, a bit hungry, and didn't allow himself to sit anywhere near Alys, he ought to be able to stay awake and guard his lady.

'Twas the longest night of his life, or so it seemed. Once the sliver of moon had set and the sky begun to glow a ghostly gray on the horizon, Padrig forced his aching body into motion. He'd had plenty of time to think, and had decided to try to enlist Lord Rannulf to help Alys. He was a powerful man with many valuable connections of both blood and friendship. If he were willing to bestir himself on Alys's behalf, perhaps she could avoid her father selling her off to the highest bidder.

Whether the life she'd lead after that would include Padrig, 'twas difficult to guess. That, too, was within Lord Rannulf's power to change. If he chose to help Padrig—help *them*—they could possibly be together.

However, if Lord Rannulf chose to punish him for the disaster this situation had become, Padrig might count himself fortunate to hire himself out as a mercenary in some backwater conflict in the wilds of France.

All he could do was try to make things right for Alys, he reminded himself as he woke her and settled her into the saddle for another grueling day of travel.

As he led the mare down the road at a fast walk, he tried not to hope too much that the life he sought for Alys would also include him.

* * *

Alys shifted to sit sideways in the saddle. 'Twas late afternoon, and she'd lost feeling in her legs around midday. They'd been traveling since before dawn, and she'd been uncomfortable as soon as Padrig helped her up onto Arian. She ached from head to toe, in some places more than in others, but considering the battering she'd endured from the storm, especially her right shoulder, 'twas a wonder she didn't feel worse.

And at least, unlike the others who'd gone into Winterbrooke, she was free.

Padrig had the more difficult task on this journey, especially now that they'd left the road for this narrow goat path that wended through hillside and valley. 'Twas a beautiful place, rugged and untouched, but it was also very rough ground to climb over. He'd quite the task, to keep Arian moving without tumbling them all over a steep embankment. As long as he didn't injure himself or the horse, he assured her, they'd be at l'Eau Clair in time for supper.

At least this time, they'd make it inside the keep.

She was glad they'd not made it inside the last time, however, though she could not help but feel great guilt over having escaped the others' fate.

Other than her physical discomfort, and her unceasing worry for Rafe, Dickon and everyone trapped inside Winterbrooke, it had been a surprisingly wonderful day, for she'd had the chance to share the time with Padrig.

He was an interesting man, inherently kind and unfailingly good-natured, with a sometimes playful, sometimes biting sense of humor. All those aspects of him came into play as they shared their hopes and dreams.

As they considered the possibility they might be permitted to have a life together.

They *would* be together, she vowed. She did not know how or where, but the dreamer inside her had given way to a determined woman, a woman with a goal.

A realistic goal, unlike the vague girlish dreams she'd so recently abandoned.

There would be no nunnery for her, that was a certainty. She shook her head in disbelief. How she'd ever believed she could find her future there was beyond her ken.

These last few days had begun to show her the real Alys Delamare. In reality, the most detailed character she'd ever created—a true work of fiction—was the Lady Alys who had ridden away from l'Eau Clair.

Her time with Padrig had revealed to her her true self, a woman with flaws aplenty, but with a capacity for love—and for passion, she thought, smiling down at the man who inspired that passion—she'd never before realized was an integral part of her nature.

She stared out over the wild countryside, her heart light with hope for the future, but her spirit heavy as she considered the struggles ahead of them to gain the life they sought.

The inevitable conflict with her father, and perhaps Lord Henry as well, as she took control of her own fate.

The battle to see Padrig keep what he had, not to lose everything because of her.

Arian stopped suddenly, starling Alys from her reverie. Alys shifted in the saddle and began to slip sideways, but she caught hold of the mare's mane and righted herself without jarring her right arm too badly.

"What is it?" she asked Padrig. He'd wrapped the reins round a stunted tree and was walking toward a sharp drop-off at the edge of the steep hillside. Suddenly he turned and ran back to her, grinning.

"Padrig, what is it?" she demanded. He shook his head and didn't answer. Instead he reached up and swept her easily from the saddle into his arms. Settling her more comfortably within his hold, he strode back to the overhang.

She couldn't help but glance down at the sheer drop-off below. Fighting the urge to squeeze her eyes shut, she wrapped her arms tighter about his neck. "Now will you tell me?"

"Look," he said, turning slightly so that she had an unimpeded view of the valley and the rolling hills beyond. "Do you see that bit of red there, to the left?"

It took a moment to find the slash of crimson in the vast sea of greenery spread out before them, but finally she spied it, not too far in the distance.

"'Tis the banner atop the keep at l'Eau Clair," he said, his voice alight with excitement. He hefted her higher in his arms and kissed her. "Didn't I tell you, *'m asgre?* We'll be there in time for supper!"

Chapter Twenty-Five

With Alys seated sideways before him, Padrig rode Arian at a brisk trot along the road leading to l'Eau Clair Keep. The village ahead lay quiet in the late-afternoon sun, but there was a group of lads playing in the fields alongside the road who caught sight of them. Recognizing Padrig, they raced over to greet him and began a noisy clamor as soon as they saw the dried blood spattered over his armor and Alys's dress.

Padrig slowed Arian to a walk, but didn't pause to answer their shouted questions. Several of the boys raced ahead of them to the keep, shrieking news of their arrival the entire way.

He shook his head and nudged Arian into a slow trot. "Lord Rannulf will think the Welsh have arrived at his gates," he said, his lips quirked in a smile.

Alys glanced up at him and returned his smile, her expression more serene than he'd seen it in days. "'Tis only one Welshman and his lady," she said. "How much of a danger can we be?"

He bent to nuzzle the soft, sensitive spot behind her

ear, savoring the warm scent of her. "You, milady," he murmured, "are more dangerous than any adversary this Welshman has ever faced."

Straightening in the saddle, he urged Arian beneath the portcullis and into the bailey, where a crowd had already begun to gather. They pressed close, their numbers and their noise making Arian sidle nervously.

Padrig, concentrating on calming the mare, realized the throng had abruptly gone quiet. He glanced toward the stairs leading from the great hall and saw Lady Gillian, Lord Rannulf hot on her heels, hurrying down to the bailey.

Padrig gave Alys's hand a squeeze, then dismounted as the crowd parted to let their lord and lady through. Once they'd stopped before him, he bowed politely. "My lord. Lady Gillian."

"What happened?" Lord Rannulf demanded, waving his hand to encompass Padrig, Alys and the mare.

Lady Gillian had already approached the horse and stood staring up at Alys. "Alys Delamare?" She reached out to Alys and took her hand. "Dear God, child, look at you. Are you hurt?"

"No, milady," Alys said. "'Tis not Padrig's blood, either."

Lady Gillian turned on Padrig. "I don't know what happened to you, nor who is responsible for it. But you get her off that horse and into the keep *at once!* We'll talk inside."

"Aye, milady," Padrig said, already moving past Lady Gillian and lifting Alys from the saddle. He knew that tone of old. Despite his age and responsibilities, there were still times she spoke to him as though he were fourteen and newly come to her keep.

And he still jumped to obey her, as he always would.

Alys, her face gone so pale that every scratch and bruise that marred her skin stood out, slid into his arms and looped one hand behind his neck to hold on. She didn't look frightened, he was glad to note. Perhaps her pallor was from exhaustion, or perhaps 'twas Lady Gillian's commanding presence overwhelming her.

"Carry her to my solar," Lady Gillian directed before turning away to order that food and hot water be brought there, as well.

Lord Rannulf threw his hands in the air and took a step toward the stairs. "My work here is done, I see." He stopped and turned to Padrig. "You and I will talk directly, Sir Padrig, as soon as my lady is through with you."

Padrig nodded. "Of course, milord." He watched Lord Rannulf stride away, wishing he could follow him now, tell him everything and get it over with.

But clearly, he'd been dismissed for the moment. Padrig glanced up at the sky, already beginning to grow vibrant with the colors of sunset, and fought down his impatience. Though he might wish to leave for Winterbrooke at once, he knew they'd not be able to leave l'Eau Clair till morn, for there wasn't enough of a moon to light their way.

They headed across the bailey and started up the stairs. Alys laid her head on Padrig's shoulder, apparently not bothered by his disgustingly filthy hauberk. "I can walk, you know," she whispered, her breath making her hair move against his neck, the innocent motion sending a chill down his spine. "You should put me down."

"Nay, 'twill do me no harm to carry you," he whispered back. He grinned. "I like to do it. Besides, would you have me face her displeasure?" He cast a brief glance down at Lady Gillian, following several steps behind them up the stairs. "You know what she's like when we don't do what she asks."

Alys grimaced. "Aye. She has the ability to make me feel guilty without a single harsh word passing her lips." She turned her head to watch Lady Gillian, as well. "I don't know how she does it, but it's very effective."

They passed through the great hall, where the servants were clearing away the tables and benches. "We missed supper," she hissed.

"We were close," he pointed out. "I'm sure Lady Gillian will feed us anyway."

A hand closed about Padrig's wrist, startling him. Lady Gillian kept hold of him and drew him to a stop. "What are you two whispering about?" she asked meditatively, her green eyes sharp as she looked from one to the other.

"Nothing, milady," Padrig said, feeling as though everything he'd thought and done these last few days was written on his face for her to read. Dear God, he hoped not! "Alys was just saying how nice 'twill be to eat decent food again."

"Indeed." Her gaze still closely fixed upon them, Lady Gillian tightened her hold on his arm, then released him. "Bring *Lady* Alys along to my solar and you shall both eat as much as you'd like." She slipped ahead of them, then paused to add, "I'm sure Lord Rannulf will wish to join us right away so you can talk." She preceded them into the chamber and went to pour wine from the ewer always kept by the hearth.

"So she can listen, she means," Alys said quietly to Padrig before they entered the room.

"She might as well listen." He carried Alys to a low

bench and settled her upon it. "She'll just ask him about it all later, anyway." Leaning close, he chuckled. "Don't tell me you'd do any different," he teased, "for I won't believe you."

"I *was* trained in Lady Gillian's household," Alys pointed out with a smile.

Two maids entered carrying trays of food and drink, followed closely by Lord Rannulf. He took two goblets from his wife, presenting one to Alys with a courtly bow, then handing the other to Padrig. "Sit, man," he ordered. "You look about ready to fall over."

Padrig waited for Lady Gillian to sink gracefully into a cushioned chair by the fire before, suppressing a sigh, he eased down onto the bench beside Alys.

The maids lit the branches of candles placed round the room and set up a small table in front of the bench, placing the food within easy reach before leaving at a nod from their mistress.

"Now, Padrig, tell me what happened," Lord Rannulf ordered. "And I mean *everything*."

Lady Gillian shook her head and chided her husband for his impatience, but truthfully, Padrig just wanted to tell it all to Lord Rannulf, make plans to set things right by returning to Winterbrooke Manor, and discover what his own fate might be.

At least Lord Rannulf let them eat while Padrig related the tale, though he interrupted often with questions for both Padrig and Alys. Alys proved a useful ally, perceptive and direct in her observations.

Lady Gillian sat and observed as was her wont, occasionally offering an opinion or exclaiming over something Padrig or Alys said.

Padrig felt drained dry by the time Lord Rannulf was

through grilling them. His overlord was well versed in the realities inherent to living in the Marches and dealing with the constant Welsh incursions. He knew what questions to ask, his comments insightful.

Though he was not surprised to learn of the situation at Winterbrooke, he was outraged about it. He got up and left them briefly, shouting for a messenger to ride out at once with a missive apprising Lord Roger Delamare of the situation.

When he returned, they heard him outside the solar, giving orders for an armed troop to be ready to ride out at dawn.

That eased Padrig's mind, though he hadn't really doubted Lord Rannulf would go back for his men. It had been several days now since the attack. Each additional day that passed could be a matter of life or death for the injured.

To Padrig's surprise, Lord Rannulf had been willing to do all his questioning with both his own lady and Alys present. Padrig wasn't certain what to make of that fact. He'd hoped for a private conversation with Lord Rannulf, an opportunity to plead Alys's case.

And his own, should he still be standing once Lord Rannulf heard everything he had to say.

They'd not yet brought up Alys's situation. Padrig, uncertain how to do so, glanced at Alys to judge how she fared now that she'd eaten and had a moment to rest. He'd done his best to avoid looking her way. 'Twas necessary to be alert conversing with Lord Rannulf. Padrig had feared Alys's presence alone would distract him, never mind that he wasn't sure he could so much as look at her without revealing what he felt for her.

She appeared well, rather pale of face and colorfully

bruised in places, but she looked completely comfortable in the FitzCliffords' company.

'Twas a bit of a surprise, for that hadn't been the case in the past, from what he'd observed of her before they'd left l'Eau Clair.

Perhaps their recent experiences had shown her the strength she'd not realized she possessed.

Lord Rannulf got up, fetched the ewer and replenished their wine. Lady Gillian settled back in her chair, her hands gripping the carved arms, and smiled. "So, my dears. Having disposed of that business for now, shall we now get to the meat of the matter?" She accepted a goblet of wine from her husband, who moved to stand behind her chair. Taking a sip, she gazed at Alys over the rim of the cup. "Have you anything you'd like to tell me, Alys?"

Alys met Lady Gillian's measuring gaze with a similar look of her own. In the past she'd never have dared to do so, but those days were long gone. "Milady?"

"The Alys Delamare sitting before me is not the same young woman who left this place less than a week ago."

Impressed, Alys smiled. "You are correct, Lady Gillian."

Lord Rannulf laid his hand on his wife's shoulder. When she glanced up at him, he sent her a questioning look, one eyebrow raised. "My love, are you certain you want us—" he pointed to Padrig and then himself "—to stay for this conversation?"

"Padrig must definitely remain. You may leave if you wish, but I imagine we'll have need of your counsel before long."

He returned to his own chair and settled back in it as if preparing to watch a joust.

"I believe, Husband, that Lady Alys left here a kitten and returned a she-wolf."

Alys felt her face heat, the sensation made worse when she noticed Padrig watching her, his lips curled in a curious smile. "If by that you mean I've grown a backbone and the will to use it, Lady Gillian, you are correct again." Edgy, feeling as though Lady Gillian was toying with her, yet not willing to be rude by mentioning it, Alys rose stiffly to her feet and began to pace the width of the chamber.

She could feel their gazes upon her, a weight hanging over her head and about to fall. She hadn't the patience to play this game.

So she would not. Drawing a deep breath, she paused in the middle of the room and faced Lady Gillian and Lord Rannulf. "What would you have me tell you, milady?" she asked, her tone more calm than she felt inside. "Do you want to know what changed? Or if Padrig is responsible?" She felt her body start to tremble, and fisted her hands at her sides in a futile attempt at composure. "I'll not tell you, for 'tis no one's business but our own." She stepped to the window and gazed unseeing at the colorful sunset. "'Tis true I'm not the person I was a short time ago. That girl would never have had the mettle to fight for herself, or for anyone else." Turning, she faced them again. "But this woman asks for your help, for myself and for Padrig. I ask you for sanctuary from my father. I—"

Noise and movement at the front of the bailey captured her attention. She leaned out the window and saw a troop of men carrying bright torches massed before the gates, a familiar banner set atop a high pole flickering in and out of sight in the wavering light.

Her stomach roiled as she glanced over her shoulder, her frantic gaze settling upon Padrig. "Dear God in heaven, 'tis my father."

Padrig rose and crossed to the window, cursing as he peered down and saw the gates swing open. Turning, he caught Alys by the shoulders. "'Tis all right, sweeting," he said to her, his voice low, urgent. "I'll not let them take you from here, I promise you."

His words gave her hope, the strength to gently take his hands from her shoulders and step out of his comforting hold.

She turned to the others, standing by the second window. "Milord, my lady." She took a deep breath and continued, "I humbly ask you for sanctuary from my father, and from any prospective husband he might have brought with him."

Lady Gillian held out her hand. "Alys, we'll protect you from any threat, you know that." She caught Alys's hand in hers and held it tightly. "But from your own father?"

Alys eased her hand from the comfort of Lady's Gillian's grasp, straightened her spine and met the other woman's sympathetic gaze. "This is not about some childish spat, milady. I ask you for my very life."

Chapter Twenty-Six

"What are you talking about?" Lady Gillian caught Alys by the hand again, led her to the bench and made her sit. "Quickly, tell us!"

Alys, stunned by her father's arrival here so soon after their own, scarcely knew where to begin. "I thought we'd have more time! 'Tis too complicated to explain it now—"

Lord Rannulf turned to Padrig. "*Has* she reason to fear for her life?" he demanded.

"'Tis very likely," Padrig said.

The conviction in his voice, his expression, the unwavering belief in what she'd told him, heartened her, gave her hope they would find a way through this morass.

He shook his head. "You should not ask me for advice, milord. I love her, and I will carry her away from here myself before I allow her father to take her."

A roar of sound built in the bailey, then ended abruptly. Into the silence shouted a voice she recognized all too well. "FitzClifford! Where the hell is my daughter?"

Alys wished she could melt into the floor and disappear.

"Bring the blasted wench to me at once," Lord Roger bellowed. "Alys! Get down here now!"

Lord Rannulf leaned out the window and gazed down at the scene below, his expression fierce. "I'll be damned if any man comes into my wife's demesne and shows so little respect for her—or for one of her ladies," he snarled. "Silence, Delamare! You've more than a young woman to deal with," he shouted. Hand on his sword hilt, he backed away from the window and drew the weapon. "Padrig, come with me."

Padrig cast Alys a reassuring look before drawing his own sword and following Lord Rannulf from the chamber.

The thunder of their boots on the stairs had barely faded away before Lady Gillian sat down beside Alys and drew her into her arms. A scant moment of her warm sympathy brought tears to Alys's eyes...tears of frustration and determination.

She returned Lady Gillian's embrace, then rose to her feet. "I'll not let my father harm *anyone* to get to me," she said, her voice vibrating with fury. "He's a vicious man, ruthless. He'll do anything to get what he wants. He always wins, milady. But he shall not succeed this time. I'll not let him."

She headed for the doorway, but barely made it two steps across the room before Lady Gillian caught her by the arm and stopped her. "*We* shall not let him."

Alys met her gaze. "Thank you, milady."

"Wait, Alys." Lady Gillian reached for the sheathed knife on Alys's belt, drew the blade free and, shaking her head, slipped it back just as swiftly. To Alys's amazement, the other woman bent, raised the hem of her gown, and drew a dagger from a sheath strapped to her leg.

She held the knife to Alys hilt-first, its long, thin blade gleaming in the candlelight. "You never know when you might need it, and your eating knife's naught but a pretty toy compared to this." She gave a rueful laugh. "I've been remiss in your training, I fear. Perhaps there are other things beyond housewifery I should be teaching my ladies."

Alys took the weapon and tucked it into her belt alongside her own, much smaller, knife. "Thank you, milady."

"Have a care, Alys, and don't be afraid to use it if you must," Lady Gillian called out to her as she ran from the room.

Her boots slid on the loose rushes covering the floor of the great hall, forcing her to slow her headlong pace. 'Twas just as well, for her body had yet to recover from her adventures. Her right arm was nigh useless, her balance uncertain. At the rate she'd been moving, she'd likely have tumbled down the stairs into the bailey.

Right into her dear father's loving arms.

She could hear men's voices shouting, but from here she couldn't discern who was speaking or what was being said. Slowing her pace further, she left the hall through the buttery instead of the main stairs outside. Using this route, she'd come out in a shadowy part of the bailey near the front gate.

She'd be able to get near her father without him seeing her coming.

She crept undetected out of servants' passageway into the area beneath the wall walk. Her father was still ranting, his shouts interspersed with Lord Rannulf's more reasonable tones. They stood in the midst of the bailey, surrounded by a restless crowd—her father's men on the side near the gate, the men of l'Eau Clair ranged between them and the keep. Torches and lanterns lit the area, flickering in the wind and lending the scene an eerie glow.

She'd come out behind her father, but could clearly see Lord Rannulf and Padrig. Both men looked furious but controlled, their swords drawn, their bodies poised for action.

Her attention was focused so intently upon the scene before her, she didn't notice the man sprawled upon the ground nearby until she nearly tripped over him.

He moaned when she accidentally nudged him with her foot. Kneeling, she moved aside so the light spilled over him, then sat back on her heels, astonished. 'Twas Rafe!

"Sweet Mary save you," she whispered fiercely. She caught hold of his arm and carefully dragged him up to prop him against the wall, grimacing at the dark stains on the dirty bandage wrapped round his wounds. "Rafe, what are you doing here?"

"Milady." He groaned, his head lolling back against the rough stones. "Didn't know if we'd find you here. I should have known Sir Padrig wouldn't let any more harm befall ye." His lips twisted into a feeble smile. "You'd best have a care—your father's lookin' for ye."

"What are *you* doing here?"

He blinked several times before he focused his eyes on her face. "Your father came just after you left. Dickon's father'd gone to yours for help when the Welsh came. He brought back an army and they routed the Welsh with nary a drop o' blood shed."

"Marie and the others?" Alys asked, her heart nigh stopping as she spoke the words.

"Alive, every one o' them."

"Thank God," she murmured, swiftly making the sign of the cross. "What of Dickon?"

"Happy to be back with his family once more," Rafe said, the words slurring together and trailing off. He sagged back against the wall and closed his eyes. "Have a care," he muttered again. "Your father's brought Lord Henry with him."

Padrig stood to Lord Rannulf's right, his sword drawn, his temper frayed beyond mending as he listened to Lord Roger's never-ending tirade. He hoped Alys remained inside and didn't hear any of it, for 'twas a foul stream of insults and arrogance fit to disgust any reasonable person.

How was it possible that Alys was of this man's blood? 'Twas beyond his ken to imagine they were related in any way at all.

Before they'd left the great hall for the outer stairs to the bailey, Lord Rannulf had paused a moment. His face and voice both had borne the unflinching air of command Padrig knew better than to ignore as he cautioned Padrig to remain silent no matter the provocation, to allow him to do the talking.

'Twas damned hard—nigh impossible—to follow those constraints when Lord Roger kept insulting the woman Padrig loved. All he wanted was to run over and grab the miserable bastard by his heavily embroidered tunic, smash his head against the nearest stone wall till he shut his foul mouth once and for all.

He understood now how Alys had so easily believed

her father capable of selling off his children to the highest bidders. From what little he'd seen of the man, 'twas clear he had nary a speck of decency hiding anywhere within his pathetic soul.

The only good thing Padrig gleaned from Lord Roger's tirade was that he'd taken back possession of Winterbrooke Manor, and that Lord Rannulf's people were safe.

For which assistance, of course, Delamare believed he deserved a reward.

Lord Rannulf had finally had enough, evidently, for he stepped forward at that suggestion and smiled.

"The only reward you're likely to get from me, you foul knave, is your life. I'd set Padrig after you like the dog you are, but the pleasure now wouldn't be worth the headache later." He laughed. "Besides, I'm sure the church—and the king as well, no doubt—would frown upon a man killing his wife's father, no matter the provocation."

Lord Rannulf's last statement rendered Delamare speechless—and he was not the only one. Padrig could only stare at Lord Rannulf in disbelief, unable to give voice to a single thought.

The man who came hurtling out of the crowd toward Padrig, sword raised, jolted him from his daze in a hurry. He'd just time to raise his sword to parry a hard thrust, else he'd have taken the blade in the throat.

Fortunately he'd not had a chance earlier to remove his mail. He needed it now! The crowd surrounding them drew back as his adversary fought like a madman, slashing and stabbing with his blade, smashing and grabbing with his fist. Padrig drew his dagger and feinted with it, forcing his opponent off balance.

The tip of the man's sword raked along the edge of Padrig's hauberk, however, and caught in his coif, which lay in useless folds on the back of his neck. The blade snagged into the heavy mesh, wrenching Padrig's head around and also pulling the other man, who refused to let go of his weapon, within reach of Padrig's own blades.

Padrig turned hard on his heel in the opposite direction and jerked the blade from his coif, then thrust hard at the other man, sending him staggering to the ground. Padrig kicked his opponent's sword away and set his own sword to the man's throat. "Do you yield?" he asked, breathing hard.

His opponent sneered, but remained silent, his dark eyes blazing with a hatred so intense 'twas unmistakable.

Padrig didn't know who the man was, but he didn't feel inclined to free anyone who had attacked him for no apparent reason. "Do you yield?" he growled.

Suddenly someone flew out of the shadows behind him and stomped down on his opponent's left hand.

A dagger hit the ground, blade flashing in the torchlight. "I wouldn't touch that if I were you, Lord Henry, unless you want to lose your hand." Alys bent over the man—Walsingham, it could be no other—and thrust a vicious-looking knife toward his wrist, pressing the point against his flesh. A drop of blood oozed from the wound and he whimpered, but his fingers still curled toward the hilt. "I mean it," she growled, her voice as fierce as her expression. "Move your hand away, now!"

The glare he sent promised retribution, but he shifted his arm as far from Alys as he could without moving from beneath Padrig's sword.

Her father moved toward her. "Drop the knife, Alys, and step back at once," he demanded. "And call off your Welsh dog of a husband."

Neither Padrig nor Alys moved away, though she straightened enough to meet Padrig's gaze over the man sprawled on the ground between them. "What shall I do, milord?" she asked Padrig, her eyes blazing. "He deserves killing for trying to kill you."

He could see the strain she tried to hide, her body shaking, her right hand limp at her side. She had used the last of her resources to come to his aid.

Still holding Walsingham in place, Padrig shifted around the man, pinned the man's arm beneath his boot and motioned for her to move aside. "Perhaps we should let Lord Rannulf deal with him," he said. He thrust his own dagger into its sheath and cast a sidelong look at his commander before leaning down to pick up Walsingham's knife. "I'm certain he has some interesting ideas of how to resolve all this," he said, shoving the knife into his belt as he stood.

He *hoped* Lord Rannulf did, at any rate. For himself, once he'd secured Alys's freedom and protection, he'd no thought of anything more than discovering the condition of his men, removing his filthy armor and getting some sleep.

All this, of course, after he learned just how Lord Rannulf planned to account for calling Alys Padrig's wife.

And worked out a way to turn that falsehood into truth.

He smiled at Alys, then called for several of the guards to take Lord Henry away and lock him up. Lord Roger Delamare he'd leave to Lord Rannulf, and let *him* explain to Alys's father how she and Padrig came to be "wed."

Afterwards he could explain it to them, as well, Padrig thought with a laugh.

But for now, his only thoughts were of Alys.

As soon as Lord Rannulf strode into the midst of the crowd and took charge, Padrig wrapped his arm about Alys's waist and led her toward the shadows beneath the wall walk. All eyes were focused on Lord Rannulf out in the bailey. No one bothered to follow them.

She leaned her weight into Padrig's hold, her body tense and shaking, yet she walked beside him with her head held high, a slight smile on her lips and hope brightening her eyes.

Gone was the Alys who scarce noted the world around her, who sought to disguise the truth of her strength and beauty.

If, indeed, she'd been aware of it at all.

It seemed to him that that quiet young woman had disappeared somewhere along the journey away from l'Eau Clair—perhaps on the morn when she'd followed him to the pool and first teased him with the true Alys, the one she'd kept hidden away.

That Alys had attracted him, but the Alys at his side tempted him to throw away his old plans for the future, to replace them with hopes and dreams he hadn't known he had.

As soon as they were concealed by the shadows, he swept her into his arms and kissed her with all the passion only she could elicit.

Gasping, she drew back and framed his face with her hands. "Do you think Lady Gillian will try to keep us apart till we're truly wed? If they allow us to marry," she added with a frown.

"They'd better let us," he said. He covered her hands with his own, raised them to rest on his shoulders and drew her close. "As for Lady Gillian, what do you think?"

"I think there are places aplenty hereabouts to work on our lessons, if we can but slip away from her notice," she said with a laugh. "Mayhap we'll have a real bed someday, but we'll find somewhere until then…"

"Until then," Rafe said from nearby, his voice dry, "perhaps you ought to find someplace else to play."

"Rafe!" Easing his arms from around Alys, Padrig crept out into the bailey and jerked a lantern from a hook by the stairs, returning to find Alys kneeling by Rafe's side.

"Let's get him into the keep and settled," Alys said, rising and taking the lantern as, their own troubles forgotten for the moment, Padrig helped his dazed second in command to his feet.

With Alys's help, Padrig helped Rafe to the barracks. His wounds had not borne the journey well, and needed to be cleaned and sewn up again. It made Padrig's body twitch in sympathy just to think of it, for he'd experienced that painful process before. However, he stayed with Rafe while Alys, with the help of a maid skilled in healing, treated Rafe's injuries.

Once Rafe was settled on a pallet in a quiet corner of the barracks, and Alys sent off with the maid to wash and change from her bloodstained clothing, Padrig sent for Lord Rannulf, then settled on the floor beside his second in command. Rafe was eager to tell everything that had happened at Winterbrooke after Padrig and Alys left. Padrig could tell the man wouldn't rest until he'd unburdened himself.

Lord Rannulf soon joined them, dropping down to sit on the floor on the other side of Rafe's pallet without a moment's hesitation. Padrig wasn't surprised to see his lord do so, since for Lord Rannulf, arrogance was merely a tool to use when necessary, not a part of his character. Rafe, however, immediately struggled to sit up against the wall behind him.

Lord Rannulf eased Rafe back down. "Rest and heal," he told Rafe. "You've served me well, Rafe. I've a new task for you, once you're on your feet again."

Rafe sent a questioning glance Padrig's way. He shrugged, for he knew nothing of any new plans involving Rafe.

The two men listened eagerly as Rafe related his tale.

"Dickon didn't know it, but when the Welsh raiding party attacked the village and Winterbrooke, his father escaped and headed north to tell Delamare what happened. Nigh a week had passed by the time he caught up with Lord Roger at Walsingham's keep and they gathered their men."

Padrig handed Rafe a cup of ale and met Lord Rannulf's gaze. "What were they up to, I wonder?"

"Nothing good," the older man replied. "Though their actions might turn out well in the end." He took the cup from Rafe and nodded for him to continue.

"They got to Winterbrooke shortly after you left," he told Padrig. "Once the Welsh saw the strength of Lord Roger's force, they surrendered with nary a fight."

"I doubt there were many Welsh within the manor," Padrig remarked. "They didn't bother with us for long, though they'd not have had much trouble taking us captive."

"There weren't many o' them at all," Rafe agreed. He laughed. "But that's not why they let us go. Peter and the others told 'em right off that Marie was Lady Alys. Since they believed she was Lord Roger's daughter, they treated her well. In fact, she's on the mend. They thought *we* were a pair of men-at-arms and a maid—not worth going after."

"How did you know 'twas safe to come out of the caves?" Padrig asked. "Had Dickon been out exploring?"

Rafe shook his head. "When his father didn't find the boy in the keep with his mother, knowing of the lad's love of the place, he first looked for him in the Devil's Lair."

"Why didn't you stay at Winterbrooke with the other injured?" Padrig asked.

Rafe made a rude sound. "Lord Roger thought to use me as a hostage if he needed one to get his daughter back," he said. "He had me tied into the saddle and brought me along on their damned trek from Winterbrooke Manor." He shook his head. "Don't know what good I'd have been if the trip killed me," he added dryly.

Lord Rannulf laid his hand on Rafe's shoulder. "You did well," he told him. He glanced over at Padrig. "You both did. Once we deal with Delamare and Walsingham—which should not take long, as each of the idiots has dug himself a deep and dangerous pit he'll not be able to climb out of—I've plans for both of you." On that cryptic note, he got to his feet. "Padrig, I expect you to join us in Lady Gillian's solar shortly."

Padrig stood, as well. "I'd thought to speak with my men who returned with Delamare." He wanted nothing more than to be with Alys, if he'd even be allowed to see her, but he could not ignore his duty.

"That can wait till later," Lord Rannulf said. "We've more important matters to deal with first." He glanced at Padrig's filthy garb. "I suggest you do whatever you can to clean up a bit, if you can do so quickly. My lady—and no doubt yours," he added with a grin, "seem to prefer we scrape off a bit of the dirt and gore before we grace them with our presence."

His heart sped up at the realization that Lord Rannulf, at least, didn't intend to keep him away from Alys. "Aye, milord." Bowing quickly, he ignored the sound of Rafe's and Lord Rannulf's laughter as he turned and strode away.

Chapter Twenty-Seven

Lady Gillian had indeed planned to keep them apart that night, but as Lord Rannulf had pointed out, there was too much to resolve about both Alys's and Padrig's situations for the discussion to wait for long.

While Padrig stayed with Rafe, Alys returned to the keep. Lady Gillian had sent word she was to join them in the solar as soon as she'd taken the time to clean up. Though it was tempting to simply find a pallet in a quiet corner of the keep, curl up beneath the blankets and hide from the morass of her father's demands, she knew she wouldn't do it. The cowardly young woman who hid from life didn't exist any longer.

Returning to the chamber she'd shared with two other of Lady Gillian's ladies, with their help Alys quickly washed, brushed out the tangled mass of her hair and changed into a fresh gown.

When she reached the solar she was glad she'd taken the time to do so, for she'd need every bit of confidence she could muster to survive the coming confrontation. The silent scene before her reminded her of those rare times when the FitzCliffords sat in judgment of some malefactor among their people. The air of gravity they both wore reassured her that they would protect her, as Lady Gillian had assured her earlier.

'Twas clear by Lady Gillian's expression that she didn't care to have the likes of Lord Roger and Walsingham tainting the sanctuary of her private rooms. Alys would rather they were elsewhere, as well, although there was much to settle before the two men left l'Eau Clair.

Left without her, she prayed.

She paused just inside the chamber. Her father and Lord Henry sat on a long bench set in the middle of the chamber. Though they remained silent, they both turned to watch her when she entered the room. She calmly met her father's angry gaze and Lord Henry's malicious glower. She'd not cower before them. If they didn't deserve her respect—and she was convinced that they did not—they certainly did not warrant her fear, either.

She would trust that she and Padrig would stay safe, and remain together through this, with Lady Gillian's and Lord Rannulf's help.

The FitzCliffords sat in their carved chairs before the fire. Padrig stood at Lord Rannulf's side; he'd removed his mail and changed his clothing, but he still wore his sword.

From the determination of his expression—his bearing—he stood ready to use it, should the need arise.

To Alys's eyes, he looked as though he'd like nothing better than to do so.

"Come, Lady Alys, join us," Lady Gillian said, motioning for Padrig to set a stool beside her for Alys. "Lord Roger, please be so kind as to close the door."

Alys crossed the room, biting back a smile as her father, his resentment obvious at being ordered about by Lady Gillian, nonetheless did as she asked.

Padrig took Alys by the hand, gifting her with a reassuring glance, and settled her upon the stool. He moved to stand by her side, hand once again clasped about his sword hilt, his expression nigh daring Walsingham and her father to object.

"Now that Lady Alys has joined us, shall we resume our discussion?" Lord Rannulf asked.

Resume? She'd thought they'd wait for her! What had been discussed—or settled—before she arrived?

Fighting down a rising sense of panic, Alys glanced swiftly at Padrig. He appeared at ease. She immediately felt reassured; they must not have decided anything yet.

Her father stood and paced the width of the room, stopping before Alys. "You're not wed after all, I hear."

She raised her chin and met his accusing stare. To give him the slightest bit of power over her would be madness! She prayed he couldn't tell how his words made her heart nigh stop.

"Am I to assume you've given him your maidenhead?" he demanded, his voice low, chilling. She remained silent, unmoving in the face of his anger. He glanced from Padrig to her. "I can see that you have," he added, his disgust obvious. "Do you realize what you've done by your actions? You are mine to dispose of as I see fit—"

"As will best profit you, you mean." She'd had enough! She rose as gracefully as she could, and despite the anger vibrating through her, spoke calmly. "Dispose of? Am I a broken cup, then, to be tossed upon the midden?" she asked, casting a scathing look at Lord Henry.

Walsingham got to his feet, his smile mocking. "I will take you, milady," he said, the insinuation in his tone leaving no doubt as to his meaning, "whether you be a broken cup or no." He glanced at Lord Roger. "Though if you have been 'broken,' 'twill cost your father dearly."

Padrig's growl as he nigh leapt across the chamber drowned out Alys's cry of outrage. He was upon Walsingham before the last words left the man's lips. Seizing the front of Lord Henry's tunic in one hand, he dragged him up till his feet scarce touched the floor and wrapped the other hand about his throat. "Did you not learn your lesson in the bailey, you filthy worm?" he ground out. Walsingham, gasping, squirmed in his grasp, his fingers wrapped about Padrig's arms as he sought to free himself.

"Enough, Padrig!" Lord Rannulf said sharply, though Alys noted he remained seated.

Padrig's hold did not ease, however, and it didn't appear anyone—even her father—was going to make any attempt to rescue Walsingham.

As much as eliminating Lord Henry would please her, she feared if Padrig killed him, they would have no chance of a life together. "Padrig." She approached him and placed her hand upon his upper arm, careful to stay out of reach of Lord Henry's flailing feet. "'*M asgre,* let him go," she said quietly. "He's not worth it."

Padrig looked down at her, his gaze searching. Opening his hands, he let Walsingham drop to the floor. Turning to her, he took her hand, brought it to his lips, then, ignoring the man sprawled at their feet, led Alys back to her seat.

Her attention focused on Padrig as he resumed his

protective stance beside her, Alys started at the sound of Lord Rannulf's footsteps in the now-quiet room as he rose and crossed to stand before her father.

"Delamare, you cannot possibly wish to give your daughter to that slime," he said, casting a dismissive look at Walsingham as the man struggled to his feet. "Indeed, should you continue to attempt such folly, I'm certain I've the means to prevent it."

"You've no right to stop me, milord. She's mine to use as I wish—and I wish her to marry Walsingham. He's still willing to take her despite what she's done."

Alys had seen that complacent look on her father's face too many times before. Her fear mounting, she watched as he hitched his belt up over his sagging belly and closed one hand on the hilt of his sword. "I'll not tell you again, Daughter." He grabbed Alys by the arm and jerked her to her feet. "You shall wed Lord Henry as soon as it can be arranged."

"No!" she shrieked. She fought his hold, but he'd grabbed her right arm, sending a bolt of agony shooting through her. 'Twas all she could do to remain on her feet.

Strong arms closed about her from behind, held her upright when her father abruptly released her. Through a haze of pain, she saw Lord Rannulf toss her father aside, heard Padrig's voice murmur in her ear. "It's all right, love." He turned her to face him and gathered her close, his hand under her aching arm easing away the pain. "Neither of them will harm you ever again, I swear to you."

Footsteps pounded into the room. She glanced over her shoulder toward the door, gaping at the sight of a pair of burly guards binding her father's arms behind him. She turned to watch as two more men trussed up Lord Henry, ignoring his curses as they jerked the ropes tight.

He quieted when Lord Rannulf came to stand before him. "By Christ's bones, but you are both fools," he said, his scathing tone matching his expression as he looked from one to the other. "Did you truly believe you could discuss treason and blackmail within the confines of your camp and not be overheard? From what I hear, it was so obvious you were plotting something, 'twas an invitation to anyone you've harmed to spy upon you! How could you not realize there would be someone willing to tell everything he'd learned?"

Lord Roger growled and cursed, fighting his bonds. "Several 'someones.'" Lord Rannulf laughed. "I've evidence enough to see you both hang, milords. It will give me great pleasure to use your secrets against you."

Lady Gillian rose and joined her husband. "I'm certain it will reassure you to know, Lord Roger, that we will keep your daughter safe, find her a fine husband." She took Alys by the hand and reached for Padrig's, smiling as she placed Alys's hand in his. "I'm certain you'll have no objection to Lady Alys's marriage to Sir Padrig."

Padrig closed his fingers about Alys's and gifted her with a smile that promised dreams made real.

Alys couldn't help but smile in return, despite her father's angry glare. "Do as you wish, you ungrateful wench," he snarled. Her smile became a grin. "I wash my hands of you."

"Under the circumstances, that is no doubt a blessing," Lady Gillian said as the guards led the two men, both muttering curses and threats, from the chamber.

Once the door shut behind them, Lady Gillian returned to her chair and settled into it with a sigh. "Well now, my dears—" she sent them a teasing look "—are you certain you wish to wed, or is that fate too terrifying?"

Lord Rannulf, pouring wine into four goblets, handed Padrig and Alys each a drink, then taking one for himself, brought one to his wife. "Perhaps Padrig wishes to learn the next task I've planned for him."

"Or mayhap Alys would like to know her future husband's prospects," Lady Gillian added, chuckling.

"All I wish to know is whether my father can keep us apart," Alys said, sinking onto the bench and looking from one to the other.

Lord Rannulf shook his head. "I believe I've the weapon to strip your father and Walsingham both of their power, and their power over each other. What a twisted knot of intrigue they've woven—treason, threats against each other and an unholy desire to wrest control of their corner of the Marches from the king. That being the case, and given the fact that we give you our blessing—" he raised his goblet in salute "—and that I wish to make Padrig castellan of a fine manor not far from here, should he choose to accept my offer, I believe you've both all the permission you need."

"You may wed as soon as you like," Lady Gillian added. "If that is your wish."

"Thank you, milord." Padrig bowed and raised his goblet in salute. "Milady." He took one sip of the wine before setting the chalice on the table and turning to face Alys. His gaze was focused on her face, his blue eyes bright, his lips quirked into a smile unlike any she'd ever seen on his face. He looked free and happy, and the intensity of the way he watched her…

By the Virgin, she could not believe he would look at her like that when they weren't alone!

He took her hand and raised her from the bench. Bending close, he murmured, "Will you come out on the wall walk with me?"

Alys nodded and set aside her untouched wine. "You know I will," she whispered.

"You shall not tonight," Lady Gillian remarked from her chair.

Alys's face heated. How had she heard them?

"You've been alone enough already," Lady Gillian added, her voice wry. "I doubt you should be alone any further until you've wed."

Padrig cast Lord Rannulf a questioning look. "Milord?"

Lord Rannulf came round to the front of his wife's chair, caught her up in his arms, and headed for the door, both of them laughing. "If you keep the door open, you may have a few moments together," he told them as he carried her from the room.

"We'll be right out here," Lady Gillian called over his shoulder. "Don't be too long."

Padrig stepped closer and framed her face in his hands. "We mustn't waste a moment," he told her quietly, brushing his lips over her cheeks between words. "For you know they'll not give us much time."

Alys felt her face heat under the weight of his regard, but she couldn't look away. He cast a glance over his shoulder, then caught hold of her free hand and led her to the window.

She wrapped her arms about him and skated her mouth along his jaw. "Then we'd best make the most of it." She reached up to kiss him.

He returned the kiss full measure, a lover's kiss of passion and caring. Alys pressed closer to him, rising up on her toes to deepen their embrace, her need for him rising, her blood heating.

Padrig's arms tightened about her, then, his touch tender, he eased back from the kiss and dropped to his knees. "Marry me, *'m asgre,*" he said, taking her hands in his and raising them to his lips. "Share my life. I vow I shall love you always."

Her heart racing, she tugged on his hands until he stood. "As I shall love you, milord," she told him, raising her hand to cup his cheek. "I will marry you when and where you will, so long as it's soon."

"Tomorrow morn?" He slid his hands to her waist and drew her close.

"As much as I might wish it, milord, I doubt it can be arranged that quickly," Alys teased. "Will tomorrow evening be soon enough?"

He bent and brushed his lips across her cheek, sending a chill of excitement down her spine. "Aye, for I'll not spend another night away from you after tonight," he whispered.

The door swung wide, hinges creaking. They turned to find Lady Gillian standing in the doorway. Alys refused to step away from Padrig. Although she was not best pleased to be interrupted, she could not help laughing at Lady Gillian's diligence. "Tomorrow evening it shall be, my dears," Lady Gillian said with a smile. "Now kiss your lady good-night, Sir Padrig. Tomorrow she shall truly be yours."

Padrig waited impatiently in the great hall for his bride, surrounded by the people of l'Eau Clair. Somehow Lady Gillian had created a festive air in a short time. The hall was decorated with flowers and colorful banners, the tables already bowed beneath the surfeit of food.

The priest had agreed to marry them here, where there was room for all to gather....

Once his bride finally made her appearance.

Alys was a vision worth waiting for. Dressed simply in a green gown, her chestnut hair flowing loose about her; the mere sight of her as the crowd parted to let her through had the power to weaken his knees. Smiling, he held out his hand to her and led her to the dais at the front of the hall.

He couldn't stop smiling. From the moment he saw her, his heart had raced in anticipation.

Of their life together.

Of learning all the nuances of their love.

They spoke their vows slowly, solemnly, investing the words with meaning.

When the time came for him to kiss his bride, he poured all the love he felt for her into that simple kiss, hoping she'd realize the unspoken promises he made.

He would repeat those promises to her when they were alone, say the words he meant with all his heart.

That night after they'd loved, Alys gazed about the chamber that would be theirs until they left l'Eau Clair for Padrig's new command. Though 'twas small, it had much to recommend it over the cave where they'd first made love.

Though she missed the hot spring, the bed had been a wonderful luxury, one they'd made good use of, she thought with a smile.

She cuddled close to her husband, savoring his warmth and strength.

"Are you happy, *'m asgre?*" he murmured. He drew her closer still, until her head lay atop his shoulder and she could hear the steady beat of his heart.

"Aye, milord. Are you?" She propped herself up on her elbow and gazed into his eyes.

"Happier than I believed 'twas possible." His gaze never leaving hers, he smoothed his hand over her shoulder and brought his palm to rest over her heart. "Alys, I swear to you I will cherish you forever, protect you with my strength, worship you with my body and my heart."

She could find no words, merely smile and fight back the tears that threatened to flow. Finally she caught his hand in her own and brought it to her lips. "You honor me, Husband. I never thought to hear such words spoken to me, only to record them as part of someone else's story. But thanks to you, Padrig, I feel as though my life has begun anew—a tale of love and living our lives together."

Padrig cuddled her close and, picking up her right hand, gently kissed her fingers. "Once your hand is better, *'m asgre*, will you write our story?" he asked. "After all, you know how it will end."

She raised herself up on his chest and, smiling, shook her head. "There's no 'the end' in the tales I write, *'m cara*. 'Tis like our story."

He pressed a kiss to her lips. "And what is that, my heart?"

"'Tis the beginning."

Harlequin® Historical
Historical Romantic Adventure!

Schooling the scoundrel...

THE SCOUNDREL
Lisa Plumley

Daniel McCabe isn't the marrying kind
until an unexpected delivery changes
his mind. Sarah Crabtree accepts his
proposal, but *her* romance is *his* marriage
of convenience! Now she must convince
the biggest scoundrel in Arizona Territory
to let her into his bed—and his heart....

Linked to
THE MATCHMAKER #674

Lisa Plumley's "books are a delight!"
—*USA TODAY* bestselling author
Rachel Gibson

On sale April 2006
Available wherever
Harlequin books are sold.

If you enjoyed what you just read,
then we've got an offer you can't resist!

Take 2 bestselling
love stories FREE!

Plus get a FREE surprise gift!

THE ELLIOTTS

Mixing Business with Pleasure

The saga continues with

The Forbidden Twin

by

SUSAN CROSBY

(SD #1717)

Scarlet Elliott's secret crush is finally unveiled
as she takes the plunge and seduces her twin
sister's ex-fiancé. The relationship is forbidden,
the attraction…undeniable.

On Sale April 2006

*Available at your
favorite retail outlet.*